CHARLIE GREEN

and the
Underground Railroad

To Winnie and Reggie

Best Wishes

[signature]

CHARLIE GREEN

and the

Underground Railroad

MARTYN BLUNDEN

Matador
9 Priory Business Park,
Wistow Road, Kibworth Beauchamp,
Leicestershire. LE8 0RX
Tel: 0116 279 2299
Email: books@troubador.co.uk
Web: www.troubador.co.uk/matador
Twitter: @matadorbooks

ISBN 978 1788037 167

British Library Cataloguing in Publication Data.
A catalogue record for this book is available from the British Library.

Printed and bound in the UK by TJ International, Padstow, Cornwall
Typeset in 12pt Aldine401 BT by Troubador Publishing Ltd, Leicester, UK

Matador is an imprint of Troubador Publishing Ltd

To the memory of Rob Bull
a dear friend, colleague and great pilot.

A real and passionate plea
For any pilot will always be
Soar the sky high with me
Never earthbound for long cries he.

Now you soar the skies all day
Looking down as we look up and pray
Memories fade though never far away
Now your own wings have their way.

Chapter 1

Above them a scraping noise made Charlie and Ben jump and look up from their game. Both froze in their head-up position for a moment. V was downstairs with their mother preparing for dinner; Oliver was coming over as a thank you for fixing her washing machine. It had been leaking water for a while ever since it had somehow vibrated itself away from the wall. Charlie and Ben were in their bedroom when they heard the noise above them while playing a Pokémon card game. Ben slowly got to his feet. It wasn't the first time they'd heard a strange noise from the loft since they'd moved in to Pegasus Ride back at the start of the summer; before, they'd heard a quiet tapping and an occasional clicking noise.

In the silence of their room you could almost hear their hearts beating in their chests like drums. The adrenalin of fear was coursing through their veins driving the beats faster. Charlie started to breathe more quickly too, and concentrated his attention above him and watching his brother move slowly around the room. Both minds were focused on what they'd heard. Charlie put down his cards and joined Ben standing by his bed.

1

"What do you think it is, Ben?" he whispered in his ear.

"Ssh." And Ben turned his head to the side slightly to concentrate the hearing of one ear above him.

"Maybe it's a rat," Charlie whispered.

"Ssh."

They both froze again and Charlie grabbed hold of his brother as they heard another quieter rumble that only lasted a second or so, easily missed if they hadn't been listening so intently. The tension was electric. There was only an empty attic above them, with no easy access. They backed away in small steps furtively towards the bedroom door. Unseen by them it opened.

"Dinner's nearly ready, boys," announced their mother loudly.

They spun round in fright, grasped each other tightly and nearly fell on the floor.

"What's the matter with you two? You look like you've had the fright of your lives."

"Mum!" they both shouted, "Don't do that."

"I only said dinner was nearly ready."

"Yeah but… did you hear that?"

"Hear what?" she asked taking another step into their room.

"The noise from the attic?"

"Oh, not that again. I told you there's nothing up there except a small table and an old rocking chair. But there may be a rat or a mouse running around."

"Oh and it's rearranging the furniture, I suppose," said Ben sarcastically, "perhaps putting the table nearer the window, you know, for a better view?"

"No, Ben, I didn't mean that," said his mother, looking slightly displeased at the sarcasm. "I just mean we live in an old house and there may be some… well, wildlife that live here too. Remember, the house had been left empty for quite a few years before we moved in. And maybe all the wildlife hasn't moved out yet! Despite the poison the rat man put down. He said he'd put a trap down in the attic; I'll give him a call to come and get him to check it again."

"Or, we might have a secret lodger living up there, Mum."

"A secret lodger," she sighed, with a desperate look on her face.

"Yeah, remember, I told you I thought I saw a face at the window a few weeks ago," pleaded Charlie.

"Yeah, well, you were just daydreaming," scoffed Ben.

"Yes, of course, Charlie, that is possible – someone who comes through our house without us seeing them, climbs into the attic without a ladder, because we don't have one, and makes themselves at home up there."

"Well, we still heard a noise."

"I'm sure you did, but now can you come down for dinner?" Just as she finished her sentence, there was a loud knock at the door. "Ah, that's probably Oliver now." Laura left the room and made her way to the front door, but the boys both barged their way past her to get there first. Clattering down the bare boards of the stairway, none of them heard the rumble of the rocking chair in the attic.

By the time she got there Oliver was standing in the hallway at the foot of the stairs. He was neatly dressed in a blue checked shirt and dark brown trousers; it was more comfortable than colour coordinated – not a man likely to win a fashion contest! His friend in town – Adam McRoy, a man with impeccable taste – had mentioned on more than one occasion that he would gladly kit him out with clothes that made a statement. So far, Oliver had not taken him up on the offer, but then he didn't have any children to embarrass! Looking about ten or so years older than Laura, his hair was short-cropped and he sported a neatly trimmed goatee beard, which she found attractive. He thought Laura was pleasing on the eye too.

"If you'd like to go into the front room with the boys, dinner will be ready very soon."

Ben led the way into the lounge. Oliver sat in an armchair and the two brothers slumped onto the sofa. Charlie led the conversation and started telling him about the noises they'd heard coming from the attic.

"Really?" he said, with slight mock surprise, his eyes widening with interest as he shuffled fully back into the chair.

"Yeah," said Ben, "and it's not the first time. Sometimes there's a clicking noise, like you hear when you get out of a car and the engine is cooling down."

"The noises never last very long, and Mum doesn't believe us."

"Well, on the clay soil we have here, old houses like this sometimes just move about a bit as the weather changes and the soil beneath dries out – that can cause it to creak. Like when you walk on a wonky floorboard."

"Eh?" queried Charlie.

"When the soil is soaked, after days of heavy rain, it swells up; later, when it dries out, it shrinks; so the thin foundations of a house like this move with it." Oliver opened the palms of his hands to emphasise the simplicity of his explanation.

"Oh," said Ben.

"Yes, but it doesn't explain my face at the window," said Charlie.

Tilting his head to one side, with a look of intrigue on his face, he looked more directly at Charlie. "What do you mean?"

"Nothing," said Ben. "Just Charlie daydreaming again."

Charlie huffed in protest and folded his arms. Oliver held his gaze on Charlie for a moment – *Had he seen her?*

"Well, it's a funny old place up here; the light can play tricks," Oliver joked. "And our brains are programed to see faces in shapes, even with just a few shapes of shadow. For instance, I'm rubbish at art but even I can draw something you'd recognise as a face with just a few lines!"

Charlie's grim smile showed he wasn't convinced. The subject changed to the building of their tree house, but before they got very far there was a shout from the kitchen. And V appeared at the door to tell them dinner was ready.

From the aroma that danced through down the hallway, Laura had cooked a very tasty shepherd's pie. The dish in the centre of the table, topped with a potato crust, was surrounded by smaller dishes of fresh vegetables grown by Harry Hobbard in the village. By her own admission she wasn't a very accomplished cook, but could produce very flavoursome simple meals.

"Smells gorgeous," said Oliver as he entered the room. Olivia held out his chair for him and did a pretend curtsey. "Thank you, Olivia!"

The children sat down while their mother began serving the meal. There was an open bottle of wine in the middle of the table. "Shall I pour?" asked Oliver.

"Would you? Thanks." She smiled.

He carefully picked up the bottle and leant over to pour Laura's glass first. Just as the wine flowed he had an involuntary jerk of his arm and the wine sloshed over the table. He quickly raised the neck of the bottle to prevent further spillage and profusely apologised. Olivia jumped up quickly to help mop up the mess.

"Thank you, dear," said her mother as she continued to serve the dinner.

"I don't think we've lost too much," joked Oliver, continuing, but this time holding the glass as well. "I'm sorry," he said again, "I don't know what happened there." Then he felt, rather than heard, a whisper in his ear and a cool movement of air without sound. He twisted his neck to look behind him.

"Everything all right?" asked Laura.

"Yes, uh… fine," said Oliver with a guarded smile.

After they had finished their meal and were talking about nothing in particular, he asked if the washing machine was working okay now.

"Fine thanks, since you fixed it. Mind you–" Laura continued after a sup of wine, "something rather annoying happened after the first wash I did with it the next day."

"Oh, what was that?"

"The wash completed well enough, and I hung it all out to dry, but as soon as I got back inside, and as I looked from the window, a freak wind must have blown across the garden because each piece of laundry, in turn, fell from the clothes pegs onto the ground."

"Yeah!" said Charlie, with a bit of a smirk. "Mum wasn't too happy."

"Darn right I wasn't; it fell right in the dirt and I had to do it all again!"

Oliver closed his eyes momentarily and shook his head. Then he took a big swig of wine. *I must have a word,* he thought and replaced his glass on the table. He felt a whisper again.

"Behave," Oliver muttered under his breath.

"Pardon?" said Laura looking across the table at him. She'd not really heard what he'd said but Charlie, sitting next to him, had heard clearly.

"Nothing, sorry I… I was just thinking about… it doesn't matter." Charlie squinted a bit and gave Oliver a puzzled look. To defuse it and move the conversation swiftly on, Oliver raised his glass and said, "A toast to the Treetop Fort."

They all grabbed their glasses and raised them towards Oliver. "The Treetop Fort!" they chanted together.

Laura got up and started to clear the table and then told Oliver, V and Charlie to go through to the lounge, but asked Ben to give her a hand. Oliver offered to help but Laura insisted he went and sat with the children. Ben willingly assisted his mother as he always did and gathered up the plates and placed them next to the sink. Then, just as he went to pick up his mother's empty glass, a strange feeling washed over his fingers and he knocked the glass over instead. It clonked onto the table, rolled to the side and fell from the table, heading quickly to the floor. With the speed of a thrusting viper he just managed to snatch it with his other hand before it became a thousand glittering pieces on the floor.

His mother, standing at the end of the table and witness to the event, firstly exclaimed, "Ben, be careful!" as he knocked the glass over; then, with surprise as he caught it, "Oh, well done!"

Ben held up the glass in triumph. He then quizzically looked at his hand for the source of the sensation he'd experienced – like an unseen hand brushing fingers over the back of his. Several seconds passed as he inspected his hand first one way then the other.

Picking up the empty pie dish Laura asked, "What is it, Ben?"

"Nothing really, Mum, it was just… as I went to pick up your glass—"

"Don't worry. You caught it anyway. That glass has got a mind of its own today!" she joked.

"Weird things happen in this house, Mum."

"Ben! I didn't mean it. These things just happen sometimes, that's all. Come on, I'll wash up later; let's go and join the others." He wanted to say that he thought it might be something to do with Oliver but then she would ask why. And that might eventually lead to an end of his and Charlie's adventures with Jenny. He rationalised the thought; as his mother had said, sometimes these things just happen. He put it out of his mind as he followed his mum through to the front room.

Chapter 2

The following Saturday morning, 25th September, sitting in the Hobbards' kitchen, Ben was getting frustrated by Charlie's whining. They'd been arguing on their bikes on their way down to see Oliver, as they had all week, but Ben reckoned he was slowly winning Charlie over. Harry Hobbard was attending to miserable Mr Seward out front in the shop, who was complaining about not receiving a delivery from Harry. Harry's home housed the village shop, and a small corner was partitioned off to serve as the local post office which Harry was responsible for. The post office section was only open for a few hours a day when Harry was not out on his rounds or collecting the mail from the main post office in the nearby town of Cheshampton.

In the kitchen the booming voice of Stanley Seward could be heard complaining about the non-delivery of something or other. Moaning, whinging and whining was something of an Olympic speciality of garage-owning Mr Seward. Mrs Hobbard – Beryl to her friends – shook her head and raised her bushy moustache-style eyebrows – almost long enough to plait – as she pulled a tray of freshly baked cheese straws from the oven.

"That man makes Ebenezer Scrooge look cheerful," said Beryl. The moreish aroma of mature cheddar cheese straws wafted temptingly across the kitchen and through the multi-coloured plastic curtain to the shop.

"Who's Ebenezer Scrooge?" asked Charlie.

"The miserable old guy in that film, *A Christmas Carol*; the one who gets visited by the ghosts at Christmas because he's so miserable and selfish," said Ben.

"Oh yes, I remember; don't they scare him into being nice?"

"That's right, my dear. They do in the end, they do," nodded Beryl.

"Maybe they could visit Mr Seward," suggested Charlie.

"If only, my dear, if only."

Returning to their original dispute Ben asked, "Anyway, Charlie, what about it? What about we go and help rescue the slave children first and then think about your trip to find King Arthur?" With a pleading look he slumped into a chair and rested his arms on the large refectory table that occupied the centre of the kitchen.

Charlie puffed out his cheeks and sighed, "I suppose so. But can I tell Jenny where we want to go?" he said looking at Oliver. "Can I wear the helmet?" His expression changed completely, he twitched his eyebrows up and down and beamed a cute smile.

Ben dropped his head and glanced Oliver a disapproving stare. Oliver couldn't resist; Charlie's charm won in an instant. "Yes, Charlie boy, I'm sure we can let you do that, can't we, Ben?" Oliver knew Charlie wouldn't give up the request anyway; he was as persistent as the need to pee after a long car journey! Once he'd got his mind set on something he'd use all the cunning tricks a cute kid could think of.

Ben's head fell further into his hands; he closed his eyes and rested his head on the table, resigned to the idea of Charlie being in control of Jenny. "OK," he groaned, but secretly smiled at the thought of going on the journey he'd hoped for. "So long as you listen to me, Charlie, and say what I tell you to say."

"'Course I will, Ben," Charlie grinned. Oliver rubbed his hand over the top of Charlie's head and smiled too.

The shop doorbell rang out twice as the grumpy garage owner left empty handed. Harry re-joined them in the kitchen. "Apparently some part for a mower he's been waiting for hasn't turned up yet. 'Taint my fault it's not 'ere yet, but he seems to think 'tis post office's fault and by that, 'e means me." Harry sat back down at the head of the table and poured some of his tea into the saucer. Taking the saucer in both hands he swigged from the side.

Beryl tutted and shook her head. "I wish you wouldn't do that when we have company, Harry."

Harry finished the saucerful and replaced the cup on it. He ran his fingers through what hair he had left, then rested his elbow on the table and supported his chin in the palm of his hand. "Well, what have you lot decided?" Subconsciously his hand reached out for one of the fresh cheese straws, which was met with a slap from his wife.

"No you don't," she sternly remarked; "they're for the shop."

Succulent scones were also cooling on a wire rack in the kitchen. Beryl was well known locally for her baking and rarely would a visitor leave without buying one or other of her freshly baked treats. The alluring aroma was a treat difficult to resist.

"Well, I think we've agreed to take up Ben's idea to search for Harriet Tubman's lost relatives."

"I see," replied Harry. "So you gonna fill us in a bit then, Ben, 'bout this 'ere Harriet woman?"

Ben spent some time explaining that part of his history studies at school this year involved researching slavery in America in the 1800s and the American Civil War. Basically, the southern American states kept slaves and the northern states didn't, which was one of the main reasons for the war. Slaves often tried to escape to the north but were equally often caught by slave hunters and returned to their owners where they often received beatings for running away. Depending on the value of the slave, the reward could lead the bounty hunters or catchers to travel far across the country in search of escaped slaves who had a big price on their head.

One slave who was successful in getting away was a woman named Harriet Tubman. She was a very determined and resourceful woman who, having made her own successful escape to a northern free state, decided to return and assist other slaves to escape their ordeal and live a life of freedom. Over a period of ten or more years she helped hundreds of slaves escape their torment through a series of safe houses on their route (called the Underground Railroad) north to New York state or Canada. However, during the Civil War she was also enlisted in the Northern Army (known as the Yankees) to fight the southern Confederate Army, through being a spy and scout one day and a nurse the next.

She put herself in extreme danger leading troops into battle areas that she knew well yet they themselves were unfamiliar with, such as she did up the Combahee River for Col. Montgomery. She was employed by Union generals like Sherman, Stevens and Hunter. Brigadier General Rufus Saxton said of her, "She made many a raid inside the enemy's lines, displaying remarkable courage, zeal and fidelity." During the war she decided to make one last trip south because at that point the southern states appeared to be getting the upper hand and it was by no means certain that the north would be victorious. More states had split from the Union and were sympathetic to the Confederate cause.

Her last mission was to try and rescue her own sister and children still enslaved, but for some unknown reason she was unsuccessful. Ben wanted to find out why and try to make the rescue successful; after all, having rescued numerous people unknown to her, these were members of her family. There must be something they could do. The more he read about the horrors of slavery in the south, the more he wanted to make a small difference, particularly for a woman like Harriet, a woman to whom many eminent politicians of the time testified to her selfless courage and willingness to encounter more perils and hardships than any other person to serve the enslaved people of the American states.

"Well, I never..." Harry was speechless, almost, and used the distraction to try, nonchalantly, for another cheese straw. Slap! "Ow..."

"Harry Hobbard, I told you!" shouted Beryl.

Harry nursed the red mark on his arm.

"They are for the shop. You can have one later if there're some left over." The others had a laugh at Harry's expense.

"That's an interesting story, Ben my lad," said Harry.

"It does seem a good reason for a trip, Harry, doesn't it?" remarked Oliver.

"Yep, I reckon it does."

"Can I bring my pistol?" asked Charlie.

"No, you can't!" shrieked Ben.

"Aw..." Charlie moaned with a sour face.

"I think Ben's right, Charlie; that might not be too clever," said Oliver.

"But I haven't got any ammo for it," he protested.

"You're still not taking it. Start pointing that at someone during the Civil War and you might get yourself shot at."

"But what if we are captured by Indians?"

"We're not going to get captured by Indians, Charlie; not unless you do something stupid, of course. Which is why you should stay here," said Ben rather forcefully.

"Now come on, Ben, he's not that bad," said Oliver reassuringly. Charlie grinned smugly. The look that Ben knew normally won people over.

"You haven't lived with him like I have," sniped Ben.

Harry stood up. "Come on, you two, you can get on better than this."

"And if you don't, I'll make you kiss and make up myself," laughed Beryl, putting her arm around Ben. She picked up a tray of heavenly smelling cakes and went through to the shop. The thought of kissing his brother made Ben straighten up and squeeze in his face like he was sucking a lemon. Charlie recoiled at the thought too.

"Okay, okay, but no gun."

"All right, Ben."

"What sort of stuff you gonna need for this one then, Oliver?" asked Harry, rubbing his hands together in a joyful fashion.

"Well, we're going to need to make a list."

Harry turned round and pulled open a drawer in the large pine dresser that was behind him and rummaged around for a pen and a pad of paper. "Right, you call it out and I'll write it down." Harry noisily scraped his chair back into a position for him to lean on the table and start writing some notes.

"Money – we'll need some US dollars. Clothing

for the boys; I think I may have some in the shed that will be suitable for me from the time I tried to help the Pinkertons find the Jesse James gang, but I will need a US Army officer's uniform. "We'll try Adam's place first for our clothes," said Oliver looking at Ben.

Adam McRoy ran a theatrical costumers in town called 'Rock the Boat' and as well as the shop, he had a massive warehouse on the outskirts of town where more vintage clothes were stored. Adam often supplied film and television productions with a wide range of period clothing and he was an old friend of Oliver's. Adam at one time had started to learn to fly with Oliver but his busy work life sometimes involved him travelling all over the world sourcing clothing and so he never found the time to complete his training. Oliver got his clothes at bargain prices and in return he would occasionally take Adam up for a flight in his aeroplane.

"If not then we'll ask Emilie if she can help; we'll need to see her for the money anyway." Harry didn't look too impressed at that idea and his face displayed the look of someone who had just swallowed a dose of some particularly disgusting medicine and his mouth displayed an inverted smile. Just then, for no apparent reason, a cool breeze flowed through the kitchen and flicked up the paper of Harry's notepad. Harry looked for an open window and slapped down the fluttering paper. Oliver felt it too and looked around knowingly.

Seeing Harry's displeasure at the thought of going to Emilie's, and knowing full well why Harry didn't like going there, he asked, "What's up, Harry?"

Noticing Harry's displeasure at the thought of it, Charlie piped up eagerly, "I'll go."

"I'll show him where to go," Ben said quickly, having already had the pleasure of Emilie's sense of humour.

"That's fine. I'll take Charlie with me. We'll go together, eh?" said Oliver and dug Charlie in the ribs with his elbow.

"Well, we'll need to go there for a map as well as the money. She's got a great collection upstairs in the map and atlas room and she's bound to have some books on the American Civil War too. Ben, can you look into the detail of where this woman was before she set off on this last trip?"

"Yeah sure, I'll borrow a book from the library at school. I can do that next week."

Beryl bustled back into the room from the shop. "How you lot getting on, then? Got a list 'ave you, 'arry?"

Harry waved a piece of paper in the air.

"When's it to be, then?" she asked.

"Can we go tomorrow?" asked Charlie eagerly.

Oliver smiled. "We're going to need a bit more time than that to get ready."

"Can't we get it all today and you come round in the morning?"

"Didn't you hear, Charlie? I've got to get a book from school and look up where and when we need to arrive. Doh. We can't just go blasting off not knowing that, can we?" said Ben snidely. As the older brother by a few years he liked scoring points over Charlie

18

whenever he could, but the next minute he'd love him to bits.

Although he was the smallest in his class, and known as a 'widdler', Charlie was a bright lad and had an amazing vocabulary for one so young and was also good at mental maths. Another of his attributes was coming up with cunning plans to get his own way – aided by his butter-wouldn't-melt-in-his-mouth smile. What he was lacking in stature he more than made up for in guile. When the moment presented itself Charlie could wind Ben up as easy as a spider spinning a web, and he loved doing it!

"No, Charles my boy, maybe next weekend? This afternoon, if your mother is okay with it, we could go into Cheshampton and visit Emilie's Emporium and see if Adam can help with the clothing for you guys."

"And George too?" Charlie added excitedly. "I've never been to the Emporium, but Ben said it's got lots of wicked stuff there – real cool!"

"Oh yes, real cool. Cool enough to give you the shivers," said Ben with a knowing smirk. "And watch out for the snake, Charlie!"

"You never said anything about a snake before."

"I don't always tell you everything, bruv."

Charlie liked wildlife and was a so-called eco-warrior at school and encouraged the environmental 3Rs at home after coming top in the project in class. Reduce, re-use, recycle was his motto, but this also turned him into the family's biggest hoarder of junk! However, he hated snakes, slowworms and even harmless garden worms – a point not lost on his big brother. Especially the time Ben found a nest of slowworms living in the top of their compost bin. Following his discovery he'd suggested the next time the 'dirty bucket' – the name given to the bucket kept under the sink for holding the food waste before taking it to the compost bin – needed emptying, that Charlie should do it. When the time came, Ben could hardly contain himself and stood at the kitchen sink watching Charlie go to the composter.

"What are you doing, Ben?" asked Laura inquisitively.

"Oh, nothing, Mum, just looking." It was better than Ben could have expected. As soon as Charlie removed the lid and peered in, he jumped backwards with a loud shriek, tripped over and spilt the contents of the bucket all over himself. It wasn't called dirty bucket for nothing – full of food in the early stages of decomposition on its way to slime land. Ben roared with laughter. Charlie scrabbled to his feet and ran back to the house. It didn't take long for Laura to put two and two together and send Ben out to clear up the mess.

It was worth it, he thought to himself.

Charlie was nearly in tears from the fright.

"There are no snakes, Charlie," said Oliver reassuringly. But he knew what Ben was referring to.

"Is George busy on the farm today?" asked Oliver.

"Yeah, he's helping his dad cut and load up wood for the winter," said Ben.

"Ah, I wondered why he'd not come with you. And how are your mother and sister – they both well?"

"Yeah, they're fine. Mum's taken V to friends for a couple of hours this morning; something about arranging a birthday party for them together."

"Is it young Olivia's birthday soon, then?" asked Harry.

"Yes," chipped in Charlie, "it's not next week but the one after that."

"Oh, that's nice," beamed Beryl. "Would your mum like me to bake a cake for her, a lovely chocolate one perhaps?"

"Ah, my Beryl likes making a birthday cake, she does, don't you, my dear?" Beryl had suddenly taken on an even more cheerful look than normal at the thought of making a beautiful birthday cake. She wobbled her way across the kitchen muttering away about what she would do. Ben looked at her, rather bemused – *batty.*

"What about you, Harry? Have you got anything planned for this afternoon?" enquired Oliver.

"No, I'm off duty this weekend; Fred Harman is picking up and dropping off the post today."

"Well, why don't all four of us go into town, you drop Charlie and me off at Emilie's, then you take Ben to see Adam about some outfits?"

"That's a good idea. I've got some things I'd like collectin' too; I'll give you a list, 'arry," said Beryl and jollied herself across the kitchen to use Harry's pen and paper. Charlie regained his excitement about going to town, but stole a sideways glance at Ben, trying to figure out quite what he'd meant.

21

"You boys better get back home for some lunch and we'll see you around two o'clock; how's that sound?"

"Great," said Ben. The sound of four chair legs scraping across the stone floor reverberated around the room like nails on a blackboard. Oliver winced.

"We'll see you later. Come on, Charlie." They rushed outside and jumped on their bikes to race home.

Chapter 3

Dressed only in shorts and tee shirts the boys enjoyed their eager ride home, although Ben maintained a small lead over Charlie all the way. The trees displayed multi-coloured leaves down Rock Lane as their tyres crunched over the surface throwing up wisps of dust that spiralled into the air. Laura had commented to them only the day before that now they lived in the country she noticed far more the gradual change of the seasons than when they lived in a town. The gradual change was all around them here, whereas in the town you only seemed to become aware of the autumn change when the trees appeared naked of leaves. Previously she seemed to miss the bit in between – one moment the trees would be in full green leaf and the next they'd be completely barren. Winter had arrived.

This was their first season change in their new home – from summer to autumn. The boys didn't fully appreciate it but she surely did. It reflected the pace of life here, slow and steady, yet purposeful; each season had its significance. In the town it was just a rush from here to there, as abruptly and quickly as possible. It was that sort of rushing about that had killed her husband and denied the children of a father.

Here, though, they were safe from that danger, here they were safe to ride their bikes around the village; it was calm and peaceful. Olivia could walk down the lane to where she was learning to ride a pony without the fear of being run over by a lunatic two minutes late for work. They also had a massive garden to play in and build camps or dens or whatever they liked. Although the house was going to take a while to bring up to date, there was no rush. They'd also met some very nice people in the village, including the Hobbards and Oliver Bramley – who'd been introduced to Laura as their nephew – who was staying with them for a while. Of course the boys knew otherwise but they maintained the pretence with their mother.

He'd been kind enough to come up to the house and had taken the boys to show them over the old airfield. Oliver had reassured her that since the farmer, Ted Tyrrell, had bought everything – land and buildings and whatever was in them – from the Ministry of Defence, all it was used for now was grazing sheep. He told her that Ted parked up some farm equipment in a couple of the old hangars, but that was all. He conveniently failed to mention his prized possession that was stored in another. That might take a bit of explaining, with more detail than he'd wanted to go into at the time, so he overlooked bringing it to her attention!

★ ★ ★

"Hi Mum!" they both shouted as they clattered through the house.

"Good timing, boys; go and wash your hands for lunch. Give Olivia a shout too please; she's in her room."

"What's for lunch, Mum?" asked Ben. He was always ravenous, yet somehow never put on any weight, although he ate like a T-rex whenever there was meat on the table!

"Sausage sarnies and salad."

Ben's face went from elation when he heard the word 'sausage', to resignation when he heard the word 'salad'. But he still replied cheerfully, "Okay." Ahead of him he could hear Charlie shouting V's name and instructions for lunch.

Minutes later a loud crash from the bottom of the stairs followed by a howl of pain emitted by Charlie announced the boys' arrival back downstairs. Laura was only mildly disturbed from preparing lunch as Ben entered the kitchen followed by Charlie with a sour puss of a face on.

"Ben always has to win, Mum. It's not fair. I was winning till he pushed me out of the way. I think my leg's broken." Ben half looked over his shoulder unconcerned, and laughed. Observing Charlie's feigned limp Laura dismissed the idea of a fracture.

"O' course it is, Charlie," Ben sneered.

"Oh, come on, you two. Is V coming?"

"Yeah, she's just looking for Babbit." Babbit, however, was already sitting in V's chair at the table.

"Has anyone seen Babbit?" said a sorrowful V as she entered the room.

"He's in your chair, darling," said Laura, placing a large bowl of salad in the middle of the table. Olivia picked him up and twirled the ribbon that adorned his neck around her fingers and slid onto her chair. They all had their own place at the table, an unwritten rule that had begun soon after they'd moved in to Pegasus Ride at the beginning of the summer holidays. "I think he'll soon need a wash, dear."

"No, you can't do that again, he doesn't like the washing machine," protested Olivia as she clutched him even tighter.

"Well, he's getting pretty grubby and is beginning to smell like Charlie's armpits when he's been avoiding the bath."

"Urh, he does not!" Olivia shouted.

"Really, V! You like cuddling Charlie's armpits?" laughed Ben, screwing his nose up at the suggestion.

"No, I don't. It's not like that." Charlie lifted his arm and pretended to sniff. V slapped his arm down. Both boys had forgotten their argument and started giggling and teasing V.

"Well, he does smell a bit, dear, and I do need to give him a wash." Babbit spent so much time being cuddled under V's chin and nose that he inevitably soaked up any dribble or nose juice than ran out when she had a cold. So, unsurprisingly, eventually he began to pong a bit, as well as his natural white colour fading to grey.

A plateful of sweet-smelling sausages placed in front of them changed their focus of attention and Ben was first to dig in. "So what have you boys been up this morning? Did you find George?" asked Laura as she cut some slices of bread.

"Yeah, but he was busy on the farm, so we went down to the shop and saw Mr Bramley and Mr and Mrs Hobbard," replied Ben.

"And how are they?"

"They're fine and Mrs Hobbard was doing some baking so it smelt lovely in the kitchen."

"Yeah and she slapped Mr Hobbard for trying to pinch one of the cakes," laughed Charlie.

With his mouth still working its way through his third sausage, Ben asked, "Mum, can me and Charlie go into town with Mr Bramley and Mr Hobbard this afternoon?"

"What's that for, then?"

During their race home the boys had been making up a story to tell their mother as a cover-up for what they were really up to. Charlie would have to use his best innocence and charm to blag it; Ben often looked too guilty to get away with a lie. His mother would spot a ruse from Ben a mile away. His face would give the game away, but he could back Charlie up much more easily.

"Well, Mum..." Charlie slowly began, "Mr Bramley, or Oliver as he keeps telling us to call him, says that he knows someone in town who runs a sort of charity shop or somewhere with lots of clothes in it, and they've got some cowboy and

27

Indian outfits we could have, for playing in – down the garden."

"Really, Charlie?" questioned Laura.

"Yeah," he continued excitedly, "the guy asked Mr Bramley, Oliver, if he knew any kids who might be interested 'cos they needed to get rid of them."

"Get rid of them," repeated Laura.

"They got a load from a film company or something and haven't got room for them all," said Charlie with the innocence of an angel.

Laura thought it sounded a bit odd but not beyond the realms of possibility.

"Oh, I see," she said, not entirely convinced.

Ben stepped in, "We were telling him last time how we were making a fort in the garden, so when his friend mentioned the costumes, he thought of us."

"I thought it was a tree house you were building?" said their mum.

"Ah, yeah… a tree house fort… sort of place," stated Ben, staring at the last mouthful of food on his plate before unceremoniously shovelling it up, desperate not to make eye contact with his mother.

"And V and George are the cavalry, I suppose," said Laura widening her eyes and looking in Olivia's direction.

"What?" said Olivia. She'd not been paying much attention to the story and was still sulking a bit from being teased about Babbit.

"Nothing, dear; your brothers are going in to town this afternoon to get dressed for the Wild West of our back garden."

"Oh, can I come?"

"No, there's not room in the car and anyway you'd get bored," said Ben.

"No I won't," she quickly replied.

"I think it's best you stay here, V; we can find something to do." V looked disappointed but was used to her brothers doing things together without her and didn't put up much of a fight.

"Is Mr Hobbard taking the post into town, then?" asked Laura.

"No, he's not on duty today," replied Ben.

"Oliver said he would take me to the Emporium, to try and find a book on Wild West forts, while Ben goes to the charity shop with Mr Hobbard," said Charlie excitedly as he tried to wipe away the food on his face, that had missed his mouth, with the back of his hand.

"Oh, going to that old junk shop again as well. Quite an afternoon you'll be having. I hope you haven't been bothering them too much; I'm sure they have other things to do but run you two around."

"It's all right, Mum, Mrs Hobbard wanted something picked up from town anyway," said Ben confidently. It was mainly true of course so he could face his mum on this one without fear of an expression that would give her cause for concern, but it was their trip in the first place that had prompted her to ask them to collect the items!

As they were finishing their lunch their mother asked, "What time are you being picked up?"

"Around two o'clock." It was already one-thirty.

"Well, help me clear these things away and then you can get ready."

"I am ready," quipped Charlie.

"Can I have my pocket money?" asked Ben.

"Me too?"

"You, Charlie Green," his mother said pointedly, "haven't done your chores – your bed's still a mess and your clothes are all over your bedroom floor. And—"

"I'll do it, Mum, I promise. Pleeease…" he begged, showing her his dappy wide-faced grin, the grin that Ben knew would get Charlie what he wanted.

"Okay, but make sure you do."

"Yeah, Charlie!" sniped Ben. Laura went to the large pine dresser, picked up her purse and gave them each their week's pocket money. A few minutes later there was a loud knock on the front door.

Chapter 4

The semaphore-style trafficator popped out of the side of the *half-timbered* Morris Minor Traveller – so nick-named because the rear half of the car was constructed with an external varnished ash timber frame rather like a medieval house – and indicated a left turn. Moments later the gleaming automobile with the bulbous bonnet swooped round the gentle curve into Church Street and past the quaint tuck shop. To the right, bold wrought-iron gates protected the brick-arched entrance at the foot of a four-storey tower and, like the wings of a great mansion, the timber frame of Cheshampton Grammar School spread out either side. Whitewashed rendered wall panels infilled the gaps of the black oak frame, interspersed with diamond-patterned leaded lights. The jetty of the first floor was supported on ornately carved buttresses with several projecting dormer gables in the roof giving a foreboding appearance.

"I went 'dere as a boy," said Harry, nodding at the window. "Dey says the rooms in the roof are haunted – by a maid that fell down one of the narrow staircases that lead up there and broke her neck." The boys craned their necks to see up to the roof. Charlie had thoughts of the face he was sure he'd seen at the little window in the roof of Pegasus Ride.

"A penny for them, Charlie?" asked Oliver.

"What?" said Charlie, wrinkling his nose.

With one arm over the back of the seat, Oliver laughed. "Penny... for your thoughts?"

"Oh, nothing." He knew Ben would only make fun of him again if he said anything about the vision at the window

Opposite the far end of the school building – where the road narrowed to a single lane – three barrel-bellied, red-faced, rugby-shirt-wearing locals were tripping out of The Wessex Arms pub; Harry jumped on the brakes and swerved to avoid hitting one who almost fell into the road.

"England is playing this afternoon," said Oliver pointedly. A huge flag of Saint George hung from a first-floor window of the public house with more revellers bursting through the narrow doorway.

Further down, just past a thatched cottage that would have looked at home in a fairy story, Harry slowed the car and turned left into Chantry Lane. He finally stopped a few yards from the junction where the pavement was a good foot above the road level and adjacent to Emilie Bracket's Emporium.

"Mind the door as you get out," said Harry. He was very protective of his treasured Morris Minor, a car he'd owned for over forty years. Most Sundays it was treated to a hand wash and wax until you could see your face reflected in the paintwork. Cleaning and polishing the *Moggy* – as it was affectionately known – was his second most passionate pastime – next to being in his garden.

Oliver gently released the door, stepped out and then tipped the seat forward to let Charlie out from the back of the car. Unseen by them, a face at an upper-storey window of the Emporium attentively watched their arrival.

"Enjoy the Emporium experience, Charlie!" said Ben, smugly. Charlie slammed the car door shut – Harry winced as if feeling the pain of being slapped hard across the face. He let out a short sigh, then selected first gear and drove off. Ben knowingly grinned at Charlie through the back window as Harry drove away.

"Why did he say it like that – enjoy the experience?"

"Oh, don't worry about him, Charlie. Come on, let's go and see if we can get ourselves some dollars, eh?" Oliver guided Charlie up the red brick path leading to a large weathered oak door studded with prominent square-headed nails and a very purposeful looking wrought-iron door handle in the shape of a ring. Similar to a number of other Elizabethan buildings in the town, the top floor of the timber-framed building jutted out over the ground floor. Most of the windows were small leaded lights except for the two main shopfront windows which had larger panes of glass offering a customer a good view of the variety of things you could find inside.

Charlie paused to read a sign at the top of the left-hand window. 'Emilie Bracket's Emporium'. And beneath the name was written, 'Artefacts old and new – available only to a privileged few'. As Oliver turned the handle on the door Charlie asked, "Are we privileged, Oliver?"

"Oh, I think we might be, Charlie. Let's hope so anyway, eh," he smiled.

Charlie followed Oliver through the creaking door. He turned to close it, but it closed by itself, which for such a heavy door was unusual. The first thing that grabbed Charlie's attention was the smell; he flared the nostrils of his little button nose and involuntarily took a big sniff. It reminded him of the time his mum had taken them to see her great aunt. Someone who Charlie thought looked at least three hundred years old – with skin as wrinkled as the dried-up dead frog he'd once found in the garden – and sticking out beneath her dress were legs that looked like those of a chicken!

When they'd arrived his mum had told them that it was furnished exactly the same as it was when she had been taken there as a little girl, which in Charlie's mind would have been at least the Victorian times. He'd even asked his mum once, quite genuinely, if she had met Queen Victoria. Which, as she was only in her mid-thirties and that comment would have made her over ninety years old, she wasn't too pleased about!

The mustiness of old carpets sliced deep into Charlie's sense of smell and he wondered if old people lost their sense of smell as well as sight and hearing. At that moment he remembered a comment his mother had made about his great aunt – that she had found it difficult to bath or shower, so she washed up as far as possible and down as far as possible. There wasn't any mention about the bits in between getting washed!

The sound of their footsteps on the stone floor echoed down the dimly lit hallway that led from the front door. Not far from the door there was an alcove on the left with a shop counter adorned with an unattended, elegant, sparkling silver cash register, with a little notice propped on top saying 'Cash only'. Behind, a rough-looking door, hung on large, crude, handmade iron hinges, led elsewhere. A few steps further on Oliver placed his hand on a doorpost on the right and swung in. "Hello… Emilie?"

Charlie was right behind him when he felt a cold waft of air pass him.

Moments later, "Oliver!" The call of a happy female voice behind them nearly made Charlie pee himself. He spun around and saw the figure of a woman in the passage standing in front of the cash register they had just passed. No sound had been heard from either of the two doors behind them, but there she stood. She had long fine silver hair and a pair of glasses hung around her neck on a silver chain and she was wearing a blousy flower-pattern dress that reached the floor. A grey woollen shawl was wrapped around her shoulders, pinned together with a silver brooch. He looked up, down, around and nearly fell back onto Oliver. As Charlie studied her, a thin smile spread across her pale, delicate face.

"Emilie, there you are." Oliver was unfazed and stepped past Charlie to embrace her.

"How are you, Oliver? Are the Hobbards looking after you well?"

"Oh, yes, a bit too well… with Beryl's cooking, if you know what I mean!" he said, patting his stomach.

Emilie chuckled.

"And you?" he enquired.

"Well, you know, just the same as ever, keeping an eye on things. Floating about here and there," she said with a wry grin and the peculiar hiss to her voice.

Out of Charlie's view Oliver raised his eyebrows and winked.

"Good," he replied.

"And this must be Charlie, I presume?"

What a weird voice, Charlie thought.

"Ah, yeah, that's right. Sorry, yes, Charlie, this is Emilie, Emilie… Charlie." Oliver swept his arm around Charlie to bring him forward to greet Emilie.

Charlie had lost his usual bold exuberance and hung back behind Oliver, but then stepped forward to shake her outstretched hand. *Rather bony and cold for comfort*, he thought and made it a quick shake before retreating behind Oliver again. He also wondered how she knew his name since they'd only decided to come a few hours before and Oliver had never mentioned anything about phoning her but he reasoned he must have done. Charlie wasn't to know but she didn't possess a phone. She didn't need to.

"Anyway, Em, I was wondering if you had some–"

He didn't get a chance to finish his sentence. "Yes, I have." She turned around and picked up an envelope from next to the cash register. "Will these do?" Emilie pulled out a wad of notes from the envelope and handed it to Oliver. He held the bunch of notes in one hand and flicked through them with the other.

"Great; these should do the job." In his hand was about two thousand US dollars; more than enough he thought for the time they were travelling to.

Charlie was confused. His little head was spinning. Firstly, how did this lady appear behind them from nowhere, and how did she know what Oliver wanted before he asked for it? And, when they walked past the counter not a few moments before, he was sure there was no package on the counter next to the till.

Oliver slid the money back into the envelope. "What were the other things you wanted?" asked Emilie.

"Maps and–"

Again he hadn't finished when she interrupted. "Yes, yes, of course, the maps and books; follow me." She slid past Oliver and Charlie down the corridor. Charlie made sure he was following Oliver and not the strange lady. It was not much further down the passage before a narrow doorway on the left led to a steep staircase taking them up to the upper floor of the shop. At the top they passed through several little rooms before she led them into what looked like a library of maps – floor to ceiling and wall to wall with maps. "We should find what you need in here. North America, wasn't it?"

"Yes, Em, that's right, around the mid-1800s."

Emilie put her glasses on her nose and rubbed her slightly pointy chin. Charlie's eyes never left her. "What about those?" she said, pointing with a bony finger to behind her visitors. Two folded maps on the fourth shelf seemed to stick out further that the rest. Oliver reached over and pulled them off the shelf. No sooner had they opened one up to read it, and while Oliver and Charlie were still looking at it, she pointed over their heads and said, "And that one."

Another map, this time in the next bay of shelves on the third level, appeared proud of the others on the same shelf. Charlie was convinced that they'd been all level with each other when Oliver had removed the first ones. He quickly turned to face Emilie. Without giving anything away in facial expression she just innocently said, "Will they be okay, Oliver?"

After a moment's silence he replied, "Yes, yes, they're just right, just what we needed."

"Oh, I am pleased. Come this way – let's see if we can find any useful books for you."

Again Charlie was open-mouthed at what had just happened and the way she silently moved from room to room, yet Oliver seemed oblivious to it. Certainly nothing seemed to surprise him. Charlie had long got over the smell of the place and was glad that he was here with Oliver and not Ben. As they followed her into a larger room surrounded with bookshelves she suddenly turned to Oliver and said, "You'll find some books on the American Civil War over there," pointing at a shelf that seemed more illuminated than any other. Then, suddenly, for no apparent reason, she said, "Someone else needs me downstairs."

Charlie looked for the source of light but as Emilie left the room it seemed to fade away. "She must have good ears," commented Charlie.

"What?"

"The lady – she must have good hearing; I didn't hear anything," said Charlie.

"She'll like that, being called a lady, but you can call her Emilie." Oliver was not really paying much attention; he was busy pulling out books on the American Civil War to look at. Without thinking, Oliver continued reading and then said, "Oh, she always knows when someone needs help," then flicked some more pages over.

"Uh…" Charlie grunted, staring at the vacant space where Emilie had been standing and cocked his head to one side to listen for footsteps on the stairs – he heard nothing.

"This is probably a good one," announced Oliver. "*The Road to Freedom – An Odyssey of the American Civil War*; this covers both the subjects we need."

Charlie started reading some of the other book spines on the shelf and pulled one out. "How about this, Oliver?" The book's title was *Untold Stories of Slavery Escapes*.

"Yes, Charlie, well done, that looks useful too." After spending some time checking through the remaining books on the shelf, Oliver gathered up a total of five books and led the way as they both headed for the stairs, with Charlie carrying the maps. Oliver led the way down another, wider flight of stairs that turned through ninety degrees halfway down with a small open doorway leading off the landing in a different direction. The walls of the stairwell were made of dark oak panels, with one which seemed to be hinged to form a door for the passage beyond. It was a low-ceilinged, dark, narrow corridor that Charlie couldn't resist having a look into.

He leant forward through the doorway and peered into the darkness; the rest of the building seemed reasonably well lit, but this was a windowless corridor that only led to more darkness. Oliver was nearly at the foot of the stairs yet Charlie still took a few steps into the passage trying desperately to see where it led, straining his little blue eyes as far in front of him as they would go. For some reason he pursed his lips and blew a little whistle, maybe for comfort, but the sound disappeared into the hollow silence. As his eyes adjusted to the darkness he could just make out that the ceiling at the far end appeared to drop down towards the floor. He took another couple of steps and saw that it led to another set of descending stairs.

Then, at the far end of the gloom, two small greeny-yellow lights appeared near the floor – like night-time road-marking lights. Charlie looked around to see who may have switched them on. He took a step back. Then, in an instant, they raised from the floor and rushed towards him and before he had time to move they flashed past his ankles. Charlie frantically stumbled back out of the passage, tripped over, and dropped the maps. Lying in a crumpled heap on the stair landing he caught sight of a black cat disappearing down the stairs at lightning speed. Although his heart was racing, blood drained from his head and he began to 'sweat like a pig', as his mother would say. Just at that moment there was a call from beyond the bottom of the stairs. "Charlie!"

He needed no further encouragement as he was already on his way down the stairs, minus the maps. He didn't so much run down the stairs as slide his feet over each step in his haste to get down. At the bottom he found himself in a small square room with three doors – the one on the left was marked private, ahead was a room that looked to be full of old pictures and to the right was a short passage. "Oliver!" he called.

The reply led Charlie through the short passage and into the far end of the corridor that led to the front door, and there Oliver and Emilie were chatting near where they'd first met. Charlie panted his way to the pair of old friends.

"Are you all right, Charlie?" asked Oliver. "You look like you've seen a ghost." Unseen by Charlie, Emilie gave Oliver a poke in the back. Oliver smiled. The black cat appeared from behind Emilie and casually curled its body and tail around Oliver's legs like an old friend.

Charlie took a step back, his chest heaving, unsure of his encounter with the cat a moment earlier. Noticing his apprehension, "Was it Postal who gave you a fright, my dear?" Emilie hissed.

Starting to brave up a bit, "Yeah, yeah, he just made me jump a bit – that's all," said Charlie. "He… err… jumped out on me… on the stairs."

"The Rectory passage was open when I came down, Em," said Oliver.

"Oh, that's where he's been; he goes after the moles, you know."

"I thought moles lived underground?" said Charlie.

"That's right, my dear, they do," replied Emilie.

"But–" Charlie started.

"Don't worry about it, Charlie; where are the maps?" asked Oliver.

Charlie pulled a downward smile, "Err… oh. I dropped them." Oliver looked at him in expectation. "I'll… I'll go and get them."

As Charlie hesitantly walked back down the corridor Emilie called after him, "Be a dear and close the Rectory passage door, would you?"

He passed through the small room with three doors, pausing thoughtfully as to what might lay behind the one marked private, and crept up the stairs quietly with a slight increase in his heart rate. Moving even more slowly as he reached the open door in the wood panelling he peered inquisitively in. Darkness stretched before him and the passage seemed to echo silence. It gave him the shivers. Charlie fully stepped up onto the landing and reached for the door. *Why would there be moles down there?*

After closing the panel door he realised there was no obvious handle to open it again – a secret passage to where, he did not know. And right now he had lost his appetite to find out! Without dwelling any further, he gathered up the maps and hurried back to Oliver.

"Well, thank you again, Em. I think we've got everything for now."

"Would you like to come through to the kitchen for a cup of tea?"

"Thanks, but I think we should be going; I expect Harry will be along soon." Probably best, thought Oliver, as Charlie would find Emilie's kitchen a little strange to say the least!

"My pleasure, my dear; you know you're welcome anytime." Emilie leaned forward, embraced Oliver and gave him a kiss on the cheek, which he returned.

Charlie made a move for the door to avoid a similar fate and grasped the metal ring to open it. He didn't look back but strode down the path towards the road. As Oliver closed the door behind him there was a toot on the car horn from Harry as he pulled up in Moggy. Harry and Ben had a selection of clothes in the back ready for their trip. After a journey that was not long enough for Charlie to recall all his experiences in the Emporium, Harry dropped the boys back at Pegasus Ride. They took their share of the clothes and left Oliver his and the books, money and maps. They were to meet the next weekend for the trip.

Chapter 5

The week had gone slowly for Charlie but today, Saturday, he was full of excitement. In the kitchen the boys were at the window looking skywards but the sun was obscured by a grey veil with a hint of rain. Ben opened the back door and stepped out into a light breeze for a better look and felt the slight chill of an autumn wind swaying some of the treetops. Charlie went to join him but Ben ushered him back inside.

"So what do you think, Ben? Will it be all right?"

"Be all right for what?" asked their mother as she entered the room behind them with an armful of laundry, which she dumped on the table.

"Er... Oliver was coming up to help us with the tree house," Ben stammered hastily.

"I thought it was going to be a fort now?"

"Yes, that's right, Mum. He's going to help us make it," said Charlie quickly.

"You didn't say he was coming today. What time's he coming?" she replied hastily.

Since he'd arrived in the village Oliver had been to the house a few times, to help with a couple of things Laura couldn't manage on her own. She liked his pleasant and relaxed nature. He was also cheerful and very knowledgeable and strangely seemed very at home in her house.

"He said around ten, after he'd helped Harry out at the post office."

"Goodness me, that's less than an hour; you'll have to give me a hand to tidy up. I don't want him seeing us in this mess." Laura never liked anyone coming in unless the house was neat, clean and tidy. Country folk weren't always that particular – not deliberately untidy, just more relaxed about it – "Take us as you find us," she'd heard, "there're more important things in life." But Laura wasn't ready, not just yet, to succumb to that way of thinking.

The kids called it *emergency hoovering* – the panic clear-up before a visitor arrived. Laura felt she was on trial for her housekeeping skills anytime someone visited them. And today she had just discovered Oliver was coming, a man she would like to impress. Being rather isolated she mainly had the kids for company, who she dearly loved, of course, but it was refreshing to get adult company for a while – especially with such a nice man. Soon the house was buzzing with activity and it wasn't long before the drone of the hoover could be heard vibrating the floorboards and beating the dust into submission!

The noise of a vehicle with squeaky brakes pulling up outside announced the arrival of Harry and Oliver. Oliver grabbed his old leather holdall from the back seat and was followed out by George, then he closed the door and waved Harry goodbye.

"They're here!" shouted Charlie as he rushed from the lounge to the front door. Just as Oliver reached for the knocker Charlie pulled the door open, beaming a great smile from ear to ear.

"Hi Charlie!"

"Hi. Come in. The others are in the kitchen." Charlie turned and led the way, George followed and Oliver closed the door behind him and followed Charlie through to the back of the house.

Subconsciously Laura smoothed down her top and skirt, then tousled her hair and gave her head a little shake. She checked her reflection in the black glass door of the microwave – then, suddenly, it inexplicably dinged and the light inside came on. She jumped back and hit herself on the back of a chair, which spoiled her composure just as Oliver entered the room. Confused about how it had come on, Laura fumbled with the switch to turn it off.

"Hello, everyone," said Oliver.

"Hi," said George, raising his hand.

Laura stared at the impertinent machine and then readjusted herself. "Hello, Oliver, good to see you." She stepped forward and gave him a gentle embrace. A kiss would have been a bit far at this stage as she'd only met him a few times but they were both relaxed in each other's company now.

"Hello, George."

"Hi, Mrs Green!"

Oliver did the grown-up thing of rustling his hand through Olivia's hair as she was sitting at the table. She still smiled though. "And how's Olivia?" he asked.

"I'm fine, thank you," she politely replied.

"Would you like a cup of tea before you start?" Laura enquired.

"That would be nice, yes, thank you." Oliver pulled out a chair, sat down and dropped his bag on the floor. The boys joined him at the table. Laura picked up the kettle and carefully turned on the tap slightly to fill it through the spout. Keeping the spout under the gentle flow of water she turned around to address Oliver. Suddenly, for no apparent reason, a great gush of cold water squirted out of the tap and within seconds Laura looked like she'd just stepped out of the shower!

"Ahhhhr… blast!" she shouted. "I wish it wouldn't do that," she exclaimed as she fought to control the tap. She'd now definitely lost her composure and nearly her temper, and she reached out for a towel.

Oliver rubbed his chin thoughtfully. "Would you like me to take a look at that?"

"Oh, would you? Not now though, but when you have some time. I know you're here for the boys today." She wiped her face and dabbed at her soaked clothes. "It just seems to do that now and again; there doesn't seem to be any reason for it. It never happens to the others, just me." After a few moments she returned to the miscreant tap and finished filling the kettle.

Oliver knew just where to look but he couldn't say. Not just now anyhow.

"I'm very grateful to you for helping the boys; I'm no good at building things and they so want to finish their... well, whatever it is."

"It's my pleasure, Laura," he replied with a smile.

Without any further mishap Laura delivered Oliver a fine cup of tea, just how he liked it, strong with no sugar. The boys milled around the kitchen waiting in eager anticipation to get off down the garden while Laura and Oliver chatted about how the weather had been and other small talk. Charlie sidled up closer to Oliver and peeked in his cup.

Oliver smiled. "I'm nearly done, Charlie."

He downed the last of his tea, well, nearly all of it – a habit he had from childhood was to leave the last few dregs in the bottom. Tea leaves – the dread of getting a mouthful of tea leaves that lay hidden in the bottom had scarred him since he was a boy. It was ridiculous, of course, because now everyone used teabags! But it was a habit too engrained to change. "That was lovely. Thank you, Laura."

"Oh, that's no trouble," she said with a big smile and feeling more at ease now. "And you boys do what Oliver tells you, okay?" She paused and then more firmly said, "Charlie!"

"Yes, Mum," he said, not too convincingly, as he skipped out of the back door first, followed by George.

Oliver bent down, picked up his bag and looked towards Laura. "They'll be all right, I'll make sure of that."

"It's just that Charlie doesn't always concentrate on what he's doing; he gets distracted by his own imagination and storytelling sometimes."

"Yes, I've noticed Charlie never tells a short story," laughed Oliver.

Laura smiled. "See you later."

Then he left to join the others in the shed down the garden.

★ ★ ★

When they'd first arrived at Pegasus Ride the two sheds in the garden had been engulfed in green overgrowth, having been left unattended for years. Green algae had covered the windows, and the buildings had almost totally been reclaimed by nature and were secured with rusty locks and rusty hinges on the doors. During the week following their arrival, Ben and Charlie had hacked away most of the brambles and Virginia creeper that clawed its way over roofs and cleaned off most of the window algae. The first shed they'd named 'Charlie's Den' and the second they had christened 'Ben's Den' and each had a crude hand-painted sign over the respective doors to state the ownership.

Charlie's Den was like the best and the worst collection of car-boot and garage-sale antiques. It was a cavernous shed with a higgledy-piggledy collection of furniture: tables of all sorts, cupboards, a dresser, a large dark-coloured wardrobe of dubious African origin with an inset full-size mirror. A few old chairs were also dotted about. The wardrobe was filled with clothing from all ages of history and the cupboards contained old artefacts that would have been more at home in various museums. On top of and underneath the tables, boxes were stacked full of things that intrigued the young inquiring mind. Since they'd discovered it, Ben and Charlie had spent hours searching and sorting through the amazing collection and apart from throwing away some old rusty tins of food, they'd just tidied the rest up a bit.

Ben's Den was essentially a workshop, which suited him. Many tools, mainly for woodworking, hung neatly on shadow boards along one wall, with a long wooden workbench, with a vice fitted on one end, beneath. A tall stack of narrow drawers were labelled and equipped with measuring and marking equipment and other tools a carpenter would use. Ben had tidied up and swept clean the floor and bench since he'd claimed ownership. So far they'd mainly used it to cut up wood and make things for the tree house. Although Ben had woodworking classes at school, his skills were still fairly basic and he was keen for Oliver to show him more.

Ben and Charlie had already built a rough platform about ten feet up a tree that stood towards the back of their long garden. It was mainly made from old pallets that they had obtained from the farm where George lived. From a distance Oliver admired their sturdy start on the construction and nodded in approval, although the old, rather rickety, wooden ladder that was home to more than one family of woodworm wasn't really safe. It was a bit iffy, he thought to himself, when *he* last used it and that was over ten years ago!

★ ★ ★

"Looks like you've made a good start, boys," said Oliver, "but we'll have to get something extra done to show your mother, so that she still believes it's the reason for me being here."

"Yeah," said Charlie excitedly, "but first we'll go on our mission, right?"

"Let's get inside first."

Ben was first to enter Charlie's Den, followed by Charlie and George. Before he entered, Oliver glanced back towards the house and caught sight of a face at each of two windows – one in the kitchen and one at the small loft room window. The kitchen face disappeared quickly, as if not wanting to be caught out looking, but the other continued her gaze, smiling – he felt happy.

Although Oliver had been to the house a few times he'd never had reason to venture down the garden to see what they'd done with the sheds.

"Wow, this is a bit tidier than when I last left it!" he said on entering – it really had been a long time.

"Yeah, we threw out some stuff that we didn't think we would use," said Ben. "I hope you don't mind?"

"And the cobwebs!" said Charlie.

"No, well, I'd been meaning to for some time, before… well, you know, and well, it's yours now, I suppose."

Oliver heaved his bag onto the table with a loud thud. It was a light tan colour with two handles and opened at the top along its whole length. It reminded Charlie of the type he'd seen a doctor use in a film and he expected a stethoscope to be extracted! The boys waited in eager anticipation of its contents.

Oliver rubbed his hands together. "Right, the first thing we have to do is some work on your tree house building."

"Aw… I thought–" started Charlie, but Oliver interrupted.

"No, we have to look as if we are working on it, at least to start with for a little while. Then, we can go on the trip, yes? See if we can find Harriet."

"Yeah!" the boys replied unanimously.

"What have you got in the bag?" enquired Charlie with a grin.

"Hmm…" teased Oliver, "let me see." Leaving the bag firmly closed he rubbed his chin as if his memory was eluding him. Three silent faces waited for more. Oliver smiled and released the catch holding the top together – it sprung open and a book, maps and notepad were pushed out by the clothes wedged in beneath. "Just the stuff we got from town last week."

Oliver picked up and opened his notebook. "Right, well, when we are ready to go this is what we'll do. I looked at the book Ben dropped off the other day and the ones we got from Emilie's and I worked out where best to start. We will need to go to a place called Hilton Head, South Carolina, in 1862. There we'll find a hospital where Harriet Tubman is working as a nurse – she was there for some time helping to look after the wounded Yankee troops. I'll fill you in on the detail later but we will have to get changed into the clothes we got from Adam before we go. I've got the money in the bottom of my bag. Ben, can you take the maps and book in your satchel?"

"Sure." And he grabbed the leather bag off the nail it was hanging on and placed the maps and book inside.

"But first, let's get a bit of tree house built!"

Chapter 6

After around an hour of tree house construction activity, which involved mainly going to and from Ben's workshop, and measuring and cutting lengths of wood, Oliver decided it was time to go. "Okay, Charlie, can you nip in and tell your mum we're going over to Ted Tyrrell's place to get some longer timbers that I know are in one of the hangars? He said it was fine for us to have them."

"Yep, sure." And he was gone in a flash.

Within ten minutes they were in the old hangar standing alongside Jenny ready to go. Charlie had the pilot's helmet in his hand and was the last to climb in the cabin of the old biplane. Before he climbed up into the pilot's seat Oliver reminded Charlie one last time what to say.

"It's okay, I've got it," he replied, and pulled the helmet down over his head.

"Where to today, Captain?" asked the voice of the helmet.

"We would like to go to Hilton Head in South Carolina in the year 1862."

"No problem. It's Charlie, isn't it?"

"Yes, it is."

"Okay, well, you sit back and we'll be off. Is Captain Bramley with you today?"

"Yes, yes he is."

"I thought so; that is wonderful. The old team, well, new-old team, I suppose!" said the soft female voice.

Then, for the first time, Charlie thought he heard Jenny chuckle. There was an especially cheerful tone in her voice today. The old aeroplane spluttered into life and rolled out of the hangar and onto the airfield. After a bit of a wiggle she was lined up and ready to go. "Ready, everybody?"

"We're ready," replied Charlie. Oliver looked down into the cabin and gave a thumbs-up sign. The engine revved up and with a loud roar they started to rumble across the grass – the tail came up a bit first, and then a few seconds later they were airborne.

★ ★ ★

One of the many secrets about Jenny was the fact that while she was on a special mission, no one could see or hear her unless they were one of her passengers. Parked up in her home-based hangar behind Pegasus Ride anyone would just see her as an old biplane.

The hieroglyph burned into the floor of the cabin – following Oliver's selfless rescue of the old man in the desert – spelt out the enchantment. The symbols he'd seen appear in the floor after that journey had had far more meaning than he could have ever realised initially. The significance of the person he'd saved, or thought he'd saved, even the act of attempting to save such a person, he'd not appreciated. Why would he? At the time he thought the old man was just a helpless soul in the middle of the desert. At first the magic eluded him.

Oliver wasn't to know that the old man was a trusted disciple of the Babylonian god, Shamash, God of the Sun, who should have taken more care of him, as it is he who protects the poor and travellers. But the old man had split his loyalties between Shamash and the God of Love, Inanna; it had gone on for years. On that day, Shamash had ignored the old man's troubles and allowed the attack to continue. When Oliver intervened, just because it was the sort of thing he would do, Inanna witnessed the whole episode. Unable to help and protect Naram from the attackers, Inanna appealed to the ruler of all gods, Apsu, to help – just as Oliver appeared on the scene.

Apsu decided that Naram had helped so many people over the centuries that he would bring him to the land of the gods for eternity and bestow on Oliver, and his machine, the ability to carry on Naram's work. The book Naram held so tightly, the ancient *Book of Everlasting Life and Goodness*, together with the symbol of Ankh he wore around his neck and Naram himself, were transported to live beside the gods. The power of the book, however, remained on earth – embodied in Jenny. Apsu used the power of light to bring Naram to his side and transfer the power of his book to Oliver's aeroplane. The transportation by the brightest light on earth embossed a rune that précised Naram's book in ancient hieroglyphic signs into the floor of Oliver's aeroplane – endowing the aircraft with new power.

Originally the symbols meant nothing to Oliver, but he got an old school friend, who'd become an ancient language professor at Oxford University, to decipher the ancient writing signs for him. Before modern writing, as we would recognise it, evolved, pictograms were used throughout Egypt and the region called Sumer where Babylon stood. The significance of the transliteration took some time to sink in and it was not until he'd returned to his home in England that he ventured to use its power. His friend assumed that some of his RAF ground crew had been playing an April fool joke on him, and didn't take it seriously. They'd been in Egypt for some time and could have concocted the array of hieroglyphs and used hot metal to burn them into the floor. Oliver soon found out differently. He knew something strange had happened that day when he returned to base with the stranger in his aeroplane, because ever after he heard a remote voice in his head, or rather through his pilot's helmet.

It was a soft female voice; a voice he thought, quite irrationally, might be that of his mother, although he'd never heard it. A mother he never knew as she'd died two weeks after he was born. Florence Alice gave birth to Oliver but sadly died of septicaemia following complications after the delivery. It was Inanna who gave Apsu the idea of blessing the craft with Florence's voice. The God of Love, recognising the love Oliver had and the guilt he carried for his unknown mother, gave him a connection, albeit him being ignorant of the truth and reason.

Ever since the day the old man mysteriously disappeared from his aeroplane in a blaze of light, the voice from above had spoken to him and asked if he wanted to go anywhere special. On a mission of mercy, anywhere in time. On that day the light had appeared from within the aeroplane, but for Oliver the power of light to travel in time came from outside – Enlil, the God of Air and Earth, provided it.

The hieroglyph was titled with the hieroglyphic signs of a sword and a long-beaked bird which translated to 'aa akh', meaning 'great helper', and underneath was the symbol of the scarab beetle, meaning eternal life and resurrection. It also mentioned that Oliver would pass into the second holy world of his birth to serve the many for eternity as long as he followed a divine path. Oliver wasn't particularly religious but was always helpful to anyone less fortunate than himself and lived by the ethics of his Christian upbringing.

The rune, however, did contain – amongst other things – one warning: not to bring people with him from the past to his world of the living through the power endowed upon him. A warning that later events would lead him to ignore but today he was off on another trip, this time with his newfound assistants!

★ ★ ★

Up, up and away they soared, higher and higher, away from Rosemie Common and through the low layer of grey cloud that obscured the autumn sun. It was clear above, as far as an eye could see, and the air was smooth too with no turbulence to rock the old aeroplane. For a few minutes whilst they climbed even higher and flew towards the distant horizon everything was calm but gradually the power of the sun dimmed and a surreal quietness descended upon those in the cabin. It grew darker and darker as they approached a huge cloud that seemed to appear from nowhere.

Sight of the cloud below disappeared and then a deep grey fog surrounded them. It felt eerie but they all knew what to expect now. It was just a matter of time as Jenny flew on straight into the heart of it. Flash! A bright light surrounded them. Flash, again, piercing through the aeroplane, illuminating everything to the brightness of a thousand flashlights. The floor also shimmered in a glowing light as if it might be on fire. Inside the cabin they shielded their eyes from the dazzling lights as did Oliver too in his open cockpit above them. It lasted only a short time before the lightning faded and they flew out the other side of the huge cumulonimbus-type cloud and into bright sunshine where calm settled on the aeroplane once more.

Down below was a huge unending ocean one side and a coastline on the other. As they descended they could make out a number of islands along the edge of the mainland with several river tributaries going inland. Jenny swooped gracefully down towards one of the bigger islands and landed in a large field of short scrub grassland. She rolled to a stop and the cabin door popped open. Oliver climbed down from his cockpit position and joined the boys at the rear of the aeroplane. Ben handed him his leather bag with his uniform, notebook and cash in.

"Thanks," said Oliver. "Have you got the map?"

"Sure," said Ben. He opened up his satchel and passed Oliver the map.

"Wow, that was great," said Charlie excitedly, with a big grin on his face. Oliver put down the bag and opened up the old map. His eyes scanned it for a moment.

"I could see on the way down that we need to head that way to the army barracks and hospital," he said pointing over the other side of Jenny. You could almost smell the excitement in the boys, eager to find Harriet, nudging one another repeatedly. "Now, remember, we are on the side of the Yankees, the northern states, at the moment, which might have to change later. And we are looking for your uncle – George's father – who was reported wounded and taken to this hospital. What's his name, Charlie?" Oliver asked, testing him.

"George Cotterell," he said proudly. The boys laughed.

"That's right; my alias last time. I thought it would be easy for you to remember!"

Chapter 7

The walk to the hospital took them about half an hour across several fields and then onto a road leading towards the town of Hilton Head. The hospital, as well as a fairly large brick-built building, was a massive collection of tents and temporary structures that had been put up to house soldiers wounded in battle. They were amazed at the size of the camp. No one took much notice of them wandering down the road in front of the main building: three kids and a bloke in civilian clothing. A picket fence surrounded the camp and Yankee soldiers were stationed outside the main entrance, which seemed quite a hive of activity, with carts coming and going and, obviously, by the sounds coming from them, carrying injured soldiers on the way in.

They pondered for a moment on the opposite side of the road to the main entrance and then Oliver led them across and approached one of the guards.

"Who is it you be looking for, sir?" answered the private guarding the main gate, behind which stood an imposing brick building. "His name is George Cotterell," replied Oliver.

"Which regiment?"

"He was under General Sherman."

"And why do you wish to see him?"

Oliver pulled George forward. "He's this boy's father and uncle to these two," Oliver said, gesturing to Ben and Charlie.

"Okay, son, what's your name?"

"George, sir."

"Right, I'll be a moment." The soldier disappeared into a small office behind him. After a few minutes he reappeared with a piece of paper in his hand.

"I'm sorry, I can't tell you where exactly you might find him, but any of General Sherman's men are in blocks F or G. Of course he may not be here at all, I'm afraid; it's hard to keep track of everyone coming in. If there's a whole load at a time we just get 'em all in first and then worry about who they are later."

He handed Oliver the piece of paper and then asked to check in his bag. Good job Charlie didn't bring his gun, which might have looked suspicious. So might the two thousand dollars, if the soldier had opened the envelope, but he didn't.

"That's your pass to go round the hospital," he said. "If you find him let us know and we can enter it in our log."

"Sure thing," replied Oliver and they walked on through a large archway through the building into a courtyard beyond. "Right, so far so good, kids."

"Shall we split up?" suggested Charlie.

"No!" replied Ben before Oliver had a chance to say the same.

"No, Charlie, this is a massive encampment; it's best we stay together, at least for the moment." Of course they had no intention of heading for blocks F or G just when a passing private stopped to ask them where they were looking for.

"We're looking for my uncle in block F or G," replied Charlie. Ben glared at him in the demeaning way he did when Charlie annoyed him.

"Oh right, guys, you gotta head through there," he said pointing through another archway, "and then straight on past the water tower and the large wooden hut on the left marked 'Surgery'. That's the surgeons' shed, you can't mistake that; don't listen to the screams, that's the worst – the screams, sometimes all day and all night when they're busy. You'll also see the boys daubed the words 'Cutting Room' on the walls." The soldier shook his head before he continued, "Then turn right down the next lane between the tents and you'll find F and G down there."

"Thanks," replied Oliver with a bit of a false smile, thinking maybe he should have done this part on his own. The boys just looked at each other dismayed.

"Each of the blocks has a hut with a porch in the corner of the plot for that letter, where the doc and nurses of each block are based and the worst of the injured in their care. Behind that you'll find a cookhouse in another shack but the men recovering from their injuries mainly live in tents."

"Thank you very much."

Oliver led them towards the archway, and then the soldier shouted back to them, "The best place to start will be to ask in the block house; they know who they've got. The names are all pinned up on the wall."

"Well done, Charlie," said Ben forcefully. "We're not really looking for our uncle – doh! Bean head."

"It doesn't really matter, Ben; we've got to start somewhere," said Oliver as they passed through the archway and were faced with the sight of an enormous sea of tents and huts. The view was accompanied with a rich aroma, one the children would be unfamiliar with – that of rotting meat! The stench filled the air and from somewhere, as they walked along, every now and then, they'd also be treated to a waft of stinky toilets – Charlie and George pinched their noses.

"Smells like our toilet after grandad's been in it!" said George screwing his face up even further. Charlie laughed. The boys didn't realise what the rotten meat smell was but Oliver knew very well where that was coming from and he decided not to enlighten them that it was human flesh! The amputated arms and legs of soldiers were dumped on a heap before being buried at some point – until then the flies and maggots had a feast.

Just before the water tower was a hut marked with a large letter D hanging from the rustic veranda. "Okay, boys, we'll start here."

"I thought we were going to find 'F' first," said Charlie.

"Explain to him will you, Ben, while I go in," said Oliver with a little exasperation in his voice. After a few minutes Oliver re-joined them outside. "This is going to be easier than I thought," he said.

"You found her?" asked Ben.

"No, not yet, but just as the soldier said, all the names of the patients, nurses and doctors are pinned up on the wall for all to see." Ben looked on attentively while Charlie and George were ribbing each other about something. "The orderly guy in there asked me who I was looking for but not before I had quickly scanned the list to check for Harriet's name under the list of nurses and that there wasn't a real George Cotterell!"

"Yeah, that could be awkward," said Ben.

"One down, fourteen to go." They moved onto the next block house but this time they all went inside, in case the orderly wasn't as occupied as the first and Oliver didn't have time to scan the list before speaking to him. No joy there either though.

As they walked past the surgeons' hut an almighty scream rang out from within which made them all jump. Then the door opened, allowing the volume of the scream to increase, and an unconscious man was carried out on a stretcher and under the cover of a heavily bloodstained sheet they could see he had no legs. These were the days of little in the way of anaesthetics, save a dash of some alcohol, and often none was available. During an amputation the men were given something – occasionally a bullet – to bite on, to stop them biting off their own tongue whilst the surgeon hacked off a limb. More men died during the Civil War from infections, disease and malnutrition than the direct effect of battle.

Many of the nurses were untrained volunteers doing whatever they could to help, with very little equipment, and for some the shock of the condition of the wounded soldiers was too much for them. But not for Harriet, although from a slave background of ill-treatment, whether the soldier was black or white they received the same loving care as she could give. She was Hilton Head Hospital's equivalent of Florence Nightingale. However, at times she was seconded by the military to either go on an undercover spying mission or lead an assault to attack in areas where she knew the countryside well. Oliver knew this and hoped they hadn't arrived at a time when she was away.

Oliver hurried them on to the next block house – block house F. No joy. The kids' morale was beginning to sag a little and some of Charlie's earlier excitement was beginning to wane too. The next nearest block house they came to was actually H and not G, but they all trooped in anyway. The desk orderly was busy talking to someone when they entered, so they all started to read the lists. One doctor for around one hundred and fifty men and the names of ten nurses to assist him. In an instant they saw her name. Charlie and George got wickedly excited but just about refrained from jumping up and down.

"Morning, sir," the man behind the counter said, nodding his head, "what can I do for you?"

Oliver made a little cough to clear his throat. He hadn't really rehearsed this part. Should he ask for her outright? He hadn't got a reason for that in his head; that's why they'd made up George Cotterell. He didn't have an answer for the 'why do you want to see her?' Blast, what an idiot! His time for thinking was over because Charlie had started and Oliver was too late to stop him.

"We're looking for Harri–" Charlie started. Ben glared at him and George tugged at his shirt. Charlie looked at George. "Oh, no… I mean–"

Oliver took over, feeling it was about to get worse. "This boy's father was nursed back to good health by a woman called Harriet, Harriet Tubman, I believe," he said rubbing his hand over George's head. "We wanted to say thank you and we have a small gift for her."

"Well, son, you've come to the right place. Our Harriet is a wonder, to be sure," the orderly replied in a strong Yankee accent. "She's one of my chief nurses sir, an' no doubt 'bout it." He then leaned over the counter closer to Oliver, turned his head slightly sideways and whispered loudly, "Trouble is, the dammed army keeps pinching her for other things. Darn it, she's better than a lot of the doctors round 'ere," he said, making sure the one not far behind him couldn't hear his comments.

"Yes, their father said she was the best he'd had," said Oliver.

Then the orderly stood back upright and asked rather directly, "You not in the army yourself, sir?"

Oliver was ready for this one. "Oh, yes, I'm just on leave from Sherman's regiment for a short while."

"Oh, I see." He nodded. "Were you at the Battle of Shiloh?"

"Uh huh."

"My goodness, you lost a lot of boys there, terrible battle that was, awful. We had some come back here after a while to recover from their wounds; some will never be the same in the head after Shiloh," he said, proudly saluting Oliver.

"Yep, we all learned a sad lesson there and saw things no man should have to see," replied Oliver shaking his head. The orderly stood with a long sad face reflecting for a moment on the men he'd seen return from that battle.

"Sir," said Ben, bringing the conversation back to what they wanted to hear, "where could we find her?"

"Of course, I'm so sorry." He looked down at a sheet on his desk. "She's doing tents ten to twenty today." The orderly explained where they were and with that they left the block house in search of tents ten to twenty.

"Thank you, sir, much obliged," said Oliver.

The tension in the group was electric. Ben felt a shiver run down his spine, Charlie and George grabbed each other excitedly, while Oliver ushered them outside before something unwanted was said. Charlie whispered something in George's ear as they stood on the veranda outside the office before Oliver led them round the corner to their destination.

Chapter 8

After a short walk passing the open flaps of several tents where men either sat or lay on makeshift beds they came to one with a number ten painted on it. Oliver halted. Number ten was on the corner of a plot with a lane branching off to the right where he could see number eleven pitched and more beyond. "Okay, guys, this looks like the place we'll find her. Ready?"

"Yep," replied Ben and the other two nodded.

As they stood in a moment's contemplation a short stocky woman matching Harriet's description appeared from inside a tent some four or five pitches away. She carried a wooden tray and a linen bag hung from her shoulder and she paused for a couple of seconds before walking towards them.

"Excuse me," said Oliver approaching the woman, "are you Harriet?"

"Yeser, I am, dat's my name, ser," said the woman in the long black dress.

"We've come to help you," said Ben with a big smile.

"'elp me, young'un, ole Harriet 'ere, in dis 'orrid place? 'tis no place for lads likes you."

The boys spread out in a half circle around her. "No, madam, not here, not in the hospital."

"O de Lorde, nobody des call me madam, tis Harriet's my name," she laughed.

Oliver looked around nervously. "Is there somewhere we can talk, out of view?"

Harriet's posture changed to one of caution. Who were these strangers saying they wanted to help her? Help her do what? "Der be an empty tent ower der, sir," she pointed. Harriet was more than capable of looking after herself, so she had little fear of a man and three boys – just mystified as to their intentions.

Out of view in the tent Oliver introduced him and the children and explained that they had heard tales from her good friend Frederick Douglas of her missions to free slaves. As soon as his name was mentioned she relaxed completely. They also heard how she still desired to rescue her sister and her sister's children from captivity.

"Does worry me greatly, Mister Oliver," she said. "De south seems to be winning dis war, an' if it does, oh glory be, sir, nufing will be good 'bout dat, sir. But I can't leave dese ere soldiers; dey be fighting for people like me, sir. Dey sufferin' some'in' terrible too, sir."

"That's why we're here," said Charlie taking her hand. "We can help get your sister." The three boys were now standing in front of Oliver opposite her, witnessing tears starting to seep out the corners of her eyes. She wiped them away quickly.

"How you gonna do dat, den?"

"We roughly know where to look but we need your help to guide us."

"I'll need da good reason to leave ere, sir," she said, addressing Oliver.

"Please call me Oliver and the boys by name; we are all friends together."

"Yesser, Mr Oliver."

He thought that would have to do!

"I can sort that out," Oliver said. "I've got a military uniform and I'll make up a request from General Sherman to have you released for an army mission. We've got money, maps and Charlie," laughed Oliver, and he squeezed the lad by the shoulders. "And with you as well, we could be the second 'Famous Five'!"

Harriet looked bemused.

Ben shook his head. "Never mind," he said.

They sat on the empty bunks and spent ten or so minutes working out a plan. Oliver would return later in the day in his Yankee Army captain's uniform, which was in Jenny, with a request for him to escort Harriet to Sherman's command headquarters. She said the guards changed at 2.00pm but Oliver would not return until she was due off-duty at 4.00pm when it would be a bit cooler as well. The sultry heat of the day was getting to them all. There was not a cloud in the sky to shade the burning power of the midday sun. Harriet gave them a canteen of water to quench their thirst and take with them until they returned. They exchanged smiles and handshakes before leaving the tent.

Harriet rubbed her hands together and buzzed with excitement almost as much as the boys. "I just can't believe it, that you would want help little ol' me like dis. De world sure can be a lovely place, full of surprises – ebrey day." A tear squeezed out and ran down her cheek but inside happiness filled her completely. She'd almost given up hope of freeing her sister. Oliver, Ben, Charlie and George left with equal joy and jollied their way back through the camp and then away to wait until it was time for Oliver to return.

★ ★ ★

Looking every bit a soldier of the Yankee Army, Oliver rode up on a bay horse he'd acquired, with another in tow for Harriet. He approached the guardhouse and asked for Harriet Tubman and gave the guardsman a handwritten note with the forged signature of General Sherman. It had taken a few attempts to get it about right, copying it from a textbook they'd brought with them on the journey.

"Yes, sir," saluted the private on duty, as he ran back into the guardhouse. Oliver had included the word 'urgent' in the message to make sure he wasn't delayed. An officer appeared at the door of the guardhouse, pulling his hat on as he approached Oliver. They exchanged salutes. Another private hustled out of the guardhouse, tripping as he did so, and ran into the main hospital building. When off-duty all the nurses lived in dormitories on the upper floor.

"So, what's she needed for this time, officer?" asked the man who'd obviously had more than his share of pork pies and not been close to a razor recently.

"Well, I can't say. You know how it is," said Oliver, in a slightly aloof manner.

His horse began to back away so Oliver gave a wriggle of the reins and a squeeze of the legs to move him forward again. The rotund officer hitched up his trousers and puffed out his chest in an attempt to increase his importance and stepped nearer to Oliver. Then Oliver beckoned him even closer and bent down to be nearer the man's height.

The pretentious officer raised his hand to cover the side of his mouth, looked around him and whispered, "Come on, you can tell me, we're the same rank, mutual trust and all that, yeah?"

Oliver moved to a whispering distance, whereupon the recipient of his message put his hand to his ear expectantly. "I could, sure." Oliver paused, looked furtively around. The fat man smiled.

"But then I'd have to shoot you – dead."

"Very funny. Oh yeah, comedian and cocky." The smile disappeared and he stepped back in distain and adjusted his hat and posture. Oliver held on to the reins in one hand and upturned the palm of his other, in a 'c'est la vie' gesture.

"I suppose you think you're better than me cos you're in the cavalry – Captain," continued the indignant officer, adjusting his ill-fitting trousers again.

"No, not at all, Captain," said Oliver sitting upright, "but the less you know about this mission the better."

"Dangerous, is it?"

"Yeah; actually, we'll be lucky to get out alive but there's some really important information needed," replied Oliver shaking his head. He cradled his jaw in his hand and sucked in a breath through clenched teeth. "Nothing personal but if we meet again it'll probably be because I need the help of your surgeons – or at least your doctors."

"That tough, eh?"

Oliver patted his chest pocket. "Let's just say I have a letter written already for my next of kin."

"Shucks, man, I didn't–"

Oliver didn't let him finish. "We all have our destiny," he said, raising his hand.

★ ★ ★

Although the journey could be very dangerous for Harriet, she never backed away from danger herself. Her unfailing belief in God, since a young girl, always carried her through. She was fearless to the point that one time she said, "No one will take me back [to slavery] alive; I shall fight for my liberty, and when de time has come for me to go, de Lord will let dem kill me." She totally believed that her Christian God would only let her be caught (by bounty hunters) or killed when he had no more work for her to do. Oliver had no intention of putting her in that danger. He knew full well she was desperately wanted by the Confederate Army and bounty hunters alike, with a big ransom on her head now, dead or alive.

Just then, Oliver saw Harriet being escorted out of the main building towards him. She carried a small fabric bag slung on a long strap over her shoulder. Not all Yankee people shared the admiration she received at the hospital but all those here knew her worth. Although he'd not received the information he'd wanted, the guardhouse captain assisted Harriet up onto the horse provided for her. "God speed and good luck, Harriet, for we need you back here when you can," he said raising his hat, as they both rode off in the direction of Bowville.

About a mile from the hospital they met up with Ben, Charlie and George in the shade of some trees. They discussed the route they would need to use to get to Maryland where Harriet's sister lived. They would take a train from Bowville through Charleston, and then on northwards to Richmond. From there they would need to go by horse and cart and eventually take the ferry across to Maryland. The train journey alone would take at least two days but the trickiest part was the fact that Charleston and Richmond were Confederate strongholds with many soldiers in the two towns. And Oliver couldn't travel through those places in a Yankee uniform! Luckily the boys had brought his civilian clothes with them from Jenny. But there was another problem. Harriet pointed out that the US dollars they had would buy the rail ticket from Bowville to Charleston but they needed Confederate state dollars to buy the tickets to Richmond.

Oliver threw his hands up. "I knew there'd be something," he said frustratingly.

Then, after a pause for thought, "Okay, Ben, why don't you and George go back and get some with Jenny," he said.

"Why me? It's supposed to be my adventure," he protested.

"Your adventure?" asked Harriet.

"Well, I read about you–"

"Where? Who's writin' 'bout me?" she interrupted.

"You shouldn't be surprised, Harriet, after the things you've done but I'll explain later," said Oliver, holding his hand up to carry on his conversation with Ben.

"I don't want to send one of you on your own and just think what might happen if Charlie and George go," he continued, and raised his eyebrows suggestively.

"It's always me," Ben protested, "cos you're such a twerp," he said glaring at Charlie and clipped him round the ear as he stood up.

"Who's Jenny?" enquired Harriet.

"She's… eh–" started Charlie.

Oliver cut him off. "She's a friend of ours."

"So, what is it we need?" asked Ben, as he pulled George up from the ground.

"I guess we'd better have a thousand Confederate dollars. Get Harry to take you to Emilie's for it."

"Wow, massa Oliver, dat's surely a lot o' money."

"Well, just in case, eh."

76

For Ben the thought of going to Emilie's was just sinking in. He was already muttering to himself about the journey to the weird Emporium; just the thought of it filled him with shivers.

"It'll be fine, Ben. Em will sort things out for you; trust me," said Oliver, trying to console him.

"It's not the sorting out that concerns me; she just gives me the creeps, that's all."

Charlie giggled. "It's all right, Ben, George can hold your hand." The tables were turned this time.

"To save time we'll go on into Bowville, get our train tickets and meet you on the outskirts of town in a couple of hours, okay?" The train station was the Hilton Head side of town anyway and Oliver pointed out a reunion point on the map.

"Got it." Ben scowled at Charlie and scuffed his feet as he and George set off for Jenny.

Ben had gone about twenty yards when Oliver jogged up behind him, put an arm around his shoulder and whispered, "It might be a good idea to get me a Confederate officer's uniform too, you know, from Adam. I think it might be useful if we're going through Confederate territory."

"Okay," he said grudgingly.

Oliver returned to where Harriet sat quietly bemused in the shade of the tree, waving the heat away. "Dese sure are some bright dittle kiddies you 'ave, Mr Oliver."

"Yes, they are rather special," he proudly replied as Ben and George waved goodbye from the distance.

Chapter 9

Back at Pegasus Ride, Ben and George trotted into the kitchen just as Laura was putting the phone down after speaking to George's mother.

"Ah, George, just in time; come with me, I have to take you home. I'm sorry, it's your father; he's had an accident on the farm."

"What sort of accident?" enquired George worriedly.

"I'm not sure exactly but somehow he got his arm caught in some machinery and he's been taken to hospital and your mother would rather you were with her."

"Where's Charlie and Oliver?" she asked.

"Oh, they've err… gone back over the airfield for some more timber," answered Ben. "We were going down to see Mr Hobbard. Oliver asked us to go and see him, to get us something."

Laura collected her bag and car keys. "Come on, George, let's get you home."

"Olivia!" she shouted. "In the car please."

Ben hung back.

"You might as well come too, Ben, and I'll take you to the shop after I've dropped George off." This was going from bad to worse. "Anyway, what do you mean, get you something?"

"Well… err, don't worry, Mum, I can ride my bike down and–" Before he could continue, Laura insisted they all got in the car. Ben and V got in the back and George sat in the front seat. In her rush to turn the car around she backed into a fence post, *crunch.*

"Damn!" It was the second time in a couple of weeks she'd put a dent in the car. The kids knew when to keep quiet! She swore a bit more then rammed the car into gear and sped off.

While their mum was out of the car taking George in to his house, V quizzed Ben. "What's up, Ben? Where are the others?" Olivia thought they might be going on some sort of trip but had been told they weren't, just working on the tree house, and anyway she was busy with Mum organising her birthday party stuff.

"We were supposed to go to that Emporium place in town and we were going to get Harry to take us. Now this has happened."

"Mum will take you there, Ben."

"Yeah, she will, but she'll also come in and want to ask questions – too many questions."

"Where are Charlie and Oliver?" she repeated.

"We left them behind to come back and get… what we were supposed to get."

"What do you mean, left them behind?"

Ben frowned. He didn't really want to tell her.

"Are they really getting some wood or have you all been away in the plane?"

"No!"

"Why are you so worried about Mum finding something else, then?" she said with a 'maybe I'll say something to Mum' look on her face.

"All right, yes, we came back in Jenny."

"I knew you'd gone off somewhere else. Is it exciting?" Olivia's tone changed instantly.

"Look, V, I just need to think a moment."

Their mum was hurriedly approaching the car.

She jumped in and slammed the door. "Now, what is it, Ben? What is it that you so desperately need from Harry?" she said rather impatiently. She strapped on her seatbelt and started up the car while he was still thinking what to say. "Come on, Ben, spit it out." A quick look in the mirror and she pulled away in the direction of the village.

"It was a special type of fixing Oliver wanted." He pulled out a piece of paper that Oliver had scribbled on, in case he got asked. He had prepared a Plan B for Ben should he need it – a request for an alternate diversionary item. "It's a–" Ben took an extra breath, "Spratt and Winglet double action brass butt hinge assembly. He thought that if Harry didn't have one, he wouldn't mind taking me into town to get one." He gritted his teeth at the last part because he knew his mother's likely reaction.

"A what? A Spat and Winkle double butt... never heard of it," replied Laura disbelievingly.

"No, Mum, a–" Ben tried to repeat it but was cut off before he got going.

"Anyway, you can't keep pestering the Hobbards, you know, every time you need something. I know they say they never mind but..." Laura was a very proud person and didn't like asking for help unless it was really necessary and certainly didn't want to be seen taking advantage of anyone's good nature. She had still not been in the countryside long enough to realise how much most country folk were more than happy to always help out whenever they could without thinking anything of it. They knew any favour would always be returned.

"Is it something you can get from town yourself, from the hardware store perhaps?"

"I suppose so but I'm not sure..." he continued with a grimace on his face unseen by his mother belying his will-she-believe-me look. "Oliver said it was a clever old type of hinge, so... maybe..." his voice was getting slower, "the Emporium would be a more likely place?" Laura didn't really listen to Ben, she just absorbed an overview of his reply. She had other things on her mind – worried about George's father. The injury caused by an incident with a baling machine sounded awful.

"Well, I was going into town anyway, so we can all go together." She indicated left at the junction and turned towards Cheshampton. While Laura concentrated on the driving Ben and V were having a whispered conversation in the back. Whatever happened, Ben had to get back – time was now ticking for Charlie and Oliver.

Laura parked up in the town centre car park opposite the tower of the old town clock. The tile-clad tower stood about forty feet high and chimed on the hour, as it had done for over two hundred years. Beneath the clock tower was now a small office, that of the solicitors, 'Cummin and Robyou'. It had originally been the home of the town fire station equipped with a horse-drawn steam-powered fire engine but had long ago been replaced by a newer fire station at the bottom of the high street. Although there was still a small sign above what would have been the entrance doors saying how to alert the firemen, and a hand-pull lever to ring the fire bell.

"Okay, Ben, you go and get what you need and I'll take V with me. Meet back here in about an hour, okay?"

Ben noted the time on the clock. "Okay, Mum," he said, relieved that there were no more questions. It only took him five minutes to reach Emilie's Emporium, just off Church Street opposite Chantry Green. He took a deep breath and braved the footpath to the front door, twisted the handle and stepped inside. Instantly the smell reminded him of his first visit, not vile or anything, just memorably musty. But this time there was also a hint of something strange in the air – a smell unfamiliar to him. Not unlike the fragrance he experienced once when his mother took him into an Indian-themed shop selling all sorts of wood carvings and stuff from that country. He thought for a moment – no, more like the smell of the herb garden at Kew when they visited. *Strange.*

He called out, "Hello!" and listened. Silence. He paused for a moment at the brightly decorated, yet unattended, cash register. Quietly he moved further on, as if walking on glass, all the while listening intently for signs of occupation. He paused again and turned his head sideways and wished he could hear like a bat and detect any movement like they do. But all he heard were his own footsteps as he went further down the corridor and called again, "Emilie!"

"Ben, my dear boy," she hissed. It got him every time; his heart tried leaping from his chest as the rest of his body exploded with adrenalin. He spun round in a fright to see her smiling at him from behind the silver cash register. Same dress, same shawl, same glasses hung around her neck.

Once his heart had resumed its normal size and position and he'd come down from the ceiling, he spoke, "Hello, miss."

"Please call me Emilie," she said, in her unusual voice that seemed to hang on to certain letters. A hollow, almost breathless voice. "I'm sorry; I didn't mean to make you jump."

Ben put on a brave half-smile. "Emilie," he took another breath, blinked, then continued, "Oliver sent me to ask for some… er, money. Some old American Confederate dollars."

"Yes, my dear, let me see what I have." Emilie reached down under the counter and picked up a small package wrapped in a piece of grey linen cloth and handed it to Ben. He took the package and couldn't help noticing the knowing look she had in her smile.

Slowly he unfolded the linen and inside was an old brown envelope. He opened the flap and pulled out the contents. A wad of Confederate dollars – to the value of one thousand dollars to be precise. The exact amount Oliver had asked for.

"Yes, yes, this is just what we wanted," Ben said excitedly. But how–"

Emilie held her hand up. "I just guessed. Was there something else?" she said knowingly.

Guessed, guessed! He repeated in his head. *She's one scary mind reader!*

"Well, as a matter of fact–" he paused, refolded the linen wrapping and tucked the package into his pocket. Ben was slowly becoming a bit more relaxed in Emilie's presence. Maybe he was getting used to her; whatever it was, his fear was giving way to caution. "Actually, there are two things I still need." Emilie looked on with a kind encouraging face and placed both hands on the counter. "I've got to go to a shop called Rock the Boat and see Adam McRoy–"

She cut him off without even hearing what it was that Ben needed, "Yes, my dear, you will need to see Adam."

"Eh?"

"Oh, yes, I'm sorry, do carry on."

"I was told to go to Adam's for a Confederate officer's uniform but I don't know where his shop is. I've been to his warehouse on the edge of town but not the shop," continued Ben.

"That's easy, Ben, you'll find it through a passageway under the clock tower, next to the parasite's office."

"Parasite's office?" Ben questioned, screwing his face up.

"I'm sorry, my dear, just a saying, I mean the solicitors. You'll understand when you're older." She smiled. "Adam will have what you want ready for you, I'm sure, when you get there. And the other thing?"

Ben thought, *How will he know what I want?* He pulled out the piece of paper and read, "A Spratt and Winglet brass double action butt hinge assembly."

"That's something I wasn't quite sure about but come this way, I think I may still be able to help."

How was she not sure about something I hadn't asked for? Ben became deep in thought again; a worried look returned to his face as the coolness of Emilie's presence sucked the heat from his nervous body. He looked furtively around for moral support but knew he was totally alone. His original nervousness had returned but he thoroughly trusted Oliver and it was he who'd sent him here. Emilie was very pleasant and appeared to be kind-natured but the mind reading spooked him. And that was not the only thing. He had no option, though, but to follow her.

Emilie silently led him through a small room full of African and other native traditional weapons, facemasks and shields, another with Art Deco-style effects from the 1930s, through a short passage and into a room of old-looking fixtures and fittings from the Edwardian and Victorian eras.

"Let's have a look round here, Ben," she said and laid a bony arm comfortingly around his shoulders.

Ben looked to his right and Emilie's spindly, frail fingers holding his upper arm and then down to a table displaying a load of things he hardly recognised. Most of the fittings were made out of iron or brass – some quite simple and others more complicated mechanical contraptions. Emilie turned to a collection inside a tall display cabinet. "What about these?" She opened the glass door enclosing them.

Inside were numerous pairs of hinges, ornately shaped and decorated. Ben picked one up but it didn't appear to him anything special; it bent backwards and forwards. He shrugged his shoulders. Then, tucked behind a long pair of black wrought-iron hinges, he saw a pair of more complicated brass hinges. Emilie had spotted them momentarily before Ben and her hand was already reaching out for them. As his hand reached the hinges her hand came down on top of his. He jumped and jerked his hand backwards. She laughed.

"I'm sorry, I didn't mean to–"

"No, no, it's okay. It's just… your hands are cold, that's all."

"Oh, that's because I have – what you could say is – poor circulation. I've sort of got used to it now."

"My gran says she has poor circulation. Do all old people have poor circulation?" Ben asked.

"Perhaps not as poor as mine but then they are probably not as old as me." She giggled.

"If you don't mind me asking–"

"I think we should get back to looking for your… well, hinge thingy."

Emilie lifted the brass hinge assembly down and handed it to Ben. He inspected the complicated hinge assembly and then turned over a small brown paper tag attached to one end and read, "Spratt and Winglet brass double action butt hinge assembly."

"That's what you're looking for, isn't it?" smiled Emilie.

"Yes, I suppose it is," he said turning them over to inspect them more closely and work out what they actually did. Then he realised Oliver's logic. If he'd asked for a normal modern type of hinge or fixing, 'for the tree house', there might have been a risk his mother would have taken him to the hardware store herself then there would have been no reason to go to Emilie's.

"Do you think it will convince your mother?" Emilie said cheekily as if she was in on the deception, and put her arm around Ben's shoulder again.

"She's got less of a clue than me about it," he laughed and held up the strange hinge assembly triumphantly.

With the trophy in his hand he started back to the passage leading to the front door, Emilie gliding silently behind him. Ben paused at the silver till and put his hand in his pocket to get out his wallet but Emilie gestured him not to bother. "As always, it's on Oliver's account."

"Thank you," said Ben with a gratifying smile. There was still something definitely weird about her and this shop. The silence, the smells, her movement and, most of all, her way of knowing what he wanted before he'd opened his mouth. His mother sometimes seemed to have the same mind-reading ability – she called it mother's intuition – but this was so much more than that. This was mind reading in advance; she wasn't just telling him of a silly number that he was thinking of, something he had seen on the TV; this was serious telepathy or something. He wasn't quite sure but in a strange way he was warming to her.

"Well, you'd better be getting along, Ben, they'll be waiting for you." He assumed she meant his mother and V but she didn't.

★ ★ ★

He paused for a moment outside the offices of Cummin and Robyou – 'Solicitors and Commissioners of Oaths' the sign said, but he still didn't get the joke. Alongside was the entrance to a passageway that originally belonged to the old coaching inn. A simply carved timber beam bridged the entrance above and a cobblestone roadway led through to the buildings behind. On the far side of the opening was a set of stone steps incongruously leading to nowhere. They were mounting steps for visitors to remount their horse in days gone by. The shop behind them was that of John Wood – the butcher. An old-style butchers with sawdust on the floor!

Ben walked through the passage, under some rooms above and found several shops around a courtyard inside. Adam's shop, Rock the Boat, was just where Emilie had said it would be. And sure enough, he had the garment ready for him in a bag behind the shop counter. When questioned he told Ben he had received a note earlier, in the old English handwriting he'd received many times before. To be booked to the account of his old friend Oliver Bramley. Ben didn't ask any more questions, just took the bag and left. He got back to the car park in good time and sat on the brick wall that surrounded a raised flowerbed outside the car park and waited for his mum to return.

About ten minutes later his mother arrived carrying two large bags loaded with shopping. "Did you get what you wanted, Ben?" she affectionately asked, appearing now to be in a more relaxed frame of mind.

Ben held up the two brass objects with a satisfying smile. "Yes, I did."

"And what's in the bag?" she said, loading her own into the boot of the car.

"Oh... I... err... while I was waiting I just popped into the shop where we got our cowboy costumes from and as it happened the man had another he said I could have."

"I'll have to go and meet this man who gives away clothes all the time; I could do with some myself," she laughed.

"They're only old ones, Mum," he replied as they climbed into the car.

"Well, you lot often rib me about being old and classic!"

They all laughed as Laura started the car to go home.

Chapter 10

As Laura packed the shopping away in the kitchen Ben told his mum he was off back down the garden to carry on with Oliver and Charlie. "Okay," she replied.

A few moments after Ben had left, V said she wanted to go and join them.

"All right, V, but don't get in their way; you know what they're like when they're trying to get on with something."

"I won't, Mum." She ran off and caught up with Ben halfway down the garden path. "Ben, Ben," she shouted, "wait for me!"

Ben turned around and painfully said, "What do you want?"

"I want to come too. You haven't got George now, so can I come instead?"

She knew the first answer would be no. She was ready for it. "Well, if you don't let me… I'll tell mum what you're really doing." The argument went on for a minute or so but Ben didn't want his mum seeing them from the kitchen window arguing and then coming down the garden herself, so he agreed to her demand. *Little brothers and sisters*, thought Ben; *why do you always seem to get your own way?* He huffed off down the garden with V in tow – observed, not from the kitchen, but from the little window in the attic.

★ ★ ★

On the journey Ben enlightened V as to the mission this time, to which she listened intently. It was not long before they landed at a spot just outside Bowville, near the main road track from Hilton Head. The cabin door popped open and let in the heat of the afternoon in South Carolina – warm enough to cook a cake! Ben had picked up an old cotton haversack from the shed, where he dumped off the strange hinges, on their way to Jenny, and carried this with him with money and uniform safely inside. Holding V's hand in a more resigned manner he looked for the spot where he thought he would find the others. Harriet had explained about a large, cranky looking tree with a split trunk that would be an easy place to spot.

And there it was, beside the roadway some hundred yards distant. As they approached, however, he could not see Harriet with Oliver and Charlie. Oliver and Charlie stood up and faced Ben as he and V approached.

"Hi," said Charlie, "where's George?"

"Where's Harriet?" replied Ben.

"Hi," waved Olivia and smiled, dangling Babbit by his ribbon.

Oliver looked a bit downhearted and sighed, "Well, it's not good news, I'm afraid." Charlie's welcoming smile had gone and he lowered his head and stepped back.

"What have you done, Charlie? You always have to go and spoil things!" Ben said, dropping V's hand and angrily waved his arms about.

"Calm down, Ben, I shouldn't have left him on his own. So it's my fault really."

"No, that's what Mum says," and then, mimicking his mother's voice, "it's not his fault, Ben, he's only small; you made mistakes like this when you were his age; yeah but I always got told off about it. Not Charlie, no, he–" Ben was disappearing down his own road of resentment for this side of his sibling relationship. He spun around and continued to gesticulate in all directions in what was turning out to be an endless moan. He took a deep breath to continue.

"Ben, Ben," Oliver protested, "let me finish!" He held out a hand and took hold of the boy. "I've got another plan, a plan to get her back."

"Get her back; where's she gone?" asked Ben abruptly.

"If you'll let me finish," Oliver said with a gasp and now a hint of a smile and a slight shake of the head.

"I didn't know he was a catcher," Charlie protested. He looked really sad, as if he were about to cry, his eyes growing bigger and shinier. Ben just looked at him dismissively.

"Who's caught her?"

Oliver sighed; he'd forgotten how difficult it could be to get children to listen when a group, of even only two, is in full flow! If only he were one of those clever people, those rare people, those undervalued people, he mused – a teacher – who could command the full attention of their class at any time. Respect! He'd never been a parent either, so this experience he was witnessing was not on his list of common and well-known experiences. So, ever the pacifist and not one inclined to shout, which he had heard parents use many times as a tool to resolve disputes – with limited success, he thought – he stepped back and waited, scratched his ear and observed.

The two boys continued for a few moments with half sentences, Ben attacking, Charlie defending, while V sidled round to stand next to Oliver and hold his hand. Oliver looked down at her knowingly and she returned the look with a shrug of her shoulders. Ben had not got an answer and was even more frustrated, and Charlie was now in tears, before they both realised they were the subject of a silent audience.

Oliver's expression with raised eyebrows said it all – finished? He hadn't really taken command in the way that a skilful teacher or parent might, but he now had their attention. "Why don't we all sit down and I'll explain." He offered a comforting arm to Charlie and a smile to Ben. "Now, while I went to get the train tickets, Harriet and Charlie went into a store to get some refreshments. Save a bit of time, I thought. However, while Harriet was talking to the storekeeper another man in there got chatting to Charlie. Or, I think it was Charlie who started talking to him first." Oliver looked down at Charlie.

He nodded. "Well, the guy looked like a real cowboy, leather waistcoat, hat and a gun in a holster on his belt and all." Oliver held his hand open and gestured a 'well, you know' sort of expression.

"Anyway, they're exchanging conversation and then he pushed his hat up and asked Charlie what her name was and what the two of them were doing together."

Ben looked at Charlie and closed his eyes.

Oliver squeezed Charlie's shoulders with his arm. "And of course, honest little blue-eyed Charlie told the man that Harriet and he were going to rescue her sister from slavery in Maryland. With that the man first pulled out a tattered piece of paper from inside his jacket and then his gun and took hold of Harriet. When I got back to the store all I found was Charlie sitting outside with a bag of provisions for our journey. So there was nothing I could do; Harriet had been taken. As Charlie said, Harriet had an army identity card displaying her name proudly and he had a piece of paper that was a notice of reward to return her to her owners."

"Why didn't you use the name we gave her, Charlie – Laura? We were going to call her by Mum's name if anyone asked who we didn't know – remember?" sighed Ben.

"I know, I just forgot." Charlie started to cry again. "He seemed like a nice man; he even let me hold his gun." Ben made the sighing sound of a slowly deflating balloon.

At the time there was great controversy over the whole slave issue; differing states of America had different laws, and the overriding federal law was being undermined by the Confederacy. What was okay in one state was outlawed in another. The Union Army, or Yankees as the southerners called them – who were effectively fighting to end slavery – occupied small enclaves and some larger areas of southern states, but the Confederate Army also threatened Washington, the Union capital. Within some of the border states even the people within the state often did not agree on how to deal with the slave issue. Should there be slaves or should they be freed? The agriculture of the southern states depended immensely on the army of people enslaved there and many landowners were reluctant to have to pay for labourers to bring in the harvests. They also felt that as they had bought slaves in the first place they were their property. Slaves were traded in market places like cattle and few people in the south thought anything wrong of it – except the slaves. So the bounty hunter walked off with Harriet unmolested.

★ ★ ★

"So, what do we do now?" asked Ben.

"Well, the good news is that he, the man with Harriet, is heading the same way as we were going anyway – Maryland. But he's got a head start as we couldn't go without you and George. Ur, well now, Olivia."

Ben got up. "Let's get after them, then."

"Yes, that's what we are going to do, now you're here, but we are going into Confederate territory in Charleston and beyond to Richmond, where they are more on the side of the slave catcher than the slave releaser. We'll have to come up with a plan on the way. Did you get the Confederate Army officer uniform?"

"Yes, and the money."

"Good, come on then, let's get to the train station and tell us what happened to George on the way."

Chapter 11

Bowville Station was a plain affair, no platforms as such, a ticket office, a waiting room and goods depository, and a telegraph office. There were several railway sidings where waiting trains could be marshalled before leaving on the single track north or south. They could see two locomotives in steam with smoke rising from their chimneys and men walking around the locomotives inspecting them, each waiting on a siding track. A bell rang somewhere in the station – near the telegraph office, they thought. A pair of dings on the bell repeated three times. Apparently it was the three-minute warning of the next train into the station. A man dressed in a railway company uniform paced up and down alongside the track in front of the main building shouting for people to clear off the track and stand clear of the line.

As he drew near, Oliver approached him. "Is this the next train to Charleston?" he enquired.

"Well, yessir, it should be. It should've been here an hour ago but the water tower at Shallow Creek had been shot out a bit and they had to suck up water from the river." He marched off shouting at some soldiers still milling about on the line outside the telegraph office. Then their attention was drawn to a louder bell, repeatedly clanging, coming from their left in the distance. And above some buildings and slightly around a bend they could see smoke squirting into the sky. As it got closer they heard the rhythmic beat of a steam railway locomotive.

Slowly the engine hauled the train of six coaches into the station then, with a screech of brakes and a loud hiss of steam, it ground to a halt. And finally the bell stopped clanging. The two boys stood in awe at the sight; like many little boys they loved *real* trains and for a moment forgot their reason for being there, just ogling the locomotive. It also seemed to allow Ben to let go of his anger and frustration at the recent events with Charlie; he put his arm around his brother's shoulder. "Wow, Charlie, isn't this great? A real steam engine."

"It's wicked, Ben, really..." He was speechless. One of the enginemen climbed down from the locomotive and started checking and oiling parts of the shiny wheel linkage in front of them. Standing close, it towered above them like a huge latent breathing monster of an engine. That was the difference between a modern train and this; this seemed alive, with steam hissing from various parts and heat radiating from the central boiler. It was said that engine drivers talked to their locomotives and they believed the loco talked back! As if it was a real living thing and not just an inanimate object.

After a few moments oiling the linkage the engineman turned around and went to the rear of the tender behind the locomotive – which had a massive pile of logs inside – and disappeared between it and the first carriage. Then, a minute or two later, he stepped back out into view and after a couple of shouts the loco pulled forward, slightly away from the carriages. As the man, dressed in a set of blue bib and braces, returned to climb the steps of the loco, Ben asked, rather concerned, "I thought this was going to Charleston?"

"It is, sonny; we're just going to pull up to get some water while they load the train." Having climbed the steps to the footplate he turned around and leaning over the side said to the gawping boys, "Would you like to come for the ride up there and back?"

"Wow, would we?" said a very excited Charlie turning to his big brother.

At that point Oliver and V joined them and Oliver heard the offer. They both looked at Oliver for approval. "Go on. We're going to get in the first carriage. Come and join us when you get back." It was good that Ben and Charlie were getting on okay again. It didn't usually take long and something like this would renew their bond.

With the loco refilled with water and reattached to the rest of the train, Ben and Charlie joined Oliver and V. After a few rings of the loco bell the train jerked into life and pulled out of the station.

"We got to do that," said Charlie.

"What?" asked V.

"Ring the bell!" he smiled. Gradually the train picked up speed but never got really fast, not by modern standards, but it was way faster than a horse could gallop. There weren't many people in the carriage with them so Oliver explained the plan he had in mind to retrieve Harriet from the clutches of the bounty hunter.

When they rolled in to Charleston it was early evening. This was a much bigger town and an important port for the Confederate cause. It was heavily garrisoned and protected by Confederate troops although, as Charlie pointed out, many seemed to be wearing worn-out clothes and not the smart uniforms of the soldiers they saw at the hospital. Luckily for them Harriet had already told Oliver of a safe house they could go to with her to stay overnight if they needed to.

The secretive movement of escaped slaves relied upon travelling from one 'safe house' to another. For actual slaves this usually meant travelling at night to avoid being seen. On her missions of mercy, Harriet travelled northwards at night using the pole star for guidance and they couldn't normally use the railways; they had to walk the hundreds of miles to freedom. There was a whole network of safe houses connected by well-worn routes. It was known as the Underground Railroad. The safe houses were code-named 'stations' and those who guided the people during their trek were 'conductors'. The existence of the system was known to the catchers; they just didn't know where the underground railroads and stations were and who the conductors were, although some had their suspicions.

They needed to find the home of a man named Edward Franklin, on Morgan Street. He'd only met Harriet twice before but knew well of her exploits and many of her associates. They disembarked the train and headed in the direction Harriet had given them, towards the dock area. Morgan Street was off Cumbernauld Road which was the main road to the docks. Morgan Street was a wide avenue lined with trees on either side and about halfway down on the right was a large white-painted house set back from a white picket fence. Nailed to a tree in the garden and facing the road was a sign, Sussex House. It was a gesture to the birth county of his parents in England. Edward was a Quaker lay preacher and a respected town businessman, a printer by trade.

Oliver ushered the children before him and then Ben knocked at the door. Footsteps approached from within and a middle-aged coloured woman opened the door.

"Good evenin'," she said and curtseyed before them.

"Good evening," said Oliver, over the heads of the children. "We are looking for Mister Franklin. Have we come to the right house?"

"Oh, yesser, you surely 'ave. Who shall I sey is wanting 'im?" she said politely with a slight lean of her head.

"He doesn't know me but I've got a message that is only for him."

The housekeeper looked a bit bemused but left them standing at the door and walked off shouting,

"Misser Franklin, Misser Franklin, ther's sommers to see yer."

"Who is it, Daisy?" they could hear.

"Dunno, sir, dey didn't give der name, jus says dey gotta message for you."

A little louder now they heard the man's voice say, "Don't worry, I'll go."

The face of a tall slim man appeared from behind the door. He wore wire-rimmed glasses and sported a full beard and thin combed-back hair. He had deep-set eyes under bushy eyebrows with pronounced cheekbones and an air of authority. The sight of him was slightly scary for the children and they all leant back into Oliver. "Good evening," he said, "please come in. I understand you have a message for me."

This he was used to. He often received strange coded messages but they were normally from known 'conductors' on the Underground Railroad – here were some complete strangers. He had to be cautious. "Come into the parlour and have a seat," he said welcomingly. The children seated themselves on one of the plush sofas of deep red damask in the large, well-decorated front room. Oliver remained standing and introduced them all. Mr Franklin greeted all, including little V, with a handshake.

"Now," he said, "what is this message you have for me?"

"Charlie, do you want to tell him?" said Oliver.

Charlie stood up and concentrated on getting the message right. "Minty says there's trouble on the line and now she can't talk to you."

"I'm sorry, I don't anyone called Minty," he replied in an apologising manner.

Without knowing the full story Ben rapidly assumed they were at the wrong house and dashed a concerned look at Oliver, who read his expression clearly and just raised a hand in signal to wait.

"Oh, I'm sorry, the daughter of Grumble must have made a mistake. We'll go back a station." Ben and V looked at each other curiously as Charlie repeated, parrot-fashion, correctly his strange message.

Edward sprung up from his chair with a wide-eyed expression and approached Oliver. "Where is she? What is the problem?" Oliver smiled and Edward enthusiastically shook Oliver's hand again.

Edward grabbed Charlie by the waist and hoisted him up with a strength he did not look like he possessed. "Well done, my boy!" he exclaimed. "A word wrong and I would have asked you to leave empty handed."

Harriet's mother was known as Grumble and Harriet was known as Minty. She'd given them the message to say just in case anything happened to her – always thinking ahead – and they desperately needed Edward's assistance.

Ben and V stood up and shook his hand again too.

"Daisy," he called at the top of his voice. "Daisy."

"Coming, masser." Daisy appeared from an adjoining room.

"Daisy," he said, holding out a hand to her, "these people come with news of Harriet."

Her face instantly lit up like the dawn on a bright new day. "Oh, Misser Franlin," she said, "where is she?"

"Well, that's what I'm about to find out and I thought you'd like to hear. Please take a seat."

"Oh, yesser, massa," she replied. She then straightened her full-length apron that hung from around her neck and sat down in a wingback chair opposite the children.

Oliver began the story, as he had with Harriet, that they were from New York and were here to help her find and rescue her sister, something she'd not been able to do alone. And he went on to explain what brought them to Edward's door and the unfortunate event that led to Harriet's capture. Before her capture Harriet was going to escort them to Edward Franklin's house for a stopover but now Harriet was elsewhere. Where exactly, they did not know, only the direction in which she was being taken.

Daisy jumped up. "Oh! Gosh, masser, dey den gone and got Harriet. What debber nex'? Dey be wippin' 'er good and hard, dey will, wen she get back." Daisy held her face in her hands and starting crying like something possessed. "She'll bleed for a week!"

"Now there, Daisy, stop that. I'm sure it's not going to come to that. We'll think of something," he said looking straight at Oliver.

"Yes, they won't get that far, will they, kids?" said Oliver confidently.

"No, mam, they won't," said Charlie going over to comfort her too. V joined Charlie on the other side.

"We have a plan," said Ben proudly and handed Oliver the bag he was carrying.

"I have a surprise for you," Oliver said, and pulled out the Confederate officer's uniform from the bag.

Almost instantly Daisy's eyes nearly cleanly blew from her head. "Oh, masser, you dun bin tricked! No officer of Mr Davis gonna be 'elpin our Harriet." She screamed and fearing it had been a clever deception quickly backed away across the room in horror.

She was referring to Jefferson Davis who was an American politician and a US representative and senator for Mississippi, and President of the Confederate States of America during the American Civil War. He campaigned for a slave society to be continued and extolled the values of the planter class. Before the war, he operated a large cotton plantation in Mississippi and owned more than one hundred slaves. Daisy was scared that they had been deceived and these visitors were acting on behalf of the Confederate state militia. Spies – to seek out sympathisers like Mr Franklin and turn him over to the authorities.

Edward stood upright at the sight of the uniform and looked surprised and distressed.

"No, no," protested Oliver, holding up his hand, "it's not what you think."

As quick as he could he grabbed his bag and extracted the Yankee soldier's uniform as well.

"Sorry, wrong one. Look, I have both," he said holding them aloft.

"Oh, Mister Franklin, what ebber next?" Daisy cried and clasped her hands either side of her face.

The tension in Edward Franklin's body language relaxed. "I think you'd better explain," he said encouragingly, gesturing in Oliver's direction. "And then you'd better keep that out of sight in this town," pointing at the Yankee officer's uniform.

Thinking there was more to this than met the eye he called out to Daisy – who'd almost fled the room. "Daisy, I believe we should take these people at their word. Come back." Daisy returned and stood next to him whereupon he placed an arm comfortingly around her shoulder. He appeared to be both master and friend.

Oliver apologised again for scaring Daisy and explained the need for the two uniforms – to assist his travels through either the northern or southern states. And then asked them to be seated again.

He then continued, "I understand from Harriet you are a printer, sir."

"That is correct; I have my business in the centre of town," he replied, rubbing his knees and sitting further back in his chair.

"For our plan to work, that is going to be very useful, actually vital!" continued Oliver. "Would you like to carry on, Ben, as it was your suggestion?"

"Yeah, Ben thought it up, sir," Charlie said, looking up at Edward and patting his big brother on the back.

"Well, sir, when I was reading about Harriet, as well as being a conductor on the Underground Railroad, over the past couple of years she's been working for the army of the north." Edward nodded in agreement but also wondered where on earth he would have read such a thing. Daisy had stopped crying and was getting herself a little more composed.

"Since the start of the war she's mainly been a nurse but has also been venturing into Confederate-held territory to scout and spy on their army using her knowledge of the area from her Underground Railroad work, and her ability to navigate through the fields and woods at night unseen."

"Oh, my Harriet, wat d'you dun?" cried Daisy. "Is dis true, Misser Franklin?"

"This is just pure speculation," he said in a very authoritative voice, "and rumour, spread by Colonel PT Beauregard of the Confederate Army. I've heard the stories myself but there's no proof and I believe they're made up to help save the face of poor soldiering on behalf of the Confederates."

It was one thing to be an escaped slave, only the slave owner had an interest in her return for that, but accused of being a spy was another matter altogether. All of the southern state militia would be on the lookout for a known spy and anyone with a connection to her would be suspect too. Franklin knew very well Harriet's abilities and most, if not all, of her actions but he wasn't about to let on that he knew. Not just yet anyway – these people still had to prove themselves to be who they said they were.

Ben had politely paused to allow him to finish but then continued, "Well, anyway, they have posted up a reward for her arrest and delivery to headquarters in Richmond and–"

Franklin interrupted Ben again, "Yes, I've seen a poster myself but I don't believe it. I know Harriet is a brave, courageous and determined young woman but that was before the war, liberating her kith and kin from their torment. I know I've not seen her for a while; that's because she's been over at the hospital at Hilton Head using her wonderful skills to save lives, whatever their colour."

Of course, Oliver, Ben and Charlie knew her whole life story, not that they could reveal that to Franklin or Daisy, but Oliver interjected. "The excuse we used to get her away from Hilton Head Hospital was for a special mission."

"I assumed, sir, you meant a nursing mission?" queried Franklin.

Oliver leant back in his chair. "No, the officer in charge on the guardhouse knew what I meant when I rode up and requested her release but few others do outside the officer corps. The spying missions she goes on are particularly secret."

Leaning forward and lowering his voice, "If this is true," he paused a moment and moved closer to Oliver, "then, sir, how did you come by the information?"

Oliver had to think quickly. He wasn't quite expecting the Spanish Inquisition-like situation he had here sitting in his comfy chair! He thought hard for what seemed to him an age of silence but was only seconds. Then Ben came to his rescue. Ben had studied more of the subject of the Civil War at school.

"It was Mr Seward, sir; he is a friend of my father's and he is something to do with the Union government."

Franklin slapped his hand down on the arm of the chair. "Mr Seward!" he exclaimed. "Okay, well of course, he is a close friend of Harriet's too. Now it all makes sense."

"So," said Daisy, confused, "Misser Franklin, is it true? Des Harriet be der spy too?"

"If it's from Mr Seward, then yes, Daisy, it's true."

"Oh, Lordy, she den so brave," cried Daisy and gesticulated with her hands before clasping her head again.

"I'm sorry, my boy, for doubting you. Please continue." He turned to Daisy and said, "We have got some special little helpers here, Daisy, no doubt about it."

"Well," Ben continued, "we thought if you could print up an official-looking letter from a Confederate government official to detain Harriet and transport her to Richmond, which would overrule the bounty hunter's rights to her, then Oliver could be the officer detaining her." Edward Franklin gave an accepting nod.

"The bounty hunter never saw Oliver so he doesn't know him so, in his officer's uniform," Oliver held it up again, "he could get Harriet away from the catcher."

Edward stood up and gave them a clap. "Well, my boys, and girl, you seem to have a great plan to get her back."

"So long as we keep Charlie quiet!" joked Ben with a cynical smile.

Daisy joined in the cheer and jiggled her arms in glee. "Will it work, Mister Franklin, will it work?" He stopped clapping and offered a hand to Ben. Ben grinned with pride and shook the hand.

"That sounds like a very clever plan indeed, my boy; well done. You had me worried for a while there though!" The towering man looked down on Ben, then sideways at Daisy and smiled at her. "It seems like I have some work to do. Would you get my coat?"

"Will it take long to print it?" asked Charlie.

"No, once I've set the printer I can print several in no time – give you a few spares. Just in case!"

"Good idea. I'll have to practise forging a signature," said Oliver. Daisy entered the room with Edward's coat. He pulled on the full-length black coat and picked up a holdall.

"I'll go now and print something off while no one else is about. It'll take a little while so Daisy will show you where you can stay for the night and I'll see you all in the morning."

Henry, Franklin's resident gardener and groom, had prepared his master's transport and a few moments later a pony and trap could be heard creaking as quietly as it could over the cobbled surface of Morgan Avenue in the direction of the centre of Charleston.

Chapter 12

After a good night's rest they were all awoken early due to the clattering of horses and a cacophony of shouting outside in the street. Charlie drew the curtains back and saw a number of soldiers in grey visiting other houses down the street and then there was a loud banging on the front door of Sussex House. Daisy answered it and was faced with two Confederate Army soldiers looking agitated. "Get the master of the house," they commanded before she'd had time to say anything. Daisy turned and hurried up the stairs and called for Mr Franklin. He appeared hastily from his bedroom still wrapping a dressing gown around himself.

"Whatever is it, Daisy? What's all the commotion?"

"Soldiers, massa, dey want you, an' dey don't sound too 'appy neeber."

Oliver and Ben came out of their rooms at the same time and joined them on the landing. They exchanged bemused smiles and then Edward started down the stairs. Oliver and Ben followed but kept a discreet distance behind and stopped halfway down.

One of the soldiers knocked vigorously and impatiently again on the door and shouted some incoherent, incomprehensible sounds in a strong southern dialect.

"I'm coming," Edward shouted back. A few seconds later he pulled the door fully open and faced the soldier.

"There's a new conscription order been issued by President Davis; it calls for all available men to be drafted, unless they have a written warrant of absence."

In his position as town councillor and magistrate, Edward knew of and had such a warrant.

"Of course, Sergeant," said Edward, recognising the man's rank; "one moment."

Edward stepped behind the door and from a drawer took out his warrant. It gave his name, address, age, occupation and reason for exemption from the draft. He handed it to the gruff-looking sergeant. He very slowly read the letter, embarrassingly confirming with the private beside him a few words that he could not read and then handed it back.

"Okay, but what about him?" he said pointing to Oliver standing halfway up the stairs. By now Charlie and V had joined Daisy, with V holding her hand, looking on from the top of the stairs.

Edward turned around. "Oh, ah him; he's with me. I mean, he is important to my work."

"Maybe so, sir, but who is he and does he have a warrant of absence?" said the trooper in a rather condescending manner. If only they'd had more time or warning Edward could easily have forged a letter for Oliver. There was no escape. Oliver moved down and towards Edward at the front door and held up his hand in a resigned fashion. He was thinking exactly the same thing.

"It's Oliver, sir, Oliver Bramley," he said to the cocky sergeant.

"Surprised someone as fit as you, sir, has not already enlisted." Oliver stood in silence for a moment and let the uneducated rather coarse sergeant have his rant at him about men not serving for the great cause of self-government for the southern states.

When he thought he'd finished, Oliver made no excuses and simply asked if he could say goodbye to the children on the stairs and collect some things to go with them.

"Okay, but be quick about it; we've got to catch the early train to Petersburg." The sergeant turned and shouted some more indecipherable instructions to his men in the street.

Meanwhile, Oliver gathered the children around him, told them where he was going and that they should follow. "Look, kids, I haven't got time now but I'm sure you can come up with something by the time you get to Petersburg. Look for me there." V started to cry. "Take care of them, Ben. I know you'll think of something."

"Sure thing," said Ben taking a deep breath and puffing out his cheeks and putting an arm around Charlie.

"Yeah, we'll sort it, Oliver," said Charlie confidently.

Daisy wrapped her arms around Olivia and comforted her. Oliver jogged up the stairs to the room where he'd spent the night.

"Hurry up!" shouted the irate sergeant. "We haven't got all day."

Edward guessed what Oliver had gone to do. "I'm sure he won't be much longer, my good man."

The sergeant tucked his chin into his chest. "Slackers, his kind," he replied. Oliver had not said a word in reply to the sergeant's interrogation. He was about to get a shock.

The sergeant turned around to face the street and observe the movements of the other house searchers. Oliver approached silently behind him dressed in his full Confederate captain's uniform. "I'm ready, Sergeant," he announced.

Without turning to face Oliver the sergeant started off again, believing he had a raw recruit behind him and now effectively under his command. "Come on, Bramley, get your lazy backside down to the street and join those other four renegades who thought they could dodge the action." The private standing beside him, but in full view of Oliver – now displaying a senior rank – was wincing at the words of his ignorant sergeant. He tried to stop the next outburst from his superior by poking him in the side but the sergeant had already started on his next flow of verbal abuse – something he was particularly adept at.

"Sergeant," his assistant loudly and positively said, interrupting and breaking his flow of words.

"What, Rigsby?" he protested. Then he turned around and saw Oliver dressed in a smart captain's uniform, standing quietly and smugly in front of him. He nearly fell back down the steps at the sight. Oliver's uniform was smart and distinguished, quite the opposite of the rugged sergeant's battered attire. He saluted and stepped back at the same time. "Sir," he said, standing more upright than before, "I didn't know; please forgive me."

"Well, you didn't really give me time to explain did you, Sergeant? I've just been on a short period of leave after the Battle of Shiloh. As a regular I've been in this since the beginning and I'm well aware of the situation at Petersburg. Shall we go?" said Oliver straight-faced, finishing with a twist of his head.

Of course, the day before he'd told an officer of the north he'd been at the Battle of Shiloh, on their side. Now he'd fooled a Confederate that he had been on their side! But Oliver had read about the battle in *Battle Cry of Freedom* and knew of some of the events and statistics that were an outcome of the battle – just in case he was asked.

"Yes, sir. Of course, sir. I, I didn't mean..." His voice tailed off as he hurried down the steps. Meanwhile his colleague was wetting himself with laugher on the inside and couldn't keep the smirk off his face. He'd received the rough end of the sergeant's tongue many times. Oliver gave him a nod, out of sight of his sergeant; he'd met people in uniform like this sergeant before. 'All brash, bully and bunkum,' his commander had said when he served in the British Royal Air Force.

The three of them joined a group in the street and marched away, with the sergeant apologising profusely and following closely on Oliver's heels. As they disappeared down the street Edward closed the door and led the children into the front parlour again.

"Well, this is a fine mess we gotten into," announced Edward as he took his seat. "I can't leave Charleston at the moment myself, I'm afraid. I'm needed here for my work, so it really is up to you now," he said addressing them. They each came up with a suggestion of a solution, even little V. They discussed the merits of each one for some time but none seemed wholly practicable for three kids to get away with. Daisy brought in some breakfast, which they enjoyed whilst continuing to explore ideas.

Then Ben asked, "What age do they recruit boys into the army?"

"Originally it was seventeen but I have heard of boys as young as fifteen getting in," replied Edward, "but don't you even think of that. Don't you realise how dangerous it is? No, that's not right."

"But we gotta try something, Mister Franklin," pleaded Charlie. He was now feeling responsible for both Oliver's and Harriet's disappearance. He sighed loudly and a worried frown drew lines across his face. Ben slouched in a chair, deep in contemplation, scratching the back of his head. V looked mournfully at Daisy who put a comforting arm around her. Babbit was keeping close company too. Silence of thought filled the room until the scrape of a chair broke it. Edward stood up.

He raised a pointed finger. "But, Ben, my lad, you could get away with being a runner."

"A runner… what's that?" answered Ben and Charlie together.

"A runner is normally a lad who takes messages from one command post to another. He's not a combat soldier but either runs, hence the name, or rides between the commanders with letters. They're really important when the telegraph is out of action or there is no telegraph station. Can you ride a horse, boy?"

"Well, after a fashion. I'm not very good. We need George for that but he did teach me a bit about it."

"Who's George?"

"Never mind, he's not here. I'll manage."

"We just need to think of the right message to send him," said Edward. The room descended into silence once more and the crickets outside could be heard through the open window.

After a few minutes it was V who was first to speak. "What about a special mission, like the one we did for Miss Harriet at the hospital?"

"Eh," said Charlie.

"Of course," said Ben. "Oliver never said what the mission was, just that it was a special mission. A secret. He just told them she was required for duty, not what the duty was to be."

"Yeah, why can't Captain Bramley have a special mission to go on? Great idea, V!" cheered Charlie.

"I see. Yes," said Edward smiling. "So, I guess you'll want me to forge another document to say Oliver is needed on a special assignment?"

"Yeah, then I could take it to him as a – what did you call them – a runner?"

"That's right. It'll mean leaving Charlie and V somewhere, while you go and deliver the message – runners don't have their younger brothers and sisters tagging along," laughed Edward.

"We'll be okay, won't we, V?" said Charlie as he finished the last of his breakfast. V nodded.

Edward left the parlour and went to his study. After about fifteen minutes he returned with two folded pieces of paper. He sat at the table again; Ben, Charlie and V eagerly drew in closer over the table to see. The first sheet he unfolded was a very professional forgery of a certificate for Harriet Tubman's release into the officer's custody, and for her escort to the central offices of the Confederate government. It then went on to explain that she was to be taken to the supreme court for trial for the crime of treason. Ben took hold of the thick paper and almost trembled as he held it.

It appeared so… official. For the first time he was beginning to realise the seriousness and potential consequences of Harriet's work. It reminded him of stories his grandfather had told him, about female secret agents dropped into France during the Second World War and the immense bravery they displayed – now all but forgotten. His grandfather was in something called the Special Operations Executive during the war but he had kept it a secret and not talked to anyone about it until the last few years of his life. He'd said he personally knew many brave women that, in the end, lost their lives because they were caught spying on the enemy.

"Luckily," said Edward, "I printed a few spare copies of the letterhead I'd forged, so here is another with a message, supposedly from Central Office, to release Oliver for a special operation too, this one signed by Robert E Lee." He smiled. General Lee was a superior commander of the Confederate Army and ultimately the supreme commander.

"How do you know the signature is correct?" asked Charlie.

"I had a request, or rather a demand, from him myself last year to print some army posters, free of charge, which was signed by him. The bill for it, he said, was to be settled after the south had won the war!"

"Will they?" asked Ben.

"Who knows at this stage but I'm keeping the letter safe just in case and that's why I have Lee's signature to copy!" he said smugly.

★ ★ ★

For the next hour or so Edward educated Ben on what he knew about a runner's role and how to deliver the message. Just outside Petersburg was a large Confederate Army camp; it was another one of their most important towns to defend and they were reinforcing it against an attack from the Yankees – which they feared might happen sometime soon. They would need to continue their journey alone by train to Petersburg, which was just south of Richmond on the same railway line. Harriet would already be well ahead of them up the line and any chance of saving her rested with Oliver, who was also now separated from them and may not necessarily stay at Petersburg very long.

There were many different battle regions all over the country. Unlike a more conventional war between two nations, with one single battle line to fight on, the American Civil War had skirmishes going on all over the place. One particular valley with its towns or railroad junctions might be under the control of the Yankees and then similarly elsewhere, not far away, could be under the control of the Confederates. They even fought and swapped control of the same piece of land several times, particularly important places like Manassas, or Bull Run – which was the same place but named differently on each side!

Most of the fighting was carried out in the southern states, so it was the Yankee Army that sent brigades of men penetrating into enemy territory to seize strategic strongholds, sometimes destroying the homelands by burning what was of no use to them, or stealing horses, food and hardware that was. After all, this was war and each side ferociously believed in its own cause. A sad fact of the war was that it sometimes set brother against brother and previously friendly neighbours against each other – depending upon their point of view.

Chapter 13

Charlie, Ben and V prepared themselves for the journey and Edward took the three of them to the train station in his horse-drawn cart. The cart was quite a posh affair – also known as a surrey – with two cushioned bench seats facing each other in the back, sheltered from the sun by a fabric canopy over the top. Henry drove them the half a mile across town in the mid-morning heat at a slow trot. People seemed to be going about their business as normal but as they neared the station – not far from the dock area of the town – the movement of army wagons carrying all sorts of supplies and more groups of soldiers marching along the road was predominant.

Henry drew the surrey to a halt outside the booking office and remained on his driver's seat but turned and bade each one farewell with a bow and a half wave of his hand. Edward escorted them into the station and purchased tickets for their journey, to Petersburg, but ultimately to Richmond as well. It was busy and they joined a queue of around ten others waiting to buy tickets. V was intrigued by the ladies' dresses, with the appearance of full-length ball gowns of beautifully patterned crinoline.

Several of the women waved fans in front of their faces to fend off the stifling heat of the morning and all wore some form of hat. At the front was a short, old, bald man arguing with the ticketing official about something. His verbal abuse of the poor official was being accentuated by the accompanying incessant tapping of the man's walking stick aggressively on the counter. Ben looked at Edward with a questioning expression on his face.

"Moaning about the price of his ticket," said Edward.

The value of the Confederate dollar had dropped considerably in the recent weeks and the old man was having a right old moan about the price increase in his ticket from the previous week.

Then the ticketing man stood up and said loudly, without shouting, "Please, sir, there are ladies behind you, would you please adjust your language? There's nothing I can do about it. That is the price. Do you wish to travel or not?"

The old man half turned around and most of the ladies in the queue bowed their heads and hushed some displeasure at the vulgar language he'd been using. He slammed some notes down on the counter.

"Thank you, sir," said the ticket man as he sat back down. Then he pushed a ticket into the Edmundson machine, which punched the correct date into the card, and handed the man his ticket.

"It's the way it is at the moment, Ben," said Edward. "The effects of the war, I'm afraid." The old man stomped off making a particularly loud noise with his stick on the wooden floor of the booking office. The queue then gradually reduced more quickly and calmly.

One of the ladies engaged in a conversation with V over her dress. Then she spoke to Edward and seeing he was obviously well-attired himself commented, "Oh, sir, she's so delightful, you must take her to Swansons on Calderwood Street; they have the most wonderful dresses for young girls and they are practically the only shop in town now with the material to make them." V beamed at the thought and rocked from side to side clutching Babbit tightly to her chest.

Edward put his hand on V's shoulder. "We'll have to see next time you visit, eh?" The two ladies bought their tickets and clucked about dressing young girls as they made their way out to the platform.

Ben had offered Edward the money for the tickets but he would have none of it. They were going off to help Harriet and he insisted he paid. He was not aware of the cash stash Oliver had left them with. He had actually left them with all the money as well as the maps and the Union Army uniform – all he'd taken with him in his bag was his civilian clothing. They waited quietly with Edward for half an hour with only the occasional conversation. Charlie kicked his heels against the bench seat and V snuggled up to Ben. Although excited about rescuing Oliver, the boy's mood was more subdued than the day before and the boys didn't have the same enthusiasm for the steam locomotive when it pulled into the station.

A bell rang out in the station and a short while later the clanging of the locomotive bell announced its arrival. They left the waiting room and stood by the side of the tracks as it chuffed slowly through the station, the boys' heads turning as it went by. It stopped with a familiar squeal of brakes and hisses of steam from the engine. Several people disembarked the carriage in front of them but they had to wait for one last person heaving a large trunk off before they could board. Edward climbed the steps to the carriage platform and led them through to find a seat – away from any soldiers – in the middle carriage of the train. Between the locomotive tender and the carriages was an open box wagon manned by a number of armed soldiers ready if there was an attack, and several more occupied the rear row of seats in the last carriage. Generally the civilian trains were left alone by the opposing armies but occasionally – if thought to be carrying soldiers – were at risk of being attacked by snipers.

Having satisfied himself they were safely seated on the train, Edward shook the hand of each of the boys and gave V a little kiss on the forehead. When the locomotive bell rang out he took one final look around the carriage and then made his way to the exit. The guard blew a whistle, waved his flag and then a hiss of steam and a large belch of smoke started the train on its way. Edward waved goodbye and the kids enthusiastically replied likewise. The huge puffs of smoke, punched into the air by the locomotive, began to increase in tempo as it slowly started to pull out of the station. The rhythmic click-clack sound of the train in motion gradually got faster as they left the area of the station, till it became a clickerty-clack, clickerty-clack, accompanied by the slight rocking motion of the carriages. It took several minutes to get up to full speed, which Ben reckoned was about forty miles an hour on the straight level track leaving Charleston – later in the journey, during a long hill climb, it would be much less.

As the train sped up, the open windows allowed a pleasing fresh breeze to blow through the carriage and cool them from the increasing heat. The countryside rumbled past and nothing much was said for the first few miles. Then Charlie piped up, "Would you like to play 'I Spy'?"

"Can I go first?" said Olivia quickly. She slid closer to the carriage window leaving Babbit on the seat and cranked her head from one side to the other.

Ben pursed his lips, "Suppose so." Then he looked nonchalantly around the carriage to find a suitable target for his turn. "Go on then, V." She was still thinking about it when there was a great squeal of brakes and the train screeched to a stop with the bell ringing madly.

The quietness of the carriage was shattered by shouts and screams of the passengers scared of what the rapid braking might mean. A man, who had been standing in the aisle, crashed to the floor next to Ben, striking his head on the corner of the seat as he fell. His hat went flying through the air and threatened to decapitate a prim lady sitting two rows away. She let out a shriek and turned to view her assaulter but also had to brace against falling on the floor herself. V was thrown into Charlie's lap which knocked the wind out of him as her head hit his stomach. He slightly slowed her impact by grabbing her shoulders but they both cried out more with surprise than pain. Ben steadied himself on the back of the seat, leant over and helped V back to her seat.

"What's happened, Ben?" she asked looking worried.

"I don't know, V – some sort of emergency, I guess."

An old lady who had been knitting fell across to the opposite seat and nearly speared a poor unsuspecting traveller with her needles. Luckily they harmlessly stabbed the seat beside him. A shot ran out from the rear of the train and two men at the rear of the carriage pulled out their pistols, yanked open the door and stepped out onto the open platform at the back.

After initially coming to a stop the train rocked backwards slightly as all the carriages buffeted against one another. Following the shouts and screams of the rapid braking, a cacophony of conversations broke out as people regained their seating. The man on the floor pulled himself up – a cut to his forehead leaked blood down the side of his face which he started to dab with a handkerchief. The near-speared man pulled the knitting needles out of the upholstery and helped the old lady back to her seat – although the needles were now seriously bent into a useless 'L' shape!

Then the train conductor appeared through the open rear door of the carriage and hurried through – he stopped to check the floored man, who was now sitting on the edge of a seat and was not too badly injured, and he assured him he would return to help. Just before he left the carriage he turned and asked if anyone else was hurt. Apart from some muttering no one actually seemed harmed and he continued to the next carriage.

"Is it a Yankee?" someone shouted.

"No, it's just a buffalo on the line," said a man who'd stuck his head out of a window. Even if it had been Yankee soldiers attacking the train the civilians in the carriage would not have been in much danger so long as soldiers weren't with them – making them a target too. They would have been in more danger if the train had struck the wandering animal, with the possibility of being derailed and the carriages turning over. It had happened before but most locomotives were fitted with a metal frame called a 'cow-catcher' at the front to prevent this happening. A sense of relief flooded the compartment when the reason for the stop was announced.

Charlie jumped on the seat and peered out of the window, then turned his head halfway back into the carriage, "I spy with my little eye… something beginning with B…"

"Oh, I wonder what that is, Charlie?" sighed Ben as he helped V regain her seat and picked up Babbit from the floor.

The two men who'd gone outside armed with pistols ready returned to their seats. "Panic over;

just a buffalo looking for an argument with the train!"

Several minutes later the loco bell announced they would soon be underway. The carriage jerked into action as the steam monster slowly belched and puffed into life. They resumed the journey towards Petersburg with fields and rolling open plains as far as the eye could see. Every now and then the bell would ring out, for no apparent reason, but always as they approached a station. To pass the time they played a few 'I Spy' games and others that they usually played on long car journeys.

Having got bored with games Charlie started making jokes about people and their appearance. V cuddled up with Babbit and chatted about getting a dress like the ladies they'd seen at the station. Charlie made jokes about that too. V got in a mood about it but Ben made Charlie apologise and within a few minutes they were all friends again.

The train chuffed on, stopping at stations and sometimes remote water towers dotted along the route, and the countryside changed from open fields and scattered trees to hilly, forested landscape with the railway winding its way along the side of a valley, slowly climbing higher and higher. This was when the train slowed the most; they could hear the hard rhythmic puffing from the locomotive thumping its way along, gasping for breath, struggling to keep forward motion, all the while disgorging an increasing amount of smoke.

V stared out of the window at the slowly passing trees. "Why's it going so slow?"

"Yeah, I could run faster than this," exclaimed Charlie.

"No you couldn't," retorted Ben.

Well, an athlete might have been able to but Charlie would have struggled with his little legs – he wasn't far off the mark though, it was certainly no faster than a horse could easily canter.

Charlie joked, "Shall we offer to get off and push?" They all laughed. The pace slowed even more and the monster up front blew out huge chuffs with an increasing amount of effort – smoke engulfed the carriages behind. At speed the smoke cleared the open wagon with the soldiers in but now they were left choking and wiping grit from their eyes. The train steadied at something like a fast walking pace – chuff-chuff-chuff – it was like the ticking of a clock. This was a time when the soldiers would be at their most vulnerable to snipers in the trees. Blinded and helpless – an easy target.

"I could run faster than this!" exclaimed Charlie again.

"I think I could too," agreed Olivia.

Suddenly a gunshot rang out and birds scattered out of the treetops. Heads in the carriage turned this way and that. Ben pulled Charlie away from the window. V joined the huddle. One of the armed men at the rear of the carriage ran through to the front and threw open the door and disappeared into the next carriage.

"What is it, Ben?"

"I don't know, V." The knitter lady turned and beckoned them over. There were no more shots – the train continued its painful progress.

"Thought he saw something," said the gunman as he entered the carriage. "Just nervous trigger-finger – shadow in the trees. These boy soldiers." He shook his head.

"Didn't think it would be anything, not up here," said the kind lady comfortingly.

After another couple of minutes at this pace, the locomotive seemed to find some more energy. The puffs became quicker with slightly less wheeze to them and the smoke reduced; the track was levelling out at the top of a climb. They had a fantastic view across a valley to more tree-lined ridges in the distance. Slowly but surely the momentum picked up. The conductor entered their carriage – he'd already checked their tickets and seemed to remember where everyone was going, stopping at each seat and giving them a clue as to how long it would be to their destination.

When he got to the kids, he told them it would be about another half hour as they coasted down to Petersburg. "We'll pick up a good speed now," he said.

"Why did it get so slow?" asked V, not understanding the effect the uphill climb would have.

"Well, unfortunately, young lady, we have an old, tired, worn-out locomotive up front and if it wasn't for the skill of the driver and his fireman, we might not have made it up the hill at all!"

"Shouldn't you give it a rest, then? Get a younger one?" she asked.

The conductor laughed, "Yes, that would be a good idea; it's just a bit tricky at the moment. The army keeps pinching all the good ones for their heavy goods trains."

"That's not fair," she replied. He rubbed her little head and shook his at her innocence.

"Luckily for us we have the best driver around to look after us – Mr Casey Jones. He knows these hills better than any and how to nurse the best out of 'Old Faithful'."

"Old Faithful?"

"That's what we named her."

"Is that really the engine's name?" asked Charlie.

"Well, it is now; since she's been brought out of retirement. Until a couple of weeks ago she'd been sitting at the back of the yard in Charleston, waiting to be scrapped. Cos of the shortages they've had to bring her back onto the line; so long as they keep old Casey driving her she'll pull through."

He doffed his cap and moved on to the next seat. It was not long to go to Petersburg so Ben explained what they were going to do when they got there. Although they had picked up quite a few soldiers on the way, none were near where they sat. In a low voice Ben talked through the plan with Charlie and V, just in case the other passengers might hear what he was saying. They'd been told to trust no one. Especially Charlie! The younger two listened carefully to Ben's instructions.

The engine bell always rang out as they approached a station but as they approached this town the bell of the locomotive seemed to ring longer and louder than before. A few soldiers appeared at the front and shuffled through their carriage towards the back, obviously in high spirits, and pointed to a sea of tents on the edge of the town.

After they had left the carriage Charlie asked, "Do you think that's where Oliver will be?" His head and hands rested against the glass of the window.

"That's what Mr Franklin said we should look for," replied Ben staring in the direction of the huge military camp. It was surrounded by a wide ditch and barbed wire fences with observation towers at intervals around the perimeter. They could see a number of formal buildings overlooking the encampment and a stockade filled with horses. Dust clouds hovered where horses and wagons were moving about within the complex. Some were covered prairie wagons, others just open carts. V and Ben joined Charlie close to the window as the train slowed further. Others in the carriage began to gather their belongings together and make ready to leave the train.

V sat back down. "I hope they've got some more shoes for those poor soldiers," she said, nodding in the direction of those who had just left.

"Yeah, their uniforms were really tatty too," said Charlie.

The Confederate soldiers may well have been in high spirits but for some the shoes they wore were only shoes in name, for very little of the shoes they wore existed – no more than pieces of leather held together with cord. Others wore cloth on their back that was more akin to a pauper's clothing than that of a soldier preparing for battle.

V said she felt sorry for them.

"That's not our problem," replied Ben. "Anyway, they'll probably get new uniforms at the camp."

The Confederate Army was desperately short of supplies of most things required for a sustained fight, clothing included. Many men did not have a smart uniform of grey but made do with whatever they'd brought from home. By contrast the northern soldiers were well kitted out and well supplied with equipment, as the northern states had the majority of the manufacturing facilities and the southern states were predominantly farmers.

"And boots?" V jiggled her feet about. She had a smart pair of lace-up *Dr Martens* which looked out of proportion for her delicate frame. But she loved them. As they were black she also got away with wearing them to school, which delighted her, and more recently her mother invented a new nickname for her – Boots! It was a name that, later, was to stick with her. For now she just wanted the soldiers to have proper boots or shoes that actually covered their feet.

"Probably," replied Ben.

Ben and Charlie also sat down just as the conductor came through announcing, "Petersburg, Petersburg Station," which he kept repeating.

A lump rose in Ben throat. "Guess this is it, guys."

The carriages came to a shuddering halt as the brakes squealed their intention to stop the train. A great hiss of steam came from somewhere up front and the bell finally stopped clanging. Ben led them to the end of the carriage, out onto the open platform and down the steps to get off. The station was a busy place with many groups of soldiers milling around and civilians with cases and boxes getting off the train. Smartly dressed porters were marching up and down alongside the train with their trolleys and barrows, taking care of passengers' baggage. One official, without a barrow, hurried – rather monkey fashion but without using a knuckle-walk – towards the three of them standing incongruously at the foot of the carriage steps as they did not know which way to go. He was around fifty years old, thin and bandy-legged, as if he'd spent years on a horse and his legs had never recovered. He had little feet and thin hair combed across a bald patch. Crow's feet clawed at the corners of his eyes and deep furrows were ridged across his forehead, although the rest of his face looked warm and welcoming.

Was he someone they could trust? They had yet to find out.

Looking at Ben, "You look a bit lost, young sir," he said, pushing his chin forward with a grin and a shrug of his shoulders at the same time. In one hand Ben held tightly on to his bag that contained the Yankee uniform and thousands of Union and Confederate dollars, and V in the other.

Charlie spoke up first. "Hello," he said attracting the man's attention.

He bent down slightly, touched Charlie's arm, smiled and returned the greeting. A thought of, *now what do I say*, rushed through Ben's brain. It had been so clear, now it was mush. Why do people keep trying to be helpful? Just leave us alone, is what he wanted to say, but he knew he couldn't.

Charlie rescued him for a bit longer. "Is Mr General Lee here?" he asked.

"Oh, my son," he replied, standing up as straight as he could, which was not particularly straight at all, "do you mean our brave and glorious army commander?"

"Yes."

"Why, do you know him?"

"No, but he's very famous, isn't he?"

"Well, I guess he is, but no, he's not here; not as far as I know at any rate."

Still stalling for time Charlie continued, "I wanted to meet him; my father's in his army somewhere."

"Oh, I see, son; can't help you with that one. Your best bet would be to go to the barracks over that way." And the porter pointed out the direction to go.

"Thanks," replied Charlie.

"But where else will you be needing to go – you look a bit lost?" he said, shuffling from one foot to the other.

By now Ben had thought of something to say. "It's okay, thank you, we're here to stay with our aunt. She'll be along to collect us shortly. I was just making sure we'd got everything off the train before we go to the front of the station to wait for her."

"Oh, yes, of course you want to make sure of that. Can I carry your bag for you, young man, and show you where to wait?" The porter made a grab for it and Ben hurriedly backed away.

"No, no. It's okay, really. I'm fine with it," Ben said hastily.

"So long as you're sure, son. I'm more than happy to help. Anything you need with the railway, you just ask." He winked. "Just ask old Will."

"Old Will?" queried Charlie cheerfully.

"Yes, young sir, that's it; Willard Chaplin at your service." The man cheerfully lifted his cap slightly with his thumb and forefinger. "But you can call me Will," he said with a nod. He looked down at V and smiled, which deepened the feet of the crows.

"Well, it was nice to meet you but if you're sure there's nothing else I can do for you, I'd better be getting along."

Now gripping his bag tightly with both hands, Ben smiled and shook his head affirmatively.

The man lifted his cap again in acknowledgement and walked away. He'd only waddled a few paces before he turned around. "Don't forget, if you need me, I'll be here about somewhere." Then he raised a hand – that had obviously seen many days' hard labour – at someone calling for a porter at the next carriage and jogged off towards them.

"He seemed a nice man," said Charlie.

"Yeah, I liked him too," agreed V.

"Yeah, well... remember, Charlie, you trusted someone before, look where that got us." Ben raised his eyebrows and put on a fat smile.

"I know, but he seemed… different; he had a kind face."

"Yeah, Ben, a really nice man," repeated Olivia. Old Will had picked up two heavy bags from a lady standing beside the next carriage and was on his way back in their direction. A prim lady walked ahead of him with a floral umbrella to shade her from the heat of the sun. As he passed them he hunched his shoulders, grinned and raised his eyebrows. The thought crossed Charlie's mind that maybe it was because he carried lots of heavy bags that his legs had bent in the middle.

"See," said V.

"Whatever," sighed Ben. "Come on, let's go; we need to find what we're looking for." He made off for the station exit leaving Charlie and V muttering to each other. "That means you two, too."

They headed towards the main station building that stood in the middle of platform buildings that stretched out either side. The brick-built, three-storey-high square building had a wide overhanging roof, clad in timber shingles, with a bell tower reaching up above. Inside, the central atrium went to the full height of the third floor, which was large enough to park a steam locomotive, with the bell room above, had the ticket office on one side and a goods depository on the other. Doorways off each side led to waiting rooms and in an archway was a small shop. As they entered, a family bustled past in the opposite direction – as if late for a train. Old Will was entering through the opposite doors, minus the bags he'd been carrying.

He didn't see them at first and went to help someone at the booking office window but as they passed by him on their way to the exit he winked at them. They all smiled back and even Ben began to think this kindly, old, odd, ape-shaped man might become a friend.

Chapter 14

There was quite a throng outside the station booking hall entrance and Ben decided pretty quickly what they should do next.

"There're too many people here – let's go further into town."

A steady stream of soldiers headed down towards the army camp they'd seen from the train. In groups of two or three and occasionally many more, the partly uniformed clusters of men drifted down the main street. Coming away from Fort Richmond was a wagon train headed by a pair of smart-looking officers on horseback, followed by a better dressed company of soldiers than they'd seen before. They briskly marched in time singing loudly and waving salutes at other bystanders. Optimism oozed from the procession – like a cheery parade on a day of national celebration. Charlie and Olivia looked on with excitement; Ben just hoped they weren't too late to find Oliver. He took a deep breath and wiped the sweat from his head.

After the convoy had gone Ben took V's hand and led them towards the centre of town. Near a small park they found a covered shelter about twenty feet square with some benches underneath. Opposite stood a row of shops and a typical western-style saloon. "Come on, guys, let's make camp here."

V and Charlie ran up the three steps leading into the shelter. With great delight they stomped and clattered on the floorboards. Ben stepped up and waved them to join him. On the far side sat two women chatting; both looked up with scorn on their faces at the disruption of their peace.

"Oi!" shrieked Ben.

"What?" Charlie and V eyed Ben with a *'what, me?'* expression.

Ben put his finger to his lips and swivelled his eyes at the other occupants of the bandstand. "Come on, we'll sit here." He smiled at the ladies and held out his arm to gather in his siblings. Ben grabbed Charlie by the arm to help him forcefully to a seat as far from the ladies as possible.

Charlie shook off Ben's grip. "What's up with you?" he groaned.

Ben half looked over his shoulder – the local gossips were back in action and ignoring the children. "We're trying not to attract attention… remember!" he whispered loudly through gritted teeth. Charlie wobbled his head from side to side and pulled a face – pushing the bottom of his mouth out with his tongue. Ben gave him a hard stare back. V sat silently.

"Okay," Charlie sighed.

"I think the best thing for you two is to wait here for me to return."

"But why don't we just come with you?" Olivia asked with a slight frown.

140

"Because I'm supposed to be a runner – working for the army. I wouldn't have a little girl with me if that were the truth… would I?" Olivia looked down at her feet and hugged Babbit more tightly. Charlie glanced across at the chatterers, engrossed in their own conversations and occasionally laughing to themselves.

"What if he's not there?" asked Charlie.

"Then I'll try and find out where he's gone – I have got a brain." Ben impatiently shifted around then dropped his bag to the floor. "I'm going to need you to look after this, Charlie. Can you do that? Do you think, just one little thing? It's very important."

Charlie bent down and heaved the bag onto the bench. "Sure, Ben."

Ben put his face to within a few centimetres of Charlie's. "And whatever you do, don't open it. Got it?" He poked him in the chest to reinforce the message. Charlie pushed him away.

"Yes, Ben… don't open it," he flippantly replied.

"I'm relying on you – if anyone sees what's in there…" He looked over at his little sister. "Keep an eye on him, V."

Olivia took a sideways look at Charlie – and smirked.

"Yes, Ben. Me and V will wait here for you."

"No wandering off, understand? I'll be as quick as I can."

"Yes, Ben," Charlie obediently repeated.

Ben shot V another look too. "Yes, Ben, we'll stay here till you get back."

Satisfied he'd made his point clear, Ben set off for the army barracks.

"Better start running then, Ben," said Charlie with a grin.

Ben ignored him and retraced his steps to the station and then followed a group of soldiers down the road to Petersburg Barracks. The railway line they'd arrived on curved off to the left; on the right were mainly commercial buildings with one particularly large warehouse sporting an impressively tall industrial chimney. Smoke and smell poured from the top.

The road led to the entrance of Fort Petersburg; the sign over the entrance was bounded either side with timber watchtowers and tall metal gates which were open. Surrounding the camp was a barbed wire fence with smaller lookout towers dotted at intervals around the perimeter, each one manned by several riflemen. A little way in front of the fence line was a wide trench and a short distance in front of that was row upon row of spiked poles pointed outwards at about chest height. They were intended to stop cavalry charges by impaling the horses if they did. Behind the barbed wire fence were ramparts of earth behind which the defending soldiers stood, armed with rifles, muskets and cannon. Although Ben thought the Confederate soldiers carried rifles, in truth most were still carrying muskets – a short-range weapon which was slow to reload through the muzzle and was fired by a flintlock mechanism.

After at first pausing to take in the scene, he cautiously but confidently moved towards one of the sentries at the side of the open gate. "I have a message for the commanding officer," he said and held up a wax-sealed folded piece of paper.

"Okay, young'un, report to the duty sergeant over there." And he gestured to a small wooden hut inside the camp which stood near the entrance to a large brick building. Fort Petersburg's main office block was only two storeys high but had an imposing entrance with pillars each side reaching up to roof level supporting an elegant porch. He paused again for a moment trying to muster more confidence before entering the hut marked 'Fort Richmond Pass Control'. A smaller sign read 'All visitors must report to the Duty Sergeant'. He took a deep breath and stepped through the open door. Inside it contained little more than a simple rough wooden desk behind which sat a bearded man in a sergeant's uniform and some piles of paper in a wooden tray. Standing beside him was another soldier. He ignored Ben's presence while he finished writing something before handing it to a waiting soldier, who then disappeared out of the door at a trot. The sergeant grabbed another paper from the tray and continued to ignore Ben. Ben stood patiently and silently for a few moments wondering if he should say something. Then, without lifting his head from his work, "Well, what is it, son? What do you want?" the man said rather impatiently.

"I have a letter, sir."

"Well, whoopy do for you." And he carried on with reading what was in his hand. The smell of a hardworking man had already assaulted his nostrils when Ben first entered the hut – as if the man had not left his desk for a week. He took a step back to be closer to the open door – and fresh air. A few more moments went by before he plucked up enough courage, "Sir?"

"What!"

Ben held up the letter.

"As if I haven't got enough to do. Come on, I haven't got all day; give it here."

"I don't think it's a letter for you, sir," said Ben nervously.

"What do you mean, not for me?" He stared at Ben furiously. "If it's not for me, why are you bothering me about it?"

"Sor, sorry, sir, I was told to report here. It's for the commanding officer, sir," said Ben shuffling slightly closer to the desk and handed him the sealed paper.

The grumpy sergeant turned it over a couple of times looking for more information other than 'The Commanding Officer from Central Office'. "Well, it should say who, not just Commanding Officer," he huffed.

"I'm sorry, sir. I was just given it, to deliver here from Central Office." A slight tremble was beginning to creep into Ben's voice and he curled his toes up inside his shoes.

"I can see that, son! Well, you need to take it in to Captain Murray," he shouted, "inside the admin block. He looks after General Hill's affairs – he's the commanding officer here. And he ain't in any good mood at the moment; been cooking my backside already this morning. So good luck with that if it ain't addressed correctly. I'll watch out for you leaving the building at a lot faster pace than you go in and that's for sure!"

Captain Murray was a fastidious man about process and procedures and he was already under pressure from higher up the command chain to organise a battalion of men for a counter-attack somewhere under General DH Hill's command. And he didn't suffer fools gladly.

He handed Ben back the letter and told him to go to the first-floor second room on the left, from the top of the stairs. It was a short walk from the hut to the main entrance between the fancy Doric columns that held up a flat portico above but far enough for the adrenalin coursing through him to raise his heartbeat. He stepped aside as two officers exited the building and then walked through the open double door. Inside, a wide staircase was set back from the doorway by about three metres, with passages disappearing down each side. Corridors also led off either side of the entrance door along the front of the building in both directions. Ben looked both ways and then warily climbed the stairs. At the top, corridors again led either side across the building with the odd chair parked outside a door.

He did as he'd been told and turned left. Further down the corridor someone came out of one room, crossed the corridor and entered another. All the doors had signs on them and the vaulted ceiling let light in from somewhere above. He could hear talking in one room as he passed but otherwise it was only the sound of his footsteps on the bare floorboards that echoed down the corridor.

The plaque on the second door proudly announced that it was the room of Captain IT Murray. Just as he went to knock on the door it opened and a giant of a man stood in the doorway. His nose was disfigured and he had a long scar across his face and, more significantly, only one arm. His left sleeve was pinned to his shirt. He barged past Ben, almost without noticing him, and bellowed down the corridor. A man's name, Ben thought, but he could not determine it through the accent. He shouted the name again which seemed to bounce off all the walls to the end before returning in a muffled echo. A door, three doors down on the other side, opened and a diminutive young man hurried out towards them.

"Sir–" Ben started, then paused for some recognition that he was there, "I believe I have a letter for you." The man looked down as if Ben were dirt on his shoe.

"What?" he shouted. Ben nearly fell backwards with the blast.

He held up the letter. "A letter, sir," he stuttered; "I think it's for you."

"What do you mean, you think it's for me?" he said at a volume that might have been heard a mile way. "It either is, or it isn't." Ben started to raise the hand in which he held the letter, when it was suddenly snatched from his grasp.

"Just got to read the blasted name on it, sonny," he boomed.

Timidly, Ben continued, "Well, it's for the commanding officer but I was told to bring it to you."

"Damned right you should," he said studying the outside of the document.

The man from three doors down had now arrived; he stopped and saluted, "Sir."

"Wait there, Solinger." The soldier abruptly placed his arms by his sides and took a step back against the wall, looking like a quivering wreck. He looked straight across from his side of the corridor to the other in a frozen gaze. The captain ushered Ben into his room, "You'd better come in, boy," and closed the door behind them with enough force that the door nearly came straight through the frame! He broke the wax seal and opened the letter and read the contents.

"Well, this is most irregular. First of all, it's not addressed to the commander by name and now I see there's no regulation request number." He waved the paper at Ben, "Where's the damn request number?" he said in a voice with enough puff to drive a steam engine.

"I don't know, sir. I just got told to deliver it," said Ben, hoping as his mother sometimes said, 'Oh, don't worry dear, his bark is worse than his bite.' Although at this point in time Ben thought that given a little encouragement this goliath might just bite someone's head off – literally.

"Yeah, boy... but from where? We caught one of them damn Yankee spies here only three weeks ago. You'll not be trying it on with me, will ya?" he said, staring straight through Ben and out the other side of the building. His face was turning a brighter shade of red and he rubbed his leaking forehead with a handkerchief to wipe away the sweat from it.

"No, sir, not at all, sir. I can assure you this came from the Command Central Office in Richmond, sir," Ben replied, trying with all his might to subdue his trembling. He curled his toes again and his pulse was racing like the wind in a hurricane.

His one and only fist thumped down on his desk like Thor's hammer. "Simple rules – why can't they just stick to 'em? Damned irregular, that's what it is! Assuming this is true, and I'm gonna get it checked first, boy, mark my words I'm getting it checked, somebody's butt is going to get kicked for this." *Checked*, thought Ben, *what does he mean checked*? His mind started racing as fast as his heart beat. How was he going to get it checked? What did he mean? This could be the end of the road for Ben if he were found out to be an imposter.

This guy obviously wasn't in a good mood – just as the sergeant had said. Ben did not know it but this Scotsman had settled in South Carolina after a career in the British Navy. He'd been a successful captain of several warships where brutal discipline was normal and he had often ordered it. It was during the storming of an enemy ship that he lost his arm to the slash of an opposing cutlass. After the Civil War broke out he'd volunteered for service but sitting behind a desk was not what he had in mind and it definitely did not suit him. Captain Murray would have felt much more at home leading a cavalry charge straight down the enemy's throat. He was fearless.

"I'm trying to organise three regiments into a force for battle and this is the second field officer in two days they've requested be released. Why don't they get themselves organised? Solinger, get yourself in here!" he boomed at the door.

Ben stood in silence looking at the floor, thinking, *Oh poo; this really isn't going so well.*

★ ★ ★

Meanwhile, Charlie had got bored, of course, and had been pacing around the town square dragging V along with him. "V, we could just go back to the station for a little while – there's more going on there – and get back here before Ben does; he's bound to be there for ages. There's nothing to do here."

"You know what Ben said – stay here," she said as purposefully as a little girl could.

"I know, but if he doesn't know, who's gonna tell 'im?" V was bored too and she didn't take much more persuading before they were on their way to the train station.

Chapter 15

On the way back to the station Charlie chatted to V about Emilie's Emporium. She'd never been there and was intrigued by what her brothers had said about the place. He told her about all the rooms and the masses of old things that were stacked everywhere and the strange little passageways joining some of the rooms and creaky stairs. And how spooked he'd been when Emilie crept up behind him and how she seemed to be a mind reader too. And how she obviously knew Oliver very well but it also seemed like there was something more than that. He told her how the cat scared him out of his skin and he nearly peed himself when it ran out of the dark passageway – a passage normally hidden behind a secret door. A passageway of darkness, to where he did not know. And when they'd got time, he was going to ask Oliver about how she walked without making any noise of footsteps too.

"Well, I'd like to meet her, Charlie, cos she gives you and Ben anything you ask for and you don't have to pay for it!" said Olivia meekly. "I think she sounds like a nice lady."

"Really! You wait till you meet her, V." After all he'd told her he was surprised she was that keen.

Charlie screwed his face up in a disapproving grimace.

"Yeah, maybe she would give me something?"

"Yeah, and maybe she'd say, 'Of course, little girl, come this way,' and we'd never see you again." Charlie paused. "Now, come to think of it..." he smirked and tapped a finger on his head. "Come to think of it!"

"Charlie," she shrieked. And thumped him on the arm.

"Only joking, V," he laughed.

Charlie lugged Ben's bag along and V followed him through the tall entrance doors into the booking hall. There were fewer people around than when they'd left and Willard Chaplin was sweeping the floor in the entrance lobby. He recognised them straight away. "Your auntie not turned up yet?"

"Oh yes, she's doing some shopping with our brother so we thought–"

"You thought," said V, correcting him.

"Yes, I thought, er... we could come and have a better look at your station."

Old Will swept the dust out the front door and rested his broom against the wall. "Of course you can. I bet you're interested in the locos, young man," he said. And then bent down a bit further still to address Olivia, "And what about you?"

She shrugged her shoulders. "They're okay, I s'pose."

"Well, it's not just the trains; I wondered what else you have at a station like this?"

The porter looked around him. "Look, I'm not too busy at the moment; why don't I show you around?"

"That'll be great, won't it, V?" She wasn't so enthusiastic but at least it was something to do. He started with telling them about when it was built and that he'd worked there since that day, just over twenty years ago. He showed them round the booking office and explained how the clunky ticket machine worked to date-stamp and punch the ticket and introduced them to the ticket master. There were separate ladies' and gentlemen's waiting rooms, cloakrooms and luggage-handling office; all of which he seemed immensely proud of. Especially how well kept they were. There was a store room, they didn't go in there, and next to it was the telegraph office.

He paused before entering to announce, with a sweep of his arm, "The latest in modern telegraphy."

V had been getting rather bored by it all but when they entered this room and saw all the equipment and wires, she asked, "Is this where you keep the telephone?"

"The what?" Old Will replied.

"The telephone. I haven't seen one anywhere; is this where you keep it?"

He looked puzzled by the word. "I've never heard it called that before but this is the telegraph office. Telephone, you say; is that what you call it where you come from?"

"No, we just call it a phone–"

Charlie gave her a dig in the ribs, "Ssh"

She frowned.

The telephone wasn't invented until 1876 by Alexander Graham Bell in Boston, USA. The telegraph office used a very simple device to communicate with a series of bleeps called Morse Code, after the inventor Samuel Morse. There was no microphone or speaker, just a single spring-loaded switch connected to an electric circuit. The operator's switch or key was rather like a single piano key, on which the operator rested his finger to press and send a series of blips and bleeps down the line. Instead of striking a string to make a musical note the key had wires attached to it to connect it to an electric circuit which in turn sent a pulse of electricity to the receiving station. Either a short note or a long note could be made depending on how you struck the key. Wires seemed to run all over the desk and up the wall into, and out of, various boxes with switches on them. There were also a pair of bells and a wooden box from which a clicking and buzzing noise was emanating as they entered.

Recently, Charlie had completed a project at school which involved a very simple electric circuit – by modern-day standards – but which would not have been recognised by the operator of this device. Today it was Douglas Doolittle who sat at the desk with an elasticated sun visor on his head, tapping away on the single key in front of him. When he'd finished tapping, he looked up and acknowledged their entrance.

"I hope you don't mind, Doug, I was going to show these kids what you do."

"No trouble, Will, I'm finished for a moment anyway; help yourself," he said and got up from his chair, then walked over to the other side of the room where a small kettle simmered on top of a black pot-bellied stove. He made himself a cup of coffee and sat down at the small round table next to the stove and began reading a newspaper.

The kindly porter guided them around the reception desk to the table where the telegraph operator sat. On the wall in front was a chart with the alphabet and numbers, each one followed by a set of symbols of dots and dashes. Another had a list of place names – either towns or stations – each associated with a 'box number' and a 'dial number'. Old Will offered Charlie the operator's seat, which he eagerly took and plopped down on. "Now," he said, leaning over Charlie's shoulder, "this 'ere key is what we use to send messages along the telegraph wires. Doug," he looked in his direction, "over there," the man winked in response, "is one of our operators. When we want to send a message he taps away on it like this." Before going any further the bandy legged porter looked for confirmation from the professional operator of the electrical wizardry.

"Yeah, it's okay, I've switched off the transmission key while you're playing."

"He taps away like this." The key was spring loaded to the up position, so Old Will pressed it down a number of times to demonstrate how it worked.

"Can I have a go?" asked Charlie.

"Yeah, go on; see how it works?"

Charlie tapped away in various rhythms.

"Can I have a go?" asked V. Charlie removed his hand and let V play with the key. She wasn't quite sure what it did and soon got bored with it.

"If you look at that chart," said their guide, pointing to the wall in front of them, "you can see what you have to do to make a letter."

"So you only do a letter at a time," asked V.

"Yes, that's right, but if you're as good as Doug over there, you don't need the chart and he's real quick at sending messages." Douglas held his cup up, smiled and winked at them again.

"No, that chart is only for the likes of me to be able to use it if we need to in an emergency. If one of the regular guys isn't around," the old man continued.

"And what do these switches do?" enquired Charlie.

"You use those switches to choose where the message is sent."

"And how do you hear what is being sent to you?"

Old Will pointed to a little wooden box near the key. "That's the sounding box; it clicks and buzzes out the message for you to write down." He threw a switch and this time when he pressed the key a loud click noise came from the box. "If you just tap the key quickly you get a click and if you hold it down a fraction longer you get a buzz." His finger bobbed up and down showing the different technique for a click or a buzz. He then explained how it was easier to write down the beeps and buzzes in a row of dots and dashes as he heard them to work out what the letter was.

Across the room Douglas laughed – the professional operator could work out the letters in his head as they were transmitted and then just write those down. But it was easier for a beginner to use Old Will's two-step method. There was always a slight pause between each group of bleeps of one letter from the next to separate them.

"Listen carefully, son, and see if you can work out what letter this is." One finger of a multi-lined leathery hand tapped at the key and Charlie listened hard – click, click, click, click. Charlie looked up at the chart – "H."

"Well done!" Ben then tapped the key just once.

"E!" Charlie exclaimed.

"Right again!"

"Okay – I'm going to do three more letters in a row now."

Charlie listened hard and scribbled down the clicks and buzzes in a series of symbols and then looked at the chart in front of him.

Charlie hesitated, "Not sure."

"I'll do them all again – starting with the 'H'." The box buzzed out a series of sounds for Charlie to decode.

He went over the letters again speaking loud as he went, "H… E… L… L… O – Hello!"

"That's right!"

"Oh, well done, Charlie!" exclaimed V clapping her hands excitedly.

"You're pretty good, son; have you done this before?" asked Old Will jovially.

Charlie didn't want to say anything but his class had studied Morse code as a historical link to an electronic project on communications they'd worked on. With a modern circuit board and buzzer connected by wires, they'd sent basic messages from one classroom to another for a bit of fun. Charlie had managed to learn quite a few of the letters so well he didn't need the cheat-sheet up on the wall – he pretended to be slow for effect!

"No, just luck, I s'pose. Can I have another go – to try and make some words up?"

"Well–" The old man looked across to his friend Douglas – he nodded, "I guess it won't harm anything if you do – go on." Charlie pulled his chair in a bit closer to the desk and thought for a moment while looking at the letter chart in front of him. Then he carefully placed a finger on the Morse key and started to tap away slowly.

"What's he saying?" Olivia asked the old man.

Old Will wrote down the marks for the sounds he heard as Charlie tapped out the code. When the click box stopped sounding the old man stood staring at the chart on the wall and mouthed letters to himself as he decoded each one.

Before he'd finished working it out, the voice of the professional across the room announced the content of the message, "My sister smells of poo!"

"Charlie!" she shouted, and thumped him in the back. Charlie fell off the chair laughing hysterically.

For good measure V kicked him too while he was on the floor.

"You smell, Charlie Green, you smell of–" She was interrupted by the sound of a bell above the desk. It rang twice, then twice again.

Douglas dropped his newspaper, jumped up and made his way hurriedly across the office. "Sorry, kids, there's a message for me coming in." Still laughing, Charlie scrabbled back to his feet. Old Will gently held both Charlie and V out of the way behind Douglas's chair. A few moments later the click box started clicking and buzzing loudly. Douglas wrote down each letter, making up the words of a message on a paper pad next to the key.

"Ben and I could make up something like this at home – between our tree house and the shed or our bedroom. It would be great fun – Mum would never know what we were saying! We just need some wire and stuff."

"Oh – I think it's a bit more complicated than that, young man," Old Will said, shaking his head. "You need this new electricity stuff – where are you going to get that from?" he laughed.

"Oh, that's easy – we can use a battery."

"And where are you going to get one of those from?" Douglas asked disbelievingly. "You can't just get one at the general stores, can you?" Charlie was just about to reply when V nudged him.

"Oh – yeah – yeah, I suppose you're right – didn't think of that."

The only batteries that were available then were heavy rectangular glass containers about the size of a cereal packet, filled with acid and carried in a wooden box. At this time it was only companies like the railway that possessed them and had a means of recharging them.

"You're a really bright lad, you know; most people don't understand any of this," said Douglas as he waved his arm across the display of what was then considered modern technology. "You did all right, kid, but I think it will be quite a few years before you could have your own!"

"Come on then, kids, I think it's time we went," said Old Will. "Don't want to put Doug off his job."

"It was very nice to meet you, Mister Doolittle," said Charlie.

"Likewise, young man." The telegraph operator held out his hand which Charlie shook enthusiastically. "And you too, little miss."

They left the telegraph office and walked further on down past other station buildings, like the stationmaster's house. At the end was another small office with wires running in and out and then up to a pole at the end of the station fence. There was no sign saying the purpose of the room.

"What's that?" asked Charlie.

"Oh, that's the repeater station for the telegraph and spare operating station if there's a problem with the main one. The message Doug sends and receives passes through there but it's normally left switched to go straight through – unless, as I said, there's a problem." Old Will opened the door and Charlie peered in. As well as a telegraph desk and operating switches, shelves that lined the walls were stacked with all sorts of spare parts and railway paraphernalia. A window either side of the door let in subdued light as it was set well back under the canopy roof. "As you can see, it's also a storeroom."

Olivia squeezed her head between Charlie and the doorframe. "Cor, it's just the sort of place you and Ben would like to play in!" Charlie smiled and stepped back from the door.

The old man closed the door. "Well, that's about everything here except the trains, so if we go back to the ticket office you can go through and watch them if you want but I must be getting back to some work before the big boss sees me not doing what he wants me to." He grinned.

"Yeah… Charlie and me should be getting back anyway."

They both thanked him for showing them around and the three of them started to make their way back. Halfway to the booking hall a tall, portly man wearing a bowler hat and sporting a bushy moustache stepped out of a door in front of them. The sign of white letters on a black background alongside the door announced it was the 'Stationmaster's Office'.

"Ah! Chaplin… just the man," he boomed. The old man stopped in his tracks and stood as upright as best he could and nervously adjusted his cap.

"Yes, sir." Behind him he waved his hand – out of sight of the master – to shoo away the children.

160

"What are you doing?" He leant forward to look behind Old Will and watched Charlie and Olivia saunter away as if they'd had nothing to do with the old man.

"Nothing, sir."

"Nothing! You're not paid by the railway company to do nothing!"

"I… I didn't mean *nothing*, sir. I… I've just taken a couple of lamps down to Joe's workshop – they need new wicks."

"Oh, I see."

Charlie and V hurried down the platform. "He was a nice man," said Charlie.

"Yes, but if our Ben has got back and we're not there–"

Charlie interrupted his sister, "Yeah, yeah I know. Come on, then."

Chapter 16

Solinger entered the room and marched towards the desk, stood to attention and saluted, "Sir!"

Captain Murray picked up a file from his desk and waved it in the air, "I want you to go through these ammunition requisition lists," and then slammed the file back down on his desk. "But first I need you to escort this lad to the telegraph office at the station. He's brought a message from headquarters that I want checked out."

"Yes, sir!" came the obedient reply.

"It's probably fine but it's just not in compliance with the regulations for a headquarters demand," he said in a more resigned way.

"Yes, sir."

Ben had mixed emotions at this point; he hadn't the courage to argue the issue with the mad, red-haired Scotsman but he was worried about what else he could do.

Captain Murray sat at his desk and wrote a few lines. "I want you to get them to send this and wait for their reply."

"Yes, sir." Solinger took the folded piece of paper.

"It might take a while – why, those dopey crows at headquarters manage to send a reply – but don't come back without one. Understand? Then get on with this."

"Yes, sir."

"I could go to the telegraph office if it would help, sir," offered Ben, thinking it might help his cause. "I'll run too and make it quicker for you."

"Yes, that would be helpful, son, thank you," he replied, seeming calm. "So I send you to get confirmation of a letter that I'm suspicious of that you brought here. Hmm... let me see?" he said rubbing his chin and giving the idea false thought for a couple of seconds, but no more.

Realising how it sounded, Ben cringed and wished he'd not suggested it now.

The captain barged his desk forward as he impatiently stood up and stomped around to tower over Ben. "I might not have been the brightest bairn that was born but if you think I'm that so blooming stupid as to send you on your own to do that... Does this look like the face of an idiot?" he shouted, pointing at himself. "Well!" he shouted again with his face inches from Ben's.

Ben wanted to shrivel up and disappear down a crack in the floorboards before the explosion took place, which looked as sure as a lighted cannon. The captain's bloodshot eyes were bulging like a big-eyed tree frog – ready to burst. He shook his head rapidly, "N, no, sir, I–"

"Yes, no sir is the right answer... if you want to leave here in one piece, that is!"

Solinger took the folded note and beckoned Ben to join him leaving the room. As they hurried down the stairs Solinger said, "Jeepers, man, you sure know how to wind him up. He's like a bear with a sore head normally; he doesn't need the likes of you to light his touch paper." Solinger was only a young man himself but as a good scholar he'd been selected for office duties and therefore avoided being sent to a front-line fighting brigade. He'd worked in the quartermaster stores in Richmond before his posting here – which he'd actually preferred. It had now come to the point when every young man was expected to be bravely fighting for the cause but the only thing Solinger had to be frightened of was his commanding officer!

"Sorry," said Ben. The soldier had a certain empathy with Ben as he was often the butt of Captain Murray's temper.

"What was in the message, anyway?" Solinger probed.

"Well I…" Ben nearly fell for it and said what was in the letter but of course if it was really from headquarters, and he really was a runner, he wouldn't have known. "I don't know; I'm only the runner," he replied. "I never know what is in the messages – I just deliver them."

"What's he asking you to send to headquarters?" Ben challenged.

"I'll look in a minute." Once they were safely away from the barracks, Solinger had a read. "It's addressed to the central army office and just says, *'Please confirm the request for Captain Bramley to be released for special duty'.*"

Ben's heart sank. *We're stuffed*, he thought.

"Oh right," he nonchalantly replied. *Somehow I need to get away, grab Charlie and V and think of another plan.* He tossed both thoughts about in his head. He also thought of the trouble they'd got Harriet into. She had been better off without them interfering in her life. This was not the way it was supposed to turn out.

★ ★ ★

Charlie and V pushed their way through the booking hall which was full of people again now. A porter followed them into the hall and with a brass cone placed in front of his mouth made an almost incomprehensible announcement. His voice attracted the attention of most of the travellers. "All passengers travelling to… *mumble mumble* least two hours… *mumble* train out… *mumble* enemy action." By now all those in the hall were facing the announcer and trying to hear what he was saying.

Charlie and V continued to leave but as they reached the entrance door Charlie took a look over his shoulder and then suddenly dragged V to the side.

"Charlie, you're hurting me," she protested. He released his grip on her arm a bit but still pulled on her sleeve so that they were hidden behind the doorpost on the outside of the hall.

"Ssh," he whispered.

"What is it?"

"I think I just saw Harriet."

"Who?"

"Harriet – the woman we were supposed to be helping." He poked his head around the edge of the door. There was Harriet, seated on a bench in the ticket office, hands on her lap, with a man sitting next to her who Charlie didn't recognise. Through the crowd – at the ticket desk – he could see the man who had fooled him into revealing Harriet's identity. Olivia pulled him back so that she could have a look.

"She's sitting on the bench opposite the ticket desk."

"Is that her, next to the man with a long coat and cowboy hat?" she asked.

"Yes, V, that's the woman."

Charlie took a second look and then with his head and one arm poked around the doorframe he felt V tugging on his shirt this time. "Charlie," she hissed.

"Ssh, I'm trying to get her attention."

"But Charlie," said V desperately.

"What?"

"We're not supposed to be here, Charlie."

"I know but…" As Charlie turned round he saw what V was tugging him about. Down the road, but marching in their direction, was Ben and a soldier.

"Great – he's gonna kill me. Quick, V, follow me!" They tried to dodge the horse and cart traffic to cross the road before Ben spotted them. Too late.

"Charlie!"

He tried hopelessly to hide behind a moving wagon.

"Excuse me," Ben said to his escort, "that's my little brother and sister; do you mind if I go and say hello? I don't get to see them very often."

"I suppose not but don't be too long. I'll wait by the entrance." Solinger continued to the station entrance and leaned against the wall while keeping an eye on Ben.

He ran across the road and grabbed Charlie by the arm. "What are you doing here?"

"It was Charlie's idea. I said we shouldn't leave the town," said V.

"I'm sure it was. I can't trust you to do anything you're told."

"I've not let anyone see in the bag, Ben," said Charlie trying to rescue something from the situation.

"That's something at least." A cart had pulled up on their side of the road and Ben ushered them behind it so they were out of Solinger's view. He was chatting to a young lady anyway and not paying attention to Ben at the present. "Look, we're in a bit of trouble. I'm on my way to the telegraph office with that guy over there," pointing at Solinger, "so they can check my message out."

"Eh?" said Charlie. Ben explained the problem quickly to them – the messages and why he was on his way to the station telegraph office. And how, when they sent the message to Richmond and got a reply from head office, he was really going to be in big trouble. They were all going to be in the poo.

"Look, Charlie, you and V get back into town, *where I left you*, and I'll get away somehow. I'll think

167

of something but it isn't going to take long for my escort to raise the alarm." Ben looked worried – he needed to come up with another plan.

Calmly, Charlie smiled and said, "Don't worry, I can sort it."

"What do you mean, you can sort it?" said Ben dismissively.

"You take V with you and just somehow delay sending the message for a few minutes."

"Why? What on earth can you do?"

"Just do it, Ben. Trust me."

"Trust you, Charlie; I can't trust you any further than I can throw you."

"This time, Ben, you can, I promise," he said with a serious look you rarely saw with Charlie. He meant it.

"But what can you do, Charlie?"

"Just trust me, Ben. If your man is going to send that message soon I need to get going." Charlie scurried off and left V with Ben. He didn't go through the main entrance but found another way onto the station.

"Come on then, V; I don't know what our brother has in mind but I have to go."

"Maybe he's going to cut the wires."

Ben led V back across the road to where Solinger was waiting – still in conversation with the young lady. "How's he going to do that – with his teeth?"

"We were shown a storeroom on the station; maybe he saw something in there he could use. He's quite bright at times, if you know what I mean," said V.

"All I know right now is that we're in the sh–, never mind."

"It was a pleasure to meet you, Juliet, and I hope to see you again soon but now I must take this young lad and get down to the telegraph office," said Solinger smugly.

"Yes, I mustn't keep a soldier from his work." She smiled, gave him a cute little wave and left.

"Come on, we must get a move on," said Solinger and led the way through the entrance to the station. "So, is this your sister?" he said without turning.

"Yes. V, this is Private Solinger."

She smiled. "Hello."

"What happened to your little brother?"

"Oh… he's er… had to go off – on an errand."

"You must be a proper soldier," said Olivia. "My brother's not a proper soldier." Ben threw V a stare that said *What are you doing?*. "He just pretends to be a soldier in grey." The stare got harsher; his eyes nearly popped out of his head.

"Really?" remarked the soldier. He stopped walking, turned around and looked down at her – they'd not made it out of the booking hall yet. "Why d'you say that?"

"Well–" she began.

"She's only a girl, she… she doesn't know anything," stuttered Ben, stopping V from continuing. Ben put a hand out to V.

Solinger held Ben back with his arm. "No, I want to hear what she has to say – it might be interesting. Go on."

"Do you have a brother or sister, Mister Solinger?" she asked.

Caught slightly off guard, he said, "Er… yes, actually, I have two brothers and a sister. I did have two sisters but one died a few years ago – from yellow fever."

"Oh, I'm sorry," V replied. "What was her name? What happened?"

"Belinda."

"That's a nice name – how old was she?"

"Just turned nine; she was about your height but with long fair hair. She'd just been down to Charleston to see our grandparents." The young soldier's face looked sad; for a moment he was lost in thought – just staring at the floor. "They had an outbreak there in '58. She didn't seem too bad when she first got home – but then she got really ill. First she just had a fever, then her skin turned yellow and when she was sick it was full of blood."

"Urr – that's horrible."

"Yeah, at first she cried and screamed in pain a lot. We nursed her for several days like that, taking turns day and night. She just lay in her bed sweating and crying. We got her to drink some water from time to time but she couldn't eat and gradually got weaker and weaker. It was when the crying stopped and she became quiet, apart from the wheezing in her chest, that Mum told us…" His eyes looked hollow and glazed. He blinked rapidly.

"What, Mr Solinger, what did she say?"

He wiped away a tear from the corner of his eye. "To say goodbye to our sister – before she would not

be able to hear what each of us had to say. Before…
before she went to heaven."

"Gosh – that's terrible." Olivia reached out and
took hold of his hand. Ben wasn't sure where to look
or what to say. *At least she hasn't said what I thought she
was going to say.* He was relieved about that.

"Do you live here, in this town?" she asked
affectionately, looking up at the man nearly twice her
height.

"No, my family lives in a small place called
Brantedville." He released her hand and rubbed his
face with both hands, then shook his head trying to
regain his composure.

"Is that far?" she asked, tilting her head to one
side.

"Not far, really… but look, you were telling me
about your brother here. Something about him not
being a real Confederate soldier."

"Well, he's not."

"No," he replied, with a lot of question in the
statement.

Ben was furious. *If we weren't about to be caught out
by the telegraph message, V's going to do it here.* He put his
arm tightly around V's shoulder and tried to make it
look like an affectionate hug. Then laughed, "V!"

"No," she turned her head sideways to look at
her brother, "Ben likes to think he's a real soldier but
he's really just a post boy. All he does is take these
silly little messages all over the place – pretending to
be a real soldier – and says how dangerous it is." She
smiled smugly.

"Ah, for a moment… oh, never mind." Solinger puffed out his cheeks and looked up in the direction he should have been heading.

"What?" asked V.

"You should be thanking your brother for what he does do – every job is important," he said as he made his way towards the exit onto the platform. "This way."

Olivia looked up at Ben with a knowing smile. *Clever girl*, he thought and winked back. Charlie had said they needed to slow the soldier down a bit – V was of some use after all.

Solinger turned left out of the booking hall. Ben was about to follow when V grabbed his hand and pulled him in the opposite direction.

"Look, Ben," she said in a stage whisper.

"What?"

"Isn't that the woman you and Charlie came to help?" she said pointing to someone no more than fifteen paces down the platform.

"Gosh – it is!" Ben looked left at Solinger marching off down the platform and then back in Harriet's direction. "Ahhgh! Now what do we do?" Harriet was flanked by the two bounty hunters and there was no way he could get her attention without them noticing. Even just to let her know he was there. He looked one way then the other again.

"What should we do, Ben?"

Her question was answered when the young soldier looked behind him and found them back at the doorway. He stopped. "Hey, come on." He

172

waved them towards him. Frustrated, Ben walked away from Harriet. V followed. They re-joined their leader but on their way down the platform to the telegraph office, Olivia dawdled along to slow them down while she also asked more questions about how long he'd been a soldier here and what his first name was.

Then she dropped Babbit and made a fuss about picking him up and dusting him down. Ben grinned at her admiringly.

"Come on, please, I need to get this message sent off," pleaded the nice young man – who they now knew as Herbert.

"Yes, come on, V," said Ben pretending to hurry her along but not actually encouraging her to move any quicker. She could be a good actress when she wanted, as demonstrated by her performances in various school plays. Ben pulled V by the hand and they trailed after Herbert who was just about to go into the telegraph office. Ben jogged a few paces to catch up.

"Hello, Mister Doolittle," said Solinger cheerfully.

"Hello, Herbert." The telegraph operator acknowledged Ben's presence with a nod but didn't speak. Ben nodded back.

"I've got a message for you, to send to headquarters."

"Right ho." And Herbert handed over the paper from Captain Murray.

Then a little voice from below the reception desk brightly said, "Hello again, Mister Doolittle!" He leant forward over the desk to see where the voice had come from.

"Hello again, my dear, didn't expect to see you again so soon."

"This is my big brother Ben," she proudly announced.

"Well, pleased to meet you, young man. Old Will came in with your little brother and sister a while ago – giving them the grand tour, I think! He's a bright young lad though, isn't he? He'll go a long way when he gets older – mark my words."

"Really?" exclaimed Ben, glancing disapprovingly at V. *He'll go a long way when I get hold of him!*

V stared at the floor to avoid his eyes but was grinning to herself about the mischief.

"Yeah, your brother's quite the smart one, isn't he? He had a go on the Morse key and wasn't bad either; he seemed to get the hang of the code really quickly. If I didn't know better I'd think he'd done it before!" he laughed.

"Oh yes, quite the smart one," repeated Ben with disdain. Douglas held his hand out over the counter to shake Ben's.

V chuckled to herself.

"The message, Mister Doolittle?" queried Herbert, who was beginning to get concerned about the time it had taken him to get this far.

"Oh, yes of course, Herbert." He sat down and opened the letter and read it through a couple of times. By now Olivia had walked around the reception desk and was standing a little way behind

Douglas, watching what he was doing. He reached up in front of him and flicked a couple of switches and then pushed a different button a couple of times.

"What's that for?" asked V. Ben looked at her, mystified as to her interest, his mind still focusing on the sort of message they were likely to receive back from Central Command in Richmond.

Douglas swivelled on his chair and said, "Oh, that's to switch the line directly to the army headquarters, see?" He pointed up to the smaller chart on the wall with place names and numbers that corresponded to a row of switch numbers. "And that button rings a bell at the other end to tell them to expect a message. I think Mr Chaplin explained it all to your brother."

"Yeah, I remember him saying something about it but I didn't really understand." Herbert Solinger let out a big sigh.

"Yes, sorry, Herbert."

"It's just that I've got to go back as soon as I can to the one-armed, po-faced gorilla with an answer and he's already got out of his tree without any bananas today."

"Ah, Captain Murray, I assume." He laughed.

"Yes, the one and only!"

Douglas tapped his finger on the desk as he waited for the return bell to tell him to send his message. "Come on," he muttered, "wakey wakey. They're normally quicker than this."

"Who?" asked V.

"Army headquarters."

Moments later one of the bells on the wall above rang out a single note – the signal for him to send his message – and he started tapping away on the Morse key. It took about a minute to complete the message then after a short pause, *ding ding ding*, the bell above him rang three times. Douglas looked at it, with surprise.

"What?" he said screwing his face up and rubbing his ear. "Send it again? That's not like headquarters. They're normally pretty good at this."

"What's happened?" asked Herbert and V together.

"Nothing really, it's just they want me to send the message again. I guess they didn't get it all first time. Maybe they've got a new guy on who's not so fast. I'll send it slower this time. Doesn't usually happen with the military but who knows these days." He pushed the button to send a double bell ring again to headquarters and waited for the single return. *Ding* went the bell. And he started keying in the message, more slowly this time.

Having completed it, again he waited a while – looking at the bell – and then said, "Well, no send-it-again bell, so I guess we'll just have to wait now for them to return."

Ben struck up a conversation with Douglas about the system he used, how it worked and so on. It was the first form of electrical communication ever used and was a mystery to most people of the time, so he was impressed by the way Ben seemed to understand it. Even little Olivia had grasped the basics. However,

Ben was beginning to sweat a bit, worrying about the return message. *Should they make a run for it now? But with V, Herbert would easily catch them.* He could just visualise the words for himself. 'No such message has been sent from this office!' The clanging of a locomotive bell rang out as it pulled into the station with the accompanying hiss of steam and smoke rising above the buildings.

He signalled to V to join him and they sidled outside whilst Herbert talked to Douglas awaiting the return message. "Do you know where Charlie's gone?" he asked her.

"No." She shrugged her shoulders and shook her head. Ben looked up and down the station buildings but there was no sign of Charlie.

"The little twit, I'm going to kill him!" he muttered with frustration. Ben thought that while Herbert was distracted in the telegraph office, if they were all together, they might just be able to disappear into town. He wasn't sure what to do but the last thing they needed was for him to be arrested.

Several minutes had gone by. "Blimey, they're slow today, Herbert," said Douglas.

Then *ding, ding.* It was too late now for any escape plan Ben may have had in mind but he stood in the doorway holding on to V, ready to leg it anyway. Douglas pressed his button once and the message box started clicking away shortly afterwards. Ben scanned the station for any sign of Charlie.

"Come on, get on with it," complained Douglas, as the letters came through at a snail's pace. "Good job it's not a long or urgent message or we'd be here all day!" he joked. Finally the box stopped clicking and Douglas put down his pen. "Here you are, Herbert," and handed him the note.

Douglas made a note of the time in the message log and Herbert read the message and then went outside to speak to Ben. V gripped Ben's hand tightly and could sense his concern.

"Don't look so worried, kid, come on, I'd better go back to miserable Murray and give him the good news. Whichever way it was, he wasn't going to like it but at least with this, you're in the clear."

"I am!" he said, with a bit more than surprise in his voice. Then coughed and lowered the pitch of his voice and said with a bit more confidence, "Yes, well err… I should think so."

Herbert held up the piece of paper and read the message.

"Apparently, according to this, we should give Captain Bramley any help he wants to get on his way and don't delay him getting to the train station or there will be big trouble." He folded it up and tucked it in a pocket. "It's not the normal sort of reply we get – strange wording – but anyway I must get back and quickly."

Ben looked down at V out of sight of Herbert's gaze and gave her an, *'I don't know how that happened'* look. She shrugged her shoulders and pouted her lips.

"Do you want me to come back with you, Herbert?" Ben asked.

"No, there's no need, unless you want to see the grumpy gorilla again?"

"Not really."

"I guess you gotta be going back to headquarters in Richmond, then?" Herbert asked.

"Yeah, but I'm just gonna catch up with my brother and sister a bit longer first." Ben and Herbert shook hands. Herbert waved goodbye to V and set off down the platform.

"I don't know what Charlie's up to and I don't know how we got that message back but let's go and see if we can find out where Harriet is – we'll have to wait for Charlie outside." Ben and V went back past the ticket office to where they'd seen Harriet on the platform, just in time to see her being escorted on to the steps of a waiting carriage. There was nothing they could do, although Ben walked towards the carriage she had entered, looking up and scanning each window in turn. When they reached the last one he smiled.

Harriet was being seated next to the window and from his lowly position he could not be seen by the man seated next to her. And the other man escorting her was standing in the aisle engaged in conversation with the train conductor and was therefore distracted. He reached up and gently tapped the side of the carriage window to get Harriet's attention. It took a couple of attempts before she noticed the noise and looked round to see what it was. Ben cautiously waved. The sight of Ben gesturing to her made her jump and she sat bolt upright in her seat looking straight ahead. Her escort turned sharply and gave her a strange look as if she were a crazy. He looked her up and down but never said anything and went back to ear-wigging what his colleague was saying to the conductor.

Harriet shuffled her bottom closer to the window and, keeping her gaze dead ahead, she twiddled her fingers under her folded arm in acknowledgement. After a few seconds she slowly and discreetly turned to look out of the window – looking into the distance and not down at Ben. She tilted her head slightly to the left but moved her eyes downwards and gave a knowing blink. She smiled too. Now in sight of Harriet, V gave her a little wave as well and then held Babbit up and waved his arm at her as well. This made Harriet's whole face smile.

She had thought her cause was lost – stuck on a train with a pair of bounty hunters intent on getting their reward. Thought God had decided it was time for her to return to her homeland and the life she had had before freedom. Not that she would actually let them get that far – the pistol concealed under her dress would see to that. At some point she would make a fight of it. But now she knew this was not true. She had always been a deeply religious woman and believed her destiny was always in the hands of the Lord. Since a terrible injury she received as a young girl, she'd suffered from periods of semi-unconsciousness where she had visions of things for her to do. As if guided by an almighty being to do the deeds she did. She totally believed in fate. Now her fate had taken a further turn, with the arrival of these sweet children who were signalling to her that they were going to free her from these men.

Ben didn't know if she knew the game 'Charades' but he was trying to do the best actions he ever had to get the message across. After a moment Harriet had to look away and sit back upright for fear of busting out laughing. Suddenly Ben grabbed V and pulled her back against the carriage side, flattening her against it with his arm.

"What is it, Ben, what's up?"

"The guy talking to the conductor has just turned around and looked at Harriet; I didn't want him to see us."

Inside the carriage the catcher took his seat – opposite his friend – and said, "I dunno what you gotta smile about, lady, but then you best get all your smiling dun now cos you won't be smilin' when we gets you back home." Both catchers laughed out loud.

At first, when Harriet next turned to look out of the window, she could not see her new friends either. Then she rested her head against the window and saw them out of the corner of her eye, pinned against the carriage side. The catchers were ignoring her, engaged in their own chit-chat, so she flicked her fingers to wave Ben and V away, scared they might be seen.

She knew in her heart things would be all right. She put her hands together in prayer and placed them under her chin. She thought, but didn't mouth, words of thanks and looked upwards.

One of the catchers thumbed at her to his mate, "He ain't gonna 'elp you now, lady." And they both laughed again. Harriet ignored them and turned her head to the outside again. Ben was reaffirming his gestures and Harriet tried to lip-read his words as they backed away from the carriage when the engine bell started to clang. A guard at the back of the train was waving a flag and blowing a whistle from beside the track; as the carriages started to move he hopped on, still waving his flag.

Slowly the train puffed and clattered out of the station, bound for Richmond. Ben and V stood back and watched it leave before making their way back to the booking hall. As they entered from the platform side, Charlie entered from the road side. Grinning idiotically, yet complacently. Ben glared, "Where have you been?"

Charlie ignored the question. "Did it work?"

"Did what work?" asked Ben.

"My message."

"What do you mean, your message?"

"Well, when I left you I ran down to the telegraph repeater station and stopped the message going down the line."

"What are you on about – repeater station?" said Ben.

"While you were at the camp, that old porter gave us a tour of the whole station–"

"Yeah, I sort of noticed you didn't do as I told you to," Ben grumbled.

"Well, this time you're pleased I didn't," Charlie said smugly.

"Go on," said Ben.

"Well, he explained that all the messages from the main telegraph office pass through the repeater station, so that's where I went when you told us about the soldier taking our message to get it checked out. I stopped it being sent to headquarters. I switched off the link box which broke the link from the station here to headquarters and waited for the message to come through from Douglas, the operator in the telegraph office. Simple!" Ben ran his fingers through his hair and relaxed his cross expression.

"Then I listened to the clicks from the buzz box and wrote down the message but I didn't get it first time. Luckily there are all the same posters on the wall as the main office and one tells you how many bell rings to send for the different reasons."

"Ah," said Ben, "that's why he had to send it twice, and slowed down." Ben was slowly getting the picture.

"Yeah, I got it the second time. I wrote all the dots and dashes down then decoded them using the chart and made up my own reply in the same way."

"You clever little…" He gave Charlie a little punch first and then hugged him.

Charlie grinned from ear to ear. "It wasn't that difficult, especially after doing the electrics project at school with toggle switches, wires and stuff. I just had to make sure I cut off the headquarters line first and then listen for the clicks and write down the message."

V gave her brother a hug too. "Well done, Charlie."

"Well, it worked a treat, Charlie, and now we can go and wait for Oliver to come out of the army camp. I'll carry that bag again now." Ben picked up the bag and with their spirits lifted they walked through the station to wait for Oliver outside.

Chapter 17

As he approached the station Oliver waved, "Hi, kids." Charlie and V ran towards him eagerly, Ben following with a look of relief. "Whatever you guys did, it did the trick. The commander's secretary man wasn't best pleased, mind."

"You met Captain Murray, then," said Ben, smirking.

"Yes, but there was nothing he could do after his moaning but tell me to get off to Richmond. I pity the next guy who ruins his day!" He laughed.

They stood in a huddle outside the station, while Ben told him how Charlie had saved the day intercepting the telegraph message to headquarters, and then sent a false reply, albeit slowly, in Morse code – which made them believe the original message.

"Fantastic – Charlie, how did you know how to…"

"At school, we did Morse code in science, as a project, to help us learn about electrics and history at the same time and the old porter man showed us how the telegraph office here works – simple really!" Charlie grinned with satisfaction, proving he wasn't as stupid as Ben sometimes made him out to be. He put up a hand to high five Oliver but Oliver wasn't quite sure that a high five was the thing to do here and patted Charlie on the head instead.

Ben went on to explain the encounter with Harriet too.

"Oh, great, they must've been held up by the delays on the line. Apparently there's been some trouble on the line from here to Richmond – Yankee snipers, I believe. But I did hear at the barracks that a company of Confederate soldiers had rounded them up."

"That was the last we saw of her – leaving on a train a little while ago."

They entered the station to find that the next train to Richmond would be in about two hours. Oliver suggested they sit in the waiting room and check they had everything with them and what to do when they got there. After a short while they had it all agreed. A plan. They just had to hope the bounty hunters and Harriet would get delayed again at Richmond and not leave town until they got there.

Charlie paced around the waiting room – where initially they were the only occupants; when he wasn't pacing he sat and kicked his heels against the bench. V sat on a bench cross-legged and talked to Babbit. It wasn't long, though, before others joined them in the waiting room and gradually the other two bench seats were occupied with waiting travellers. The large clock on the wall ticked painfully slowly and time dragged by.

After staring out of the window watching a waiting train, Ben sat down next to Oliver, thought for a moment, and then quietly asked, "Oliver, I've been wanting to ask you about Emilie."

"What about her, Ben?" he said, unfolding his arms and resting his head on one hand.

"Well, both Charlie and I have been to her shop – the Emporium – and…" he paused and looked over at Charlie.

"Yes, Ben." He nodded for him to continue. Charlie moved over and sat on the other side of Oliver.

"It's just that, when I first went there, she gave me the creeps. I mean, nothing horrid or anything really, just a… a feeling." Ben hesitated and sighed slightly.

"Go on," said Oliver.

V slid over to hear what they were saying too.

"I mean, it's an amazing place with all the stuff she has in there but it also gives you a weird feeling, like it's been like that forever."

"And it smells strange – like old and mouldy," Charlie chipped in.

"Yeah, and sometimes there's a strange sweet smell – like burning flowers. Like the smell of the oriental shop Mum took me in once. She said it was hippy – whatever that means."

"And she creeps up on you when you're not looking," said Charlie.

Oliver smirked and let out a little laugh. "She is a bit mischievous, I'll give you that, but she doesn't mean anything by it. Just her way – that's all," said Oliver.

"I don't think Harry's too keen on her either. He didn't seem too happy about having to go there when we were discussing getting the stuff from her for this trip."

"Oh, Harry doesn't really mind, if he has to go he will, but she has played a few tricks on him in the past. He nearly sliced his own finger off once when she made him jump!"

"Is that it, Oliver? Is she some kind of magician, like that guy on the telly who can read your mind and hypnotise you; so you do things you don't mean to?"

"I watched him with Mum once; he was very clever," said Charlie. "A man ate a raw onion like it was an apple!" Oliver leant back on his seat and laughed again.

"Or maybe," offered Charlie, "she was once a ballerina and that's why she walks around so quietly."

"Quietly!" exclaimed Ben. "It's not just quiet, it's silent."

"Come on, Oliver, you must have known her a long time – what do you think?"

"Ah, yes… I have certainly known Emilie a long time. In a way, I suppose, longer than you could imagine, but she's not a magician or an ex-ballet dancer!"

"Are you related, then?" asked V. "Like cousins or something? My mum had an aunt she knew for longer than I could imagine. I think her aunt was Victorian."

"No, V, she wasn't Victorian, she lived in a Victorian house, that's all," said Ben.

Charlie laughed and made a face at V. Oliver couldn't help grinning either.

"No, V, not at all. We are, I suppose, quite close. She's been a good friend for a long, long time now and if you promise to keep it a secret between you three and tell no one – and as you already, obviously, know about Jenny, which no one else does except Harry and Beryl – maybe I can let you in on another little secret."

"Pinkie promise!" said Olivia, and held out the little finger on her right hand.

"Urh?" murmured Oliver.

"Pinkie promise – we tell no secrets!"

"Oh – I see!" Oliver hooked his little finger around V's and repeated the phrase. The boys copied their sister and each held out their little fingers. They moved in even closer to hear what Oliver had to say.

"Well, it all began when I went on a trip to–"

Suddenly the door to the waiting room was flung open and a porter announced that there was a Richmond-bound train leaving shortly – an extra train taking a contingent of soldiers on board – and if anyone wanted to join it they could. It was over another hour before their scheduled train was due to leave. Oliver stood up. "Yes – we'll go!"

"Okay – follow me." As they stepped out of the waiting room, *clang, clang, clang*, the now familiar sound of a loco bell sounded.

"Sorry, kids," apologised Oliver, "the sooner we get to Richmond the better."

"But what about Emilie?" pleaded Charlie.

"That'll have to wait till later. We'd better get to the train now."

Ben and Charlie let out a big sigh and dropped their heads in disappointment. They knew something was strange about Emilie but what was it that Oliver was about to tell them?

Oliver took V by the hand. "Come on, boys, if it's quiet on the train, I'll fill you in with more of the story there." Disappointed, but resigned to the situation, Ben picked up his bag and he and Charlie followed Oliver out of the waiting room. The train standing in the station had five carriages attached behind the locomotive and its tender, with a further guard's wagon at the back.

After wandering through a couple of carriages they found a seat on the near full train and made themselves comfortable. Shortly after, they were underway to the sound of the locomotive bell clanging again. It was quite hot in the carriage and as the clickerty-clack of the train wheels over the track increased in tempo, so a welcome breeze flowed through to cool them. The countryside was flatter here with more open farmland and homesteads peppering the landscape. People could be seen working and tending the crops in the afternoon sun, although some lines of cotton-wool clouds were slowly drifting across the sky.

It wasn't a long journey but Charlie got up and explored the whole length of the train and for a time tried to watch the engine men at work from the open platform at the front of the first carriage. The loco had four large driving wheels with four small ones at the front beneath the massive chimney. One of the men operated the controls to drive the machine while the other almost constantly had to feed the fire with logs from the tender. A tall column of grey smoke spewed out of the chimney, flowing back over the carriages behind where Charlie stood. He listened to the pounding, thumping heartbeat of the steam engine lugging the train along. The rhythm of the cylinder beat and the fire breath from the chimney really did make it seem like a living thing – he made a wish to be in control of one himself someday.

A few minutes later the conductor entered the carriage in which the rest were seated. "Next stop Richmond!" he shouted.

"I'll go and get Charlie," said Ben. "As much as I would – at times – not want him around, I don't want him missing when we get there."

"Yes, he actually did a good job back there – with the telegraph. If it wasn't for him–" said Oliver, pondering the thought.

As the train rolled into Richmond they felt a certain relief that they'd made it this far. After it had screeched to a halt with a big hiss of steam from the loco, they let the soldiers pile off first and then disembarked the carriage. There was quite a lot of activity going on at the station, and it was much bigger than the others they had visited – only Petersburg was close – with a wide, high overall roof spanning four railway tracks. In the centre of the roof there was a further vented raised section that let out the smoke and steam. Another train sat idle on another track, headed in the other direction – back to Richmond. Railway employees in neat blue uniforms and little peaked caps were bustling about all over the place – fetching and carrying bags and trunks.

There were a number of station buildings on both sides of the tracks with signs hanging outside most of them, yet people still seemed to have the freedom to wander about all over the tracks to get to their train. Ben, Charlie and V followed Oliver as he walked towards the sign marked 'Exit to East Street'. Although he had no more idea of where to start than they did, it looked like a good place to begin. They reached a crowded lobby area, just inside the open doorway to the street. Oliver perused the scene for a moment and then decided to put the first part of their plan into action here.

But first he told Charlie to hold on to V's hand and take a look round the station for Harriet. If they saw her they were not to speak to her but come back and wait for him and Ben. "There," he pointed, "just outside the ladies' waiting room.

Even if she sees you, just nod or something, but don't go to her. Okay, Charlie?"

"Yes, I understand, no talking." He sighed.

"Sure!" emphasised Ben.

"Yes, Ben!"

"Well, I know what you're like – you always want to be first." Charlie did like being first at everything, he was not very good at being restrained. If an opportunity arose for him to win, be the lead, or triumph at something, he would – any attainment that could be admired, considering his petit stature for his age, he'd do it. He wasn't averse to a bit of sly cheating either, if it meant victory for him! And he played the 'I'm only small' card frequently!

Once Charlie and V had disappeared through the crowd, Oliver began the theatre.

"Yes, son, you heard right," said Oliver loudly and deliberately. "That Harriet Tubman woman I'm looking for is rumoured to be hereabouts somewhere." He slyly looked around to see if anyone was listening.

"I saw a poster, sir, asking for information of her whereabouts as she was an escaped slave," Ben replied, in a similar louder-than-normal voice. They moved a few paces closer to a large crowd.

"That is also true, son, but now I have a warrant to arrest her and take her before a court for treason." A few heads began to turn.

"Treason!"

"Yes, treason – we think she's been working as a spy for those damn Yankees."

"Well, I did see someone looking like the person you described, not long ago, walking right through this station."

"You did, son?" said Oliver, keeping up the pretence. A few more people started to take an interest in what Oliver was saying.

"You're quite sure, a black woman wearing a long black dress and a bonnet on her head and two scars on her face?" asked Oliver in a very formal voice and indicated on his face with a finger where the scars were.

"Yes, sir, I'm sure I did."

"But you don't know which way this woman was heading?" asked Oliver waving his fake warrant in the air. Ben shook his head.

"Sir!" a raised voice from a nearby crowd called. And a man in a brown suit held up his arm to attract Oliver's attention and made his way through the crowd towards them. "Sir!" he repeated, "I think the boy's right; I might have seen the woman you're looking for too."

"Really, sir?" Oliver said, in slightly disbelieving voice. He was a middle-aged man carrying a neat leather briefcase near to his chest and he wore a wide-brimmed hat.

He stood in front of Oliver. "Yes, sir, from what I could hear, I'm sure I saw her with two rough-looking cowboy types and one of them was holding on to her. They were standing in front of me in the ticket queue."

"Did you happen to hear where they were going? The government would be very grateful," asked Oliver.

"Well, there are no trains in the direction they wanted to go but I heard one of them say he was going to try and find a livery yard or somewhere to hire some horses."

"Did they say where the other two would wait?"

"No, sir, but I got the impression it wouldn't be far away. They didn't seem very familiar with Richmond," the man with the briefcase replied.

"Well, thank you very much, sir, I much appreciate your help."

"Anything for our boys in grey – like you." He raised his hat as a salute to Oliver and left.

Oliver turned to Ben and in a slightly lower, yet commanding voice said, "Well, son, you might be able to help me here – I'll make it worth your while." He pretended that they had just met and shook Ben's hand.

"I'd be pleased to help you, sir." He did his best to stand to attention – like a soldier.

"Follow me, son – we're going to have a look around the station first."

Chapter 18

Oliver and Ben moved away to a quiet corner of the lobby – far enough away from prying ears. "She might not be far away, then," said Ben.

"No, I'll bet they're not far at all – could well still be in the station."

"Shall I go and find Charlie and V?"

"Good idea, Ben, but first just have a scout around the far side of the station. Charlie and V were going to stay this side of the rails, so why don't you go and have a look around over there first. I'll wait for you all here."

"Okay, Oliver."

After Ben had left, Oliver strolled over to the street exit and viewed the people coming and going outside. Richmond was a busy town, where the government of the Confederacy was based, as well as the President – Jefferson Davis. Carts loaded with goods trundled to and from the station goods yard way off to Oliver's left and apart from the troops; life seemed to be going on as normal. But these were the early years of the Civil War; a blockade of the southern state ports made it difficult to bring in fresh supplies from outside the Confederacy. Times were to become much harder for the Confederate population over the next couple of years, with many goods in short supply. The northern states were the industrial powerhouse of the US and also traded easily with other nations for supplies, yet had the ability with their navy to maintain a stranglehold on the fortunes of those who lived in the south. Today it was not obvious to Oliver how much the south was suffering – except perhaps in the state of the soldiers' dress. He returned to survey the people thronging the inside of the station complex.

★ ★ ★

V tugged at Charlie's hand and pointed to a small group of people chatting beyond what looked like a couple of chairs where men were seated getting their shoes shined by two little boys kneeling at their feet. "Psst, Charlie," she said, "look, isn't that Harriet over there?" She'd not seen her close up, only sitting on the train when she was with Ben at Petersburg Station.

"Yes!" said Charlie excitedly. "That's her." Charlie pulled V to the side and partly hid behind a newspaper stand.

"Shall we go back and tell Ben and Oliver?" asked V.

"I think we should just let her know we're here," replied Charlie, taking a second look from behind his hide.

"But, Charlie–"

Before she could say any more Charlie moved from their hiding place. "We'll just do it quietly.

Come on, V." Charlie stepped out and followed closely behind a man and a woman walking towards the shoe-shine stand – V found herself being dragged along too. The four of them looked like a man and his wife with two children following behind.

As they got closer V could see Harriet had her hands tied with a piece of rope and her minder was holding the other end. The catcher was talking and laughing with two other men having their shoes shined. Charlie and V kept themselves hidden by walking closely behind the couple. Both Harriet and the catcher had their backs to the approaching family group – not that the couple realised they had suddenly become a family group! But that's what it would have appeared to be to a bystander.

As they were about to walk unnoticed past Harriet, Charlie gave V a nudge, "Char–" she squeaked and she fell sideways into Harriet's dress. Harriet stumbled slightly herself at the impact and let out an 'ooh' sound, then turned and looked down at V crumpled underneath her. With the movement, Harriet's hands pulled on the rope, which attracted the catcher's attention. He turned round with a gruff look to see what she was doing, then gave the rope a tug in his direction.

"Oi! What you playing at?"

"Sorry, sir," she replied as she regained her posture. At first Harriet didn't recognise the little girl but still smiled at her despite the rope digging into her wrists again.

198

V beamed back. "I'm sorry," she said apologetically and started to go a bit red in the face as she unravelled herself from Harriet's dress.

"You don't have to apologise to this thing," snarled the catcher. "It was probably her fault anyway." He gave another tug on the rope holding Harriet's hands and bent down and offered a hand to help V to her feet.

"I'm okay," she said, declining the helping hand, and scrabbled herself onto her feet. Harriet took a second look at the little girl brushing herself down and who appeared to be looking around for someone else. Something about her seemed familiar, yet she didn't really recognise her. She squinted and concentrated for a moment – something in her thoughts told her she should recognise this young person.

The couple Charlie and V had been hiding behind stopped and turned around to see what the commotion was about. Before Harriet's minder could spot him Charlie dived around the backs of the couple, out of sight again. V looked for Charlie. *Where had he suddenly disappeared to? Why did he push me into Harriet?*

"Are yous ole right, little one?" asked Harriet. "I'm sorry if I dwas in yer way, young lady."

"No, no, not at all, I… I just tripped, that's all. I'm fine. It was my fault." Another sharp pull on the rope moved Harriet a further couple of paces away.

The lady who V had, a few moments ago, been hiding behind stepped forward – ignoring Harriet's presence entirely – and took Olivia by the hand. "Now, are you sure you're okay?" she asked, then glared at Harriet in disgust.

"Really, I'm fine." V shook herself and waved her arms as proof.

"Is this yours, my dear?" asked the man as he bent down and picked up a soft grey-white little cuddly toy. It was Babbit.

"Yes, thank you," she said and grasped him tightly, then checked to see if he was okay too. Turning her head from side to side she finally spied Charlie furtively moving behind the couple. She frowned at him.

Fearing he might be spotted, Charlie slowly backed away and moved behind a stout wooden pillar. A whistle blew somewhere in the station and a locomotive bell began to clang above the sound of conversations nearby. Charlie stayed hidden for a moment then craned his head around the pillar to see what was going on. V was still dusting off the dirt and the new lady friend was fussing about her. His eagle-eyes also saw someone hurrying towards them who then shouted something – looking every bit the outlaw man. As he got closer – and waving furiously – Charlie heard him as he repeated himself, "Glenn, Glenn, I've got the horses. And a cart," he shouted.

It was Don Henley, the desperado partner of Glenn Fry who was holding on to Harriet. He wore a wide leather belt sporting an impressive row of bullets and a six-shooter pistol hanging loosely at his side. He waved his hat wildly in the air, obviously very excited at his news. As Glenn turned back to face the direction of the voice calling him, Harriet took advantage to glance in the opposite direction, where Olivia was staring. And there she could just see a little face peeking out from behind a column. A face she recognised. The one which belonged to the little boy who had got her into this situation. But she also knew it had been an innocent accident. She felt good – relieved.

It was awkward for her but she nodded at him to keep away as best she could – to remain out of view. With her hands tied and too close to her captor to say anything she hoped he took the hint. His head disappeared behind the pillar.

"You can't be here in this big station on your own; who are you with?" asked the lady.

Making sure Harriet could hear her by turning slightly in her direction, "I'm looking for my…" she hesitated, "my uncle Oliver. He said to meet him at the ladies' waiting room."

"Well, you're going the wrong way for that; it's over there," pointed the lady, back in the direction from which they had come.

"Oh, thank you – he's an important officer in the army, you know," said Olivia, turning back to face the elegantly dressed lady.

"Oh, you must be proud of him."

"I am, and he looks so smart in his grey uniform," she said loudly, emphasising the word – grey.

While her escorts were distracted – busy discussing their next move – Harriet took the opportunity to listen more carefully to what Olivia was saying. Last time she'd seen Oliver he was dressed in a Yankee officer's uniform. *What was this about a Confederate uniform*, she thought?

On their journey to Richmond, Oliver had impressed on them all the importance of the colour of the uniform, especially as he had both in his bag, depending on which he needed at the time. Olivia was good with colours – a definite talent for art, her teacher had told her mother.

"Which regiment is he in?" asked the man.

"Oh, I don't know – but I think he is a captain."

"A captain – that's good." His wife nodded in agreement and approval. As this was the capital of the Confederacy everyone strongly backed the army and what it stood for – although many good men had died since the war started and many families were bereaved of fathers and sons.

Harriet looked over her shoulder at Olivia – the little girl seemed to be trying to give her a message. Charlie sneaked another peek and waved this time, then gestured a thumbs-up at V. The penny dropped – she had seen the little girl before, with Ben at Petersburg Station. *That's where I've seen her before.*

"Well, you'd better be getting along to the waiting room – to find your father."

"Yes, yes... thank you – I will." She tapped Harriet on the leg. "Sorry about–"

The lady swept her arm around V and moved her away from Harriet's position. "You don't need to apologise to her, just go and find you father – that thing is fine!" Harriet ignored the woman's contempt and smiled at Olivia. Olivia smiled back. She found it hard to understand how these people could treat Harriet, or indeed any person, in this way, but remembered what Oliver had said – 'leave it to him'.

By now Don had joined Glenn and explained he'd managed to get a pair of horses and a cart to take them and Harriet but a condition of the deal was that they would deliver some supplies to an army outpost on their way. Most horses and carts were now under the control of the army unless specifically required for reserved occupations beneficial to the Confederate cause. Don had agreed to return the cart after they'd completed their journey and would deliver the supplies to the garrison as soon as he could on his way to return Harriet to her owners.

Just as V was being ushered on her way to be reunited with Oliver, she overheard one of the men say something about 'the Johnson Road supply depot'. They were already leading Harriet away and V didn't hear anything else. Halfway to the lobby she looked back and saw the desperados – with Harriet – leaving the station by walking alongside the tracks towards a tall water tower. The smartly dressed man and woman – still standing where she left them – waved and then walked off in the opposite direction towards a waiting train. Charlie was still hiding behind the pillar but once Harriet and her two guards were at a safe distance he ran to catch up with V.

Soon after Charlie and V had returned, Ben joined them shaking his head – he'd not seen anything of Harriet.

"It's okay, Ben, these two have found her," smiled Oliver.

"Yeah, Charlie pushed me into her."

"We had to get her attention somehow."

"Oliver said we weren't to talk to her."

"Well… we didn't really and you found out where they might be taking her," said Charlie smugly, scratching his nose.

"You did? Where?" interrupted Ben.

Oliver looked around furtively and then said, "If Olivia's right it sounds like they are going to the supply depot to get the horses and a cart to take Harriet. I heard mention of the place while I was in the barracks at Petersburg; it's a large yard not far from the station, by all accounts."

"That's good news. Well done, V," said Ben. He put his arm around her shoulders and gave a squeeze. She smiled and hugged him back.

"What did they say then, V?" asked Ben.

"Something about the Johnson Road supply depot. Yes, I think that's what the man said."

"You sure? It's important, V; we don't want to waste time going the wrong way."

"Well, that's what it sounded like and we could follow them anyway."

"We'll need to catch up fast, though, because if they leave town we don't know which way they will be going," said Oliver. "Now Ben's back we need to get going. Show us where you saw her."

Charlie led them through to the boot-polish stand and pointed out where the bounty hunters took Harriet. Ben jogged up the track out of the station looking all around for signs of them and Oliver hurried the others behind. Outside the station building there were many railway tracks and sidings holding goods carriages and locomotives. Two tall water towers occupied a position alongside the tracks, one on the main line and one nearer the sidings where a locomotive tender was being filled with water. To their left was another large red-brick shed with a single track running through it. A line of goods wagons reached inside the shed where sacks of something were being unloaded from one of them.

Way over on the right, with a single track leading to it, was a circular building with a wide, raised centre section of roof – a waft of smoke emanated from one of the vents that surrounded the raised section. It was the locomotive repair and stabling shed. Horse and manpower were being used to move empty and loaded wagons around the marshalling yard and many people were busy making the goods yard function but there was no sign of Harriet and her captors. After making a solo attempt to spot Harriet, Ben re-joined the others who were now standing at the base of the water tower by the main line.

"Couldn't see her anywhere," sighed Ben. He'd run to the far side of the yard and back and now rested his hands on his knees and panted. His head drooped down, partly in exhaustion and partly disappointment. The bounty hunters were getting away again.

Chapter 19

There wasn't much of a fence to keep the general public out of the marshalling yard but they weren't supposed to be just wandering around the tracks and soon a railway worker approached them as they stood next to the tower.

"Hey, you shouldn't bring kids through here," he shouted.

"We were following someone and sort of got lost, or rather lost them. We were… err… trying to collect something of ours," explained Oliver.

"If you've got something to collect, you need to go over to the goods shed and ask them."

"Well, it wasn't exactly the railway goods depot we were looking for… it was–" Oliver was interrupted by a train coming towards them on the mainline, ringing its bell. The railway worker guided them away from the track and waved at the driver as the train passed.

"You were saying."

Charlie went to speak but Ben, who'd regained his breath now, beat him to it, "Well, actually, we were looking for somewhere called the Johnson Road depot."

"The Johnson Road Depository?" the man scoffed. "You don't want to come through here for

Johnson Road, that's down past Sickle Street, the other side of the East Street entrance. You are lost!" he laughed. Looking at Oliver, "Nah, you gotta go back through the station – out through the East Street exit. Like I said, look for Sickle Street," he said pointing.

Oliver thanked him. "Come on, kids, looks like we've been led up the garden path." V gave him a confused look. He laughed, "Don't worry, V, we'll find 'em." He grabbed V's hand and they all hurried back towards the station, through the crowds and out the East Street entrance.

"I hope you heard right, V, or we really are going to lose them again," said Ben.

"I did. I'm sure."

"Yeah, but Charlie saw them going out the other way." V hugged Babbit and looked worried that maybe she'd got it wrong.

"I don't know why they'd do that!"

"It's all right, V, they must have had a reason for going that way – but the best we've got is what you heard."

★ ★ ★

She had a tendency to easily worry about such things and had a very sensitive nature. When she was six – during her second year at school – she became so concerned that her classmates had rejected her that when she lay in bed at night she started pulling her eyelashes out. It wasn't until she'd pulled over half of them out that Laura noticed something was wrong. It was after a particularly bad day for V that Laura found her crying in her bed late at night and when she wiped the tears away Laura noticed for the first time V's lack of eyelashes.

At first she didn't say anything but after a few moments comforting her, V subconsciously began to pluck away at her eyelashes. "Why, darling?" she'd asked. V didn't really know – except it was something that happened when she worried about things going on at school. Laura couldn't believe her little daughter was under so much stress that she was doing this to herself. How could a six-year-old be under that amount of stress? Childhood was supposed to be the one time in your life that was stress free. She couldn't believe it and started crying herself. V said it wasn't because she was being bullied – just that she didn't think any of her classmates liked her, which turned out not to be the case at all. Olivia was just a very sensitive, loving, caring little girl who just wanted everyone to give her the same in return. When it didn't happen, her overactive imagination took over and invented horrors of rejection that led to her trichotillomania.

Laura visited the school at the time and found reassurance from her teacher that Olivia's relationships with her classmates appeared normal but that she would keep a close eye on her and help V understand the complex relationships children sometimes have. With reassurance that things were not as bad as V perceived she gradually overcame her problems and eventually her eyelashes grew back to shadow her beautiful eyes. However, Laura never again let down her vigilant care and attention of things that could worry V.

★ ★ ★

After a moment Ben spotted a sign on a building wall announcing Sickle Street.

"Come on, this way," he said. They dodged horses and carts to cross the busy dusty road to Sickle Street and made their way past various shops and offices in search of Johnson Road. There was still no sign of Harriet, though, as they hurried along. Then after passing two other crossing streets they saw a sign for Johnson Road – buildings several storeys high lined the road but it was not as busy as the other two streets they'd used to get here. Ben jogged on ahead with Charlie close on his heels. Oliver would have expected it to have been much busier if it was the home of an army supply depot. It didn't look right.

He scratched his chin, *This is Johnson Road but it's not as busy as Petersburg. If there was an entrance to an army depot we'd see some guards about.* Ben and Charlie were fifty or so paces further ahead of him and V was looking at both sides of the street for signs of an army building, then a man stepped out of a doorway a few yards in front of him. "Excuse me," said Oliver, holding up his hand, "I'm looking for the Johnson Road army supply depot."

The man looked a bit puzzled for a moment and then said, "Ah, I think you mean the John Swan Road Depot. That's the army depot; there is a depository further down," he said pointing, "but it's a furniture depot!"

Ben and Charlie were running back to join them just in time to hear Oliver ask the man for directions. "It's just the other side of the marshalling yard at the station. Go around the top end and John Swan Road leads down to the canal. You'll see the supply depot on your left." He raised his hat and walked off down the road.

"What did he say? It's not here?" asked Charlie. V screwed her face up and wished she'd not said anything and wanted to hide.

"That's right, Charlie, it's back where we started."

"Sorry," said V timidly.

"How's that? V said she heard them say Johnson Road?"

"Well, it was close," said Oliver. "I think they must have said John Swan Road. That's where the depot is."

"Goodness, Olivi–" began Ben.

"No, Ben, we had no idea. She just misheard, that's all."

"Yeah, but we–"

"No good crying over spilt milk," said Oliver, "We'd better hurry back and hope we're not too late." He took hold of Olivia's hand reassuringly. "Come on, it's okay."

V was nearly in tears. "It's all my fault; we'll lose her for good now," she cried.

Charlie put his arm around his sister. "Come on, V, we can run there; we're not giving up." She held Babbit tightly under her chin with the ribbon twirled around her fingers. Charlie smiled at her and gave her another squeeze, then took hold of her hand and whispered in her ear, "Let's show 'em who's quickest at running." Then he pulled her from Oliver's grasp and started to run along the pavement.

"Hey, wait for us!" shouted Ben. Oliver and Ben didn't catch them until they were about to cross East Street back at the station.

As the man said, they routed up around the goods yard and there they found the road they were looking for. Oliver for one was glad they had resumed walking, albeit at a fast pace, as he was panting like mad from the run to catch up. He rubbed the sweat off his forehead and then slowed to a normal walking pace. Further down the road there were clear signs of army activity with soldiers milling around about a hundred yards further down the road and carts being hauled out of an entrance. They stopped short of the brick-pillared entrance arch and Oliver gathered them to one side. Oliver again rubbed his head and massaged his neck. He felt hot but it was a warm day, although not warm enough to cause him to feel the way he did. He took comfort by leaning on a wall

"Are you all right, Oliver?" asked Charlie. Ben was a few steps away scanning for signs of Harriet while V also watched Oliver struggle with the heat.

"Yes… I'm fine. Just feeling a bit 'hot and bothered' as my mother used to say." He squinted and shrugged his shoulders. "Let's hope we find Harriet here, eh?"

"Why would they want to go to the army depot anyway?" asked Charlie.

"I think the army has commandeered a lot of the transport around here, particularly the horses and carts, as the Union Army keeps destroying parts of the railroad tracks. So it may be the only place to get hold of them now."

Ben had re-joined them. "Shall I go and have a look from the gate? I might be able to see what's going on."

"Yep, good idea," sighed Oliver. His temperature was rising and a red inflammation was showing on his neck. "Why not? Just go and have a quick look. We'll wait here."

Ben sauntered down to the entrance to the depot. Several soldiers loitered around the gateway chatting to each other and paid no attention to the boy kicking stones about near one of the entrance pillars. Ben could see stockpiles of cannon balls and other shells, a row of cannon, some permanent-looking brick buildings and a row of more temporary looking wooden huts on the right. He kept to the side as a couple of open wagons loaded with barrels left the depot followed by a covered wagon with two soldiers at the front. They shouted something in a strong southern accent and waved to the guards, who laughed and waved them on.

He could see some men hitching four horses to a cannon and a cart being loaded with something from one of the brick buildings but it was too far away to see what. Suddenly Ben moved quickly to hide behind the pillar. Outside one of the sheds beyond the piles of cannon balls and cannon shells he thought he could see a person sitting in the back of an open wagon. The person was wearing head gear that looked similar to that which Harriet wore and they sat with their head lowered and arms folded.

At the front a man sat higher up on the bench seat and it looked as if he was holding the reins and steadying the horses. He couldn't be sure because it was quite a distance but he believed it could be Harriet in the back. His heart raced and a burst of adrenalin coursed through his veins. He cautiously snuck another look. Still the group of soldiers laughing and joking at the gate ignored him. Ben backed away at first then turned and ran back to where the others were waiting. It wasn't far but by the time he reached them he was puffing like a steam train. His eyes said it all.

"What is it, Ben?" asked Charlie eagerly, grabbing his brother by the arm.

"I think–" he puffed, "I can see her."

"Really, who, Harriet?" said Oliver. Ben nodded, gasping for air. V smiled excitedly and jumped up and down. Charlie grinned from ear to ear.

"Yes," continued Ben, "I'm sure she was sitting in the back of a wagon with a load of barrels and there was a driver up front talking to some guys around the horses." Oliver opened his bag and retrieved the order Edward Franklin had printed for him and handed it to Ben for a moment, then removed his army hat and swept his head with his hand. Beads of sweat oozed from his brow and his face was noticeably redder than it had been only a few minutes before. He wiped his forehead with his sleeve and took the note back from Ben. All three looked on with concern as Oliver was obviously pausing before speaking.

"Are you all right, Oliver? Your neck is… well, gone all red." V looked at him with a worried frown.

"Yeah, don't worry, V – I'm fine really." But he wasn't; his throat was burning and it hurt to swallow. "Okay. If it is them I think they'll be leaving that way," he said, pointing down towards the canal. "And, if I'm right, we will also need to go that way, I think."

They would have to take a ferry and cross the river to get to Maryland – Harriet's homeland.

"Ben, could you get the map out and have a look yourself, see if you reckon I'm right?"

Ben rummaged around in his bag and pulled out a map of the area they'd got from Emilie. Charlie held out one side of the map while they studied the layout. V moved closer to Oliver and held his hand; she tried to brighten him up by wiggling Babbit in front of him and talking in Babbit language. It made Oliver smile but it didn't make him feel much better. He knew something was not quite right, he'd been slowly feeling groggier as the day had gone on.

Both Charlie and Ben were competent map readers with the skills the orienteering lessons had taught them at school and they soon sussed out where they were on the map. It helped that they had the massive station complex of Richmond behind them and the river and canal not far away. Harriet had marked on the map earlier where they would have to go to reach her sister and that was clearly in the direction Oliver had suggested.

"Yep, I reckon so," said Ben and manoeuvred the map to show Oliver.

"So what are we going to do?" asked a bright-eyed Charlie.

"Well, I think you should take Olivia and walk on past the entrance around that corner so you are out of sight of the guards. Find somewhere to wait while I take Ben and speak to the guards." Charlie wasn't impressed with the idea, he wanted to be involved, but he did understand. He set off with V and they calmly walked past the soldiers on duty at the gate and disappeared around the bend in the road. Ben tucked the map away and after a few moments he and Oliver walked down towards the depot entrance. Seeing Oliver in his officer's uniform approach, the soldiers guarding it straightened themselves out and saluted.

Addressing one of the men, "Good day," Oliver said in the most official officer's voice he could muster. His eyes were beginning to sting a bit but he knew he needed to gather all the strength he had and get Harriet out.

The soldier stood to attention and returned the salute, "Sir."

Oliver pulled a piece of paper from the top pocket of his uniform and unfolded it. "I have here a warrant for the arrest of a woman who I am led to believe might have been brought here." He flashed the official-looking piece of paper under the soldier's eyes.

"A woman?" questioned the private.

"Yes, a slave woman by the name of Harriet Tubman who may have been brought here by two bounty hunters looking for horses to transport her out of here. So, if she is here, I need to collect her."

"Yes, sir!" He saluted again. "I'll just get the gate corporal, sir." The man turned about and went into a small brick-built office by the gate. Shortly afterwards another man strolled out to speak to Oliver. He confirmed that there had been two men with a fugitive slave asking after a cart and horses, and as far as he knew they were loading up now. They had been hired the use of a wagon on the condition they deliver some barrels of food to some troops on the way and return the vehicle when they had completed their journey.

While the man read the warrant for Harriet's arrest Oliver had passed to him, Oliver looked past the corporal into the busy supply yard where men in civilian clothing and soldiers were either loading or unloading wagons, or carrying things from one place to another. A hive of activity. A large red-brick building about twenty yards from the gate dominated the foreground and had the words 'Quartermaster' painted in big letters on the side above a large sliding green door. In the distance he saw what Ben had seen. He turned his head slightly and gave Ben a thin smile from the side of his face, then winked.

"Well, sir, that looks in order." The corporal turned around and pointed in the direction of the wooden huts to the right beyond the stockpiles of munitions. "You'll find the guys you're lookin' for down at the corn sheds, sir," he drawled. He handed the letter back to Oliver which he refolded and tucked away in his top pocket. The corporal spat on the ground. "A spy, would you believe it? She looked so darn innocent too."

On hearing their corporal's words the other soldiers muttered to each other and then one said, "Let us at her, sir, we'll make sure she don't do no more spying." And then he spat on the ground too, before continuing to chew on his tobacco.

"Thank you for the offer, soldier, but I am instructed to take her back with me to headquarters and I have my young runner here to assist me in her escort." Oliver signalled to Ben to follow him as he walked through the gateway into the yard. Ben followed at a discreet pace or two behind Oliver who was trying to look every bit the superior officer. His training as an officer in the Royal Air Force when he was a young man had never left him and he knew just how to behave to be convincing to junior or senior ranks in the army. He boldly marched on looking confident, with a certain disdain for lower ranks, without appearing snobby, but every step was an effort with some microbe attacking him for which his immune system had no answer.

As they approached the corn sheds the second cowboy joined the first on the driving seat and they were just beginning to move off when Oliver raised his hand and shouted, "Hey, stop!"

"Whoa," said Glenn, who was holding the reins. The cart abruptly stopped as he pulled back on the brake lever to his side.

"What's the problem, officer?" asked a soldier standing on the raised deck in front of the door to shed no 4. Harriet was sitting with her back to Oliver and Ben's position but soon turned around when she heard Oliver's next comments.

"Is the person in the back of this cart Harriet Tubman?" She recognised the voice immediately.

"What if it is?" snarled Don.

Harriet hadn't fully turned about when she heard Oliver continue, "She is wanted by the high court of the Confederacy to answer charges of treason."

"What d'you mean, treason?"

"Spying, son," answered Oliver cocking his head slightly to one side.

"Spying!" repeated the soldier on the deck.

"Yes, soldier. And here I have a warrant for her arrest and remand into my custody." Oliver again pulled out the letter for inspection.

Don asked to see the letter.

Glenn was illiterate so Don read out the letter to him.

"Darn it, what about the reward we're supposed to get, what's owed to us for catching her? She's an escaped slave, yer know," shouted Don. His face was filled with anger. Gone were the laughing, joking smiles of a few minutes before. Now he was incensed. They'd brought her all this way and were close to getting their money, only to have her taken from them.

On the other side of the cart Glenn released the hand brake and raised his hand holding the horse whip.

"Don't even think about it, son, you'll never make it out of the yard. Those guys on the gate would see to that," said Oliver calmly. Glenn lowered his hand. "A cunning woman this one," said Oliver to the soldier; "she's caused us some trouble but not anymore."

"What about our reward money?" complained Glenn.

"I'm afraid you'll have to take that up with Lieutenant General James Longstreet at headquarters but he is away for at least another three days. He ordered her arrest."

Now facing Oliver and Ben, Harriet was doing her best at looking sullen. "I ain't dun no spying," she complained. "I'm just an 'ousekeeper."

"Shut up, woman," Don shouted, "no one's talking to you!" He climbed down from the cart and gave Oliver the letter back.

"Well, it ain't good enough, see. I wants my money. We brought 'er up 'ere from bloomin' Bowville at our expense…"

"The army appreciates the trouble you've gone to but, as I said, you will have to go to the Department for Compensation to make a claim. I will file a report as soon as I return and explain the situation."

Glenn yanked the brake hard on and jumped down to join his friend. He thumped Don on the arm. "If you hadn't spent so long joking with your old mate we'd 'ave been outa here."

Don shoved him back. "Well, you could 'ave 'elped load those barrels instead of sitting on your fat lazy butt." They continued arguing and jostling each other as they walked to the main gate.

By now several other men had joined the group around the cart with whispered voices and fingers pointing at Harriet. Ben made eye contact with her and tried to show with his body language that everything was going to be okay. He was so glad that they were finally reunited but was getting more concerned about Oliver. Although he was carrying off the officer bit very well and had fooled everyone so far, he looked in pain. Just every now and then he grimaced and either rubbed his neck or chest.

Harriet could see it too; her nursing experience told her he was not well. Moving over to address the soldier on the loading deck, "I'll need to commandeer this wagon to take her back to headquarters, I'm afraid. Could you arrange to unload this other stuff and then we'll be off?"

"Yes, sir," he sternly replied and saluted the officer.

Oliver moved away from the crowd and leaned against the side of the shed in the shade.

"Are you all right, Oliver," asked Ben.

"I thought so but I'm feeling a bit… oh… don't worry." He closed his eyes for a moment and listened while the officer in charge barked out orders. Soon the barrels were unloaded and only Harriet was left in the wagon. Oliver instructed Ben to ride in the back and pretend he was holding on to the rope that was still tied around Harriet's wrists. From the driver's seat Oliver released the brake and gave the reins a gentle shake to encourage the horse to move. The surrounding soldiers gave him a salute as he left the shed loading bay. After a few moments they passed out of the main gate and turned left. Harriet was free again.

Chapter 20

As they rounded the first bend in the road Ben leant over and untied the rope around Harriet's wrists. She rubbed each in turn gently, wincing slightly. Then she gave Ben a big hug. "My Lordy, dem I pleased to see you."

"We're pleased to see you! How are you? Did they mistreat you?" asked Oliver half turning his head.

"'twas not so bad, I've suffered much worse, dat's for sure. Once I'd seen dis ere Ben by der train, I knew I'd be saved. De Lord wasn't ready for me yet!" Harriet had unrelenting belief in destiny and, in her mind, her god decided her destiny. She had such strong belief it gave her tremendous courage in the face of adversity. Later, her bravery leading and scouting for troops during the Civil War conflict was recognised by several military commanders as exceptional. Tenacity was also an attribute that helped her move so many slaves to freedom along the Underground Railroad. She did not scare easily!

Ahead, Oliver could see two little faces poking out from behind a broken picket fence. He was happy and let a broad grin spread across his face. On seeing the cart driven by Oliver approach them, Charlie and V burst out and they nearly fell over in their eagerness to rush out towards it. "Come on, you two, jump in the back."

Harriet helped them up and they both hugged her tightly. Oliver didn't stop any longer than was needed and soon got the horses to trot down the road towards the outskirts of town.

"I'm so sorry, Miss Harriet," said Charlie, "I didn't mean to get you in trouble." His face was a picture of apology, with a sad smile. He blinked his eyes in an effort to stop his tears. Sometimes he would put this look on but this time it was for real – he knew he'd nearly ruined their grand plan and Harriet's life.

Harriet held his hands in hers. "You need to have more faith, little Charlie – I knows you didn't mean me any harm, you're too nice. You just got to get to know people a bit better, though, 'fore you trust 'em, dat's all." She smiled.

Her magnanimous attitude relaxed Charlie – cheered up by that he turned to V, "This is my sister Olivia – we call her V."

"I dun thought it 'twas – your brother told me with his hands at the train station."

"With his hands?" mused Charlie.

"Yes, I saw 'er with 'im at Petersburg, when I was on der train, and when she fell on me in the station." Harriet patted Olivia on the shoulder and made charade-like hand gestures and silently mouthed the words – 'you are good friends'. Olivia tried to reply the same way – saying Babbit liked her too. Harriet laughed and offered open arms to Olivia.

"It was Charlie who pushed me into you in the station – to get your attention."

"I can believe that, 'e seems a rite cheeky lad." Harriet jokingly poked him in the ribs. He was now returning to his normal cheery self and shrugged his shoulders up high – smiling with his whole body. Charlie and V snuggled up either side of Harriet as the cart rattled down the lane that ran downhill towards the river. From the bottom of the hill they went across a raised causeway near the riverbank and past a company of soldiers stationed to defend the city with several cannon behind an embankment. The army battery was set back from the road by about fifty yards with the cannon facing out towards the river – to protect against Yankee riverboat attack. A couple of the soldiers watched them pass but without his hat on, which he'd chucked in the back as soon as he was clear of the depot, no one could recognise he was dressed as an officer from that distance. And anyway, officers didn't normally drive wagons.

In the back Charlie and V whispered to Harriet about Oliver. After the excitement of rescuing her, Oliver had deteriorated and Ben was now driving the wagon horses under Oliver's guidance. Another half a mile up the road and Ben pulled into a small clearing under the shade of hemlock and walnut trees. The dappled shade was a welcome break from the heat of the sun. Ben moved closer to Oliver and steadied him; his head was down, bracing himself against the side of the wagon. Ben looked over his shoulder and shook his head at the others watching from the rear.

"Oliver's got worse."

"I'm okay, Ben… just give me a minute."

"What's all dis I 'ear, you ain't too well?"

"Oh, it's nothing… really."

Harriet stood up and felt his forehead. "You got a fever, you 'as."

"Can you help him?" asked Charlie, looking worried.

Harriet climbed down from the back of the wagon followed by Charlie jumping over the side. "We need to 'elp 'im down first, then I'll 'ave a closer look." They sat Oliver down, resting him up against a tree. The late afternoon sun was not as strong now but Oliver was burning up. Harriet released his tunic and undid a couple of buttons on his shirt. He closed his eyes and slumped down while she felt his pulse and placed a hand on his forehead. But as soon as she saw the rash and swellings on his neck she knew, or thought she knew, the problem. The doctors at Hilton Head called it diphtheria; she also knew they had no cure for it. Some got better, some died. She said nothing to name the disease as she didn't want to worry the children – she had an idea.

When she was a young girl the local native Indians of her homeland, the Nanticoke people, often helped the slave community with herbal remedies to ease and relieve the pain of diseases. And she was sure that she'd seen this disease treated on the plantation where she worked driving horses at the plough, but it was a long time ago. An old man dressed in a colourful beaded tunic, with a single feather attached to a bandana and a blue-painted face was a frequent visitor but his skills were mocked by the plantation owner. She'd seen it for herself though; he'd used a potion and a poultice that seemed to relieve the symptoms. But the white man did not believe in the witch doctor's (as they referred to him) medicine.

"'e's getting very sick," she said, shaking her head as she stood up. V sat down beside him and held his hand; Charlie knelt down the other side.

"What should we do?" asked Ben worriedly.

"I'll be okay; I've just got a bit of a bug, that's all." With that he rested his head against the tree, took a deep breath – which was a bit painful – and let it out slowly.

"Should we take him to a doctor, or hospital, like the accident and emergency unit?" suggested Charlie.

"Dere wat?" asked Harriet.

"Never mind him, he… he makes things up." Ben glared at him. Charlie had forgotten for a moment that this was 1862, not the twenty-first century. There was little that doctors could do in the middle of the nineteenth century except chop off damaged limbs, clean up wounds and patch people up with rough bandages. It was before the discovery of medicine as we knew it today. But some herbal potions could have a positive effect.

"There must be something we can do," said Ben.

"His best chance is if we can find old Ramukata."

"Who's he?" asked Charlie.

"'e's the greatest healer in Maryland, apart from de Lord, but I've not seem 'im in years. 'e might not eben still be alive."

"We're not that far from Maryland though, are we?"

"Is he a doctor?" asked V innocently.

Harriet bent down and rested a hand on V's shoulders. "Sort of 'e is… sort of. 'e's a Nanticoke Indian with very special powers, 'ealing powers. An' dey say 'e talks to the spirits too."

"What are spirits?" asked V.

"Dead people," answered Ben bluntly.

"Oh! How–" gasped V.

"Don't you remember Mum telling us something about her old, great aunty Lily and uncle Reg doing something like that in their front room – the room she was never allowed in when she visited the house as a little girl? Her mum told her that they reckoned they spoke to a guide – as they are called – in the afterlife, someone who could communicate messages to their dead relatives. I'm sure her mum went along once to a gathering one evening and was scared by it and never went again."

"Yeah," piped up Charlie, "I remember, Mum said it was a load of mumbo jumbo and Dad used to joke about Mum having some weird relatives on her side of the family."

V thought for a moment, *Where did Mum get that saying from, mumbo jumbo, and what did it mean? Another of her crazy old sayings.*

"Well, you don't 'ave to believe it – and you shouldn't mess with de spirit world – but if it helps, eh – we should let him give it a try," said Harriet stepping back and looking solemnly at Oliver who now had his eyes shut again. "I've seen 'im meself fix up a potion of wild flowers and berries, and I can't say its name in present company but he sometimes uses a warm yellow liquid to make an emulsion. Then 'e soaks a cotton wad in it and ties it around the swelling."

Ramukata was probably the best chance they had; they had to find him, if Oliver was to have any chance of not sinking into a coma from which he might not return. Most likely he'd picked up the disease in the hospital at Hilton Head, as it was carried in the air, or from another person while in the army camp – you could carry the disease without showing any of the symptoms. More men died in the American Civil War from malnutrition and disease than as a direct result of combat. The conditions they lived in sometimes were appalling – particularly for the men of the Confederacy. The medicine man would help anyone who sought his help – although few of the non-natives trusted the old man and his potions.

"So how do we get him to this Ram…uka?" asked Charlie.

"Ramukata," smiled Harriet. "Well, dwere not far from his homeland of Maryland; dwe need to get a ferry up de Potomac to Leonardtown. De settlement 'e lives in is den not far."

"Come on then, let's get going; he's not looking any better for a rest," said Ben.

Without opening his eyes Oliver suddenly spoke up, "I can hear, you know, and I'm not so sure about having some rain-dancing nutcase weirdo give me mashed-up wild weeds and flowers with buffalo wee soup to make me feel better." The first smile for a while stretched his lips.

"Urrh!" screeched V. The boys laughed.

Harriet was slightly offended. "'tis not weeds and... and de other thing you said dat I shan't say in front o' de children."

V giggled more and Charlie sniggered.

"You tis very sick, master Oliver and dis is dwhat we tis goin' to do."

Harriet was taking command of the situation and was not going to take no for an answer. "First, dwe mus' get 'im into his other clothes. No uniforms. 'e not gonna treat no soldier." Harriet ushered the children away while she helped Oliver change into his civilian clothes and poked his Confederate uniform into his holdall. After a few more minutes they were all loaded onto the wagon and heading off to the ferry that would take them to Leonardtown, with Ben and Harriet in the driving seat.

★ ★ ★

Curiously, Ben was right and there was a branch of their ancestors that held séances in the front room of their home – to try and communicate with the dead – and their guide was a long-deceased Native American Indian tribal chief. That was well before he was born, and therefore he had never seen it, but a portrait of the guide hung in that front room – a room where the curtains were never drawn open. The painting showed a tall, muscular man in brightly painted buckskin tunic and leggings standing proudly with a spear in one hand, the other a clenched fist across his chest. On his head he wore a spectacular headdress of white and black eagle feathers that reached down to his waist, and around his neck hung a pair of eagle's feet on a leather cord. His name was Ramuka – coincidence – quite possibly. It wasn't something that was talked about outside the close family circle of those who attended the evenings of receiving messages from departed souls. Now they were en route to meet a very similar-named medicine man – also a Native American Indian!

★ ★ ★

"There it is, Ben." Harriet pointed past the horses tied up outside the saloon and the general stores to a wooden shed and wide timber-decked platform. Tied up alongside was the river ferryboat – smoke gently rising from its twin funnels. Ben guided the wagon to a halt at the dockside. Harriet pulled the brake lever on hard while Ben jumped down and went over to speak to a man in the ferry master's hut. He explained that Oliver, his father, was very sick with diphtheria and they were taking him home – probably to die. Ben also fibbed that Harriet was their housekeeper, helping them get home. Once other travellers waiting to board the ferry heard how ill the man in the wagon was, they all kept a safe distance.

Luckily for the children they'd all been vaccinated against the disease as babies. Harriet never once worried for her own health; her religious belief was all she thought she needed. Half an hour later they were all glad to get on board the ferry and leave the dockside, although the wind was picking up a bit which caused the boat to rock about midstream. Smoke and steam poured from the funnels as the paddles churned through grey-brown river water driving them against the current of the Potomac. There was space for three wagons and horses but for this journey only one was being carried and the remaining passengers stayed well clear at the back of the boat. It did not take long to cross the river to their destination which was slightly upstream of their departure point.

The captain blew three long notes on the steam whistle as the boat approached the dock and shut off the drive to the paddles, as he'd done many times before, and the ferry gently bumped into the unloading dock. The jolt made the two horses on the front of the wagon rock back and forth a couple of times. Ben, standing between them, held the bridles firmly and talked to reassure them – and then patted each on the neck. Once the boat was roped up safely to the harbour, unloading began. Ben climbed back up onto the driving seat next to Harriet, she released the hand brake and Ben gently flicked the reins to bring the horses to life. They left the boat with a clatter of hooves and the cart wheels rattled over the planks of the gangway.

Harriet directed Ben away from the ferry dock and along the road towards the village of Nantego, where they hoped to find Ramukata. The end of daylight was approaching and the sun sat on the tops of the trees like a lost ball. Now and then a whirling wisp of wind picked up the dust from the road and swirled it around them. They'd not been travelling on this road for long when, in the distance, about half a mile away, Charlie spotted smoke rising just above the trees before the wind dissolved it into thin air. He tapped Harriet on the shoulder; she nodded in confirmation to his question. They would be in the village in the next few minutes.

Ahead, a narrower track led off the main lane. Ben jiggled the reins as they approached it and the horses turned to follow the track. It led them to the village which was formed of tepees arranged roughly in a big circle around a large open fire. Two log cabins were set back to the left with a few cattle grazing in a small paddock on one side. Some pigs seemed to be free to wander around wherever they liked and a couple of children appeared to be rounding up some chickens and herding them towards a small hut. Another group of children were playing near one of the tepees.

Not far from one of the log cabins the carcass of a deer hung from the branch of an otherwise bare tree stump – where two men were busy skinning it. A group of men sat cross-legged around the fire –

one smoking a long pipe and wearing a headdress of stiffened animal hair called a roach. As Ben drove the wagon into the village the children playing stopped their game and stared at the strangers entering their village and a shout went up from one of the men sitting at the fire. The men who'd been skinning the beast on the tree also stopped what they were doing and, one brandishing a long knife, the other a tomahawk axe, walked towards the wagon.

From their right a tall, burly native man with long, straight black hair wearing only a leather breechcloth around his waist and a red bandana on his head approached the wagon. Ben hauled back on the reins, the wagon stopped and Harriet climbed down to address the fearsome-looking man coming towards them. The native, known as Little Tree, took hold of one of the horses' bridles and spoke to her. It only took a few moments for Little Tree's face to change from a threatening, dour expression to a smile. He'd met Harriet once before when he was a boy helping Ramukata on a visit to the plantation where she worked and she'd given him some food from the farm store. Food he'd known she'd stolen for him and risked a beating for doing so if she had been found out. They embraced and he turned and led the horses towards the group around the fire. Little Tree shouted something and two of the seated men stood up and approached him.

Charlie was very excited and stood up in the back of the wagon and waved. The children who had been playing ran over to greet them and several others soon appeared from inside a tepee. V stayed with Oliver while Ben and Charlie jumped down to join Harriet with Little Tree, who was now talking to Chief Deep River in a mixture of Algonquian language (their native language) and English, which many natives now spoke. But Chief Deep River was an old warrior and preferred to use his native tongue when speaking with his own kind. A similar-aged man remained seated smoking a long, elaborately decorated pipe with an expression of scorn on his old, weathered face as he listened to the conversation. He had no care for the well-being of a white man.

After a few minutes Chief Deep River pointed in the direction of Ramukata's tent and suggested that they go and ask if he would help them. Chief Deep River smiled and raised his big hand to acknowledge friendship to Olivia who was looking on from the wagon. The chief had long black hair held back in a multi-coloured headband that had three feathers poking out the top. He wore a finely stitched, cream-coloured leather jacket adorned with tassels of cord across the front and plaits of black hair attached in long rows down each sleeve. They were mainly from the scalps he'd taken as a young warrior fighting other tribes for their land but some were also from the invading white man. Those days were long gone, however, and now they lived in peace with their white neighbours. All that was left were the stories. Very little was written down to record the native Indian history but elders would tell tales around the village fire to pass on the knowledge.

Ramukata lived apart from the rest of the village,

to the side of the clearing near the edge of the forest. Smoke drifted lazily from the top of his tepee and outside was a frame of tree branches decorated with feathers, furs and ferns and there were also animal horns sticking out from the top. The sides of his tepee had symbols and geometric patterns painted in yellow ochre and crimson red. Some were just for decoration, others held secrets, but written in a way only Ramukata, or another of his kind, would understand. To the left of his home two short, stout tree butts had been positioned upright in the ground which could be used as a crude table and about six feet above them hung a string of wind chimes, gently singing in the breeze.

As Little Tree and Harriet walked off, Charlie stepped closer to Chief Deep River. "Are you a real chief?" he asked, looking up at the once mighty man.

"Yes, son, I am. I am Chief Deep River of the Nanticoke people," he replied proudly.

"Wow! Do you fight cowboys?" he asked innocently. Ben scowled at Charlie. Deep River laughed.

"No, son, no more. We are at peace nowadays."

"Do all of your tribe live here?"

"No, some live in other villages along the river. This is head village," he replied standing up straighter and folding his arms across his chest.

"Come on, Charlie," said Ben putting his arm around Charlie's shoulders, "we should go with Harriet."

"Your father's a very sick man," said Deep River.

"Yes, he's not well at all," replied Ben sadly.

"Ramukata will fix him good though. Don't worry 'bout a thing; everything's gonna be all right. You can tell your mama 'cause I'll be standing by your side. It may seem a wonder but your trip won't have been wasted."

"It's true then, what Harriet said – he's a good doctor?" asked Charlie.

Deep River nodded. "Yeah, you'll see; if he can't make him better nobody can."

Harriet turned and gestured for Ben and Charlie to bring the wagon with them as they followed her and Little Tree.

Ben took hold of one of the horses and turned it towards Ramukata's tepee.

With a worried look Olivia asked, "Is it going to be all right, can he really make Oliver better?" Her sensitive compassion showed in the expression on her face.

"We hope so, V." Beads of sweat formed on Oliver's brow and ran down either side of his face – they had no way of measuring it but even V could tell he had a high temperature. He lay motionless in the back of the wagon with his head to one side resting against V. His neck was red and swollen, and small abscesses were beginning to form on either side. Oliver coughed.

"You need to get me to Jenny." His throat hurt like hell and burning pain shot through him when he coughed. He tried to swallow but that was as bad. He felt he was being choked, like someone was ramming a hedgehog down his throat.

"It's going to be okay, we'll soon see Mr Ramukata – he's going to make you better," Olivia whispered in his ear. Oliver put his hands around his neck and felt the swelling and the rising boils. He'd witnessed a similar condition before on a previous journey – to Africa – and he knew his best chance was to return to Jenny. A journey home would certainly cure him, Jenny's powers would see to that, but he was a long way from the safety and protection of his beloved aeroplane.

As the wagon stopped outside the tepee of Ramukata, Little Tree went inside to find him while the others gathered around the back. "Jenny's the answer!" he said in a slightly delirious voice. "I need to get back to Jenny," he whimpered.

"What's dat 'e's sayin'?" asked Harriet.

"He wants to go to Jenny," said Charlie.

"Jenny?"

"Yeah… err… she's–"

Ben interrupted Charlie, "She's the friend we told you about – when we first met."

"Oh I see; she won't be able to 'elp 'im now – 'e's too sick. She'd be a long way away back down south."

"Jenny… get me… to Jenny," pleaded Oliver sorely.

Harriet leant over the side of the wagon and felt his forehead again. "'e's got more fever now." Then she walked over to the entrance of the tepee just as Little Tree and an old man with a blue-painted face came out. Ramukata held his arms out wide and engulfed Harriet with a warm welcome. They conversed for a few moments before approaching the wagon.

"He's right, Ben. Remember when we first met him and he was all beaten up – then after we got back home in Jenny he was fine. The journey fixed him."

"We're too far away, Charlie – you heard what Harriet said – he's really ill. We've gotta let this this old man try for us. Harriet believes he can do something to help," said Ben.

Olivia hugged Oliver and a tear oozed from the corner of her eye. *Please get better, Mr Oliver.* She looked up at the imposing figure of the medicine man approaching her. He was taller than most, with a serious look on his face on which years of exposure to sun and wind had taken a toll. At first he rested his hands on the side of the wagon and looked Oliver up and down, then bent down slightly to speak to Olivia. His English was surprisingly good. "Your name must be Olivia. I hear your father is rather sick – he doesn't look too good."

"Can you make him better?" Ramukata took a closer look at the swellings on Oliver's neck and felt gently under his chin and then his forehead. Oliver opened his eyes slowly but only halfway. He tried to raise a hand and offer it to Ramukata but was too weak.

"It's okay, sir, you rest." Ramukata took hold of Oliver's hand and gently raised it but noticed him wince at the movement so laid it back down again. With the touch of an angel Ramukata felt Oliver's near-motionless chest, then slid his hand across to feel under his armpit; again Oliver flinched. His fingers could feel a puffy swelling under the sick man's tunic.

He glanced sideways to Harriet – it wasn't an encouraging look. Then looked back to Olivia with a more positive smile. "I'll do my best – I'm sure he'll pull through." Ben wasn't fooled, though; he'd seen the look the man had given Harriet – he'd all but shaken his head in gloom. Ben knew he was trying to protect Olivia. He worried.

Charlie was still innocent to the seriousness of the situation. He climbed a step on the wagon. "What will you do… to make Oliver better?"

"Bring him into my tent – I'll start straight away."

"Thank you, sir," said V.

"But first–" He pulled out a strip of coloured cloth from a pocket and wiped it over Oliver's sweating forehead, uttered some words under his breath, then kissed the piece of cloth. There were many similar pieces tied to the wind-chime frame and Ramukata walked over and tied this one on as well. He returned to the side of the wagon. "It's Harriet you should thank for bringing you here – I knew her father well and he helped me more than you'll know, so I would do anything for her. And I understand you're here to help her – so," he held his arms out wide and then patted his chest, "I cannot refuse to do the best I can for you."

A wide, wrinkled smile cracked across his face. "But I will need the help of my friends long gone too." He looked to the heavens, cupped his hands around his mouth and then closed his eyes and spoke some words in his native Iroquoian tongue. He called out a short phrase three times. Ben looked at his younger brother and hunched his shoulders.

The children had no idea what he was saying but as he did so, a cool breeze washed over them and made the wind chimes sing. The wind seemed to swirl around them while he chanted – the coloured tassels of cloth attached to the frame of the wind chimes fluttered wildly and the smoke from his tent that had been lazily rising swirled in a corkscrew above. Olivia was slightly anxious and looked to her older brother for reassurance. Ben moved over to the wagon and put an arm around her and whispered a comforting word in her ear. He wasn't sure what was happening – but had faith in Harriet and maybe the medicine man too.

The evening had been slowly darkening but now the sky was full of cloud hiding the moonlight above. As the pulsing flow of the breeze streamed past them Ben and Charlie turned their heads to follow it. Then for just a few seconds a bright glow in the centre of the darkness above them caught their eye. A circle of light sparkled brightly in the cloud and then appeared to travel down towards them getting faster and faster. Then, as strangely as it had appeared it disappeared, through the top of Ramukata's tepee. The event had only taken a few seconds – the hole in the clouds had closed and the light had gone out. The boys looked at each other, slightly spooked and mystified at what they had seen.

"What was that, Ben?" Charlie asked.

"I dunno – some trick of the moonlight?"

Harriet had come up behind them and felt their concern. "'tis okay, boys – Ramukata will soon know de best way to 'elp Mr Oliver."

Little Tree and Ramukata lifted Oliver from the wagon and took him inside the tepee. Harriet kept the children outside and reassured them that everything would be all right. After a few moments Little Tree emerged and spoke to Harriet.

"Ramukata needs to be left alone now – he will do what he can. I will take you to a hut where you can rest overnight."

"He will be okay, won't he?" said Olivia tearfully.

"Now, don't you worry about a thing, Miss Olivia, everything is goin' to be all right," replied Harriet. For once Charlie's face looked worried too; he climbed up into the back of the wagon and comforted his young sister. Little Tree took hold of the bridle of one of the horses and led it across the grass to the place where they were to spend the night.

Chapter 21

Bird song and the noise of the forest woke them as dawn broke. Ben opened one of the wooden window shutters and early morning light poured in from the treetops. The ground was damp from some light overnight rain but the fire in the middle of the camp still burned. A boy stood by poking it with a stick, then threw another log on. He'd done well in keeping the fire going through the rain. A tripod of poles held a large pot over the fire into which a woman was putting something. Ben couldn't make out what – but it looked like vegetables of some kind.

"What time is it?" asked Charlie. None of them wore a watch – something Oliver had told them to do – but Ben had tucked his in his pocket out of sight. He knew he should not let Harriet see, so he turned his back to her and cautiously slid the watch out. The hands were motionless – at somewhere just before midday. And it was definitely not that. Ben pushed the useless watch back into his pocket.

"'tis early, Master Charlie," said Harriet. She, like the others, had slept on a pile of furs on the floor and was now standing and tying a scarf around her head. "Dey live by de time of de sun here – not a clock on de wall."

Olivia wiped her eyes and rustled around to find Babbit. She gave him a little shake, stroked him for comfort and then joined Ben by the window. "I'm hungry, Ben." They'd not eaten since having some biscuits at the train station the day before – they were all feeling in need of some food.

"Me too."

Harriet walked over to Ben and V. "Don't worry, Miss Olivia, we gonna 'ave some nice corn porridge dis morning." She pointed to the cooking pot steaming over the fire. "Look, 'tis already being cooked up."

"Corn porridge!" said a voice from beneath a blanket on the floor.

"Yes, Master Charlie... corn porridge. I spoke to Little Tree last night after you'd all gone to sleep." Charlie made a yuck-face – the idea of any sort of porridge made him gag. "He also said Master Oliver gonna be sick for a few days – he'd got a real big fever last night."

"He is going to be all right, though?" said V sorrowfully.

"Yes, um, I'm sure he will – Ramukata started last night after he'd spoken to..." She didn't want to say who he'd really spoken to. She knew. He'd called on the tribe's high god Hawenniyo while they were standing outside his tepee and the high god had sent the great spirit Orenda to help. In their late night chat Ramukata had remarked that Oliver must have friends in high places – the gods – or been a really, really good man because they'd been so quick to offer help.

The saying 'what goes around, comes around' has its roots in ancient mythology, as does 'one good turn deserves another'. Oliver, under the hidden guidance of the Babylonian god Apsu, had been doing good deeds for years and had often found himself in trouble with his own race – humankind. He didn't understand the ancient gods, or pretend to, he just knew something mysterious was at work when he flew with Jenny but, also, being compassionate and generous to people was natural for him. That was partly why he and Jenny were picked. Not all gods are good though – there are 'dark gods' – ones that wish to be all powerful and control humans for badness, that stem from the badlands. This is why the spirit world should be left alone to those who know – know how to use it for good, not evil. Ramukata knew how and when to call on them for help for the good.

"Who, who has he spoken to?" asked V.

Harriet stuttered, "A... a good friend."

Charlie had climbed out of his bedding and was now standing behind V. He looked up at Harriet. "Was it one of the dead people?" Charlie never held back on a question if he wanted to know something, even if others felt it was awkward!

Olivia shivered, "Oh... that's not really true, is it?" Ben whacked Charlie in the shoulder.

"What?"

"I... I don't know, my dear. It's best we don't ask too many questions. So long as 'e makes Mister Oliver better, eh." Olivia clung to Harriet for comfort. The talk of speaking to dead people scared her. Being in the middle of a dark forest scared her – and mischievous Charlie knew it.

"Shush…" said Charlie suddenly and he stared, zombie-like, out of the window, then slowly raised his head as if being drawn upwards by an unseen object. "Yes, master, I'll–"

V clutched hold of Harriet more tightly and Babbit was nearly strangled.

"Stop it, Master Charlie, you're scaring you sister!" He got another whack from Ben. Charlie laughed.

Harriet looked sternly at Charlie. "You mustn't mess wiv de spirits, Charlie – 'tis bad thing to do." V gave him a slap and a cross look too.

At that moment the fire-boy started walking towards the cabin. "I think he's coming to get us for breakfast," said Harriet.

★ ★ ★

A little later they were all sitting around the fire with a wooden bowl of corn porridge. Harriet had whispered to them to accept it graciously and eat it all up. Eating was a communal activity and all members of the tribe either sat, or stood around the fire together to eat the prepared meal. Keen eyes looked on to watch the strangers feed. It would be considered disrespectful not to finish the food given. Chief Deep River stood proudly – like a schoolmaster – overseeing their consumption of breakfast and looking for approval.

Harriet finished first. "'twas lovely," she said wiping her lips with her sleeve. Charlie had done well, even though it wasn't smothered in the usual layer of sugar he would normally apply to his breakfast cereal! He wanted to impress. Olivia struggled the most and was last to finish after poking it around the bowl with her wooden spoon for what seemed an age. But they all managed a grateful smile and thanked the chief for the food.

On their way to breakfast Harriet had talked to the children about going to rescue her sister while Oliver was being treated in Ramukata's tepee. There was nothing they could do for him that Ramukata wouldn't do better and that's what they'd originally come for. She'd spoken to Oliver late the previous night who'd insisted they go on without him to get Rachel and pick him up on the way back. As always, he thought of others before himself.

★ ★ ★

It was not far to where Harriet's sister was held as a slave, about ten miles east, working in the household of Mrs Worthington – a terribly mean woman who was very unforgiving when a slave did something she disagreed of. She always carried a cane and was not averse to using it – she also had a vicious tongue. Her husband was not immune to the wrath of her voice either. Often slaves were punished by him simply because she wanted it. She demanded it. He was a kind man but brought up with slavery; yet he tried to treat them the best he could. This was a family where the husband and wife were on opposite sides of the Civil War argument. Many families were split in a similar way during the conflict.

★ ★ ★

"I guess you'll be leaving soon," said Deep River, "if you're to get back before nightfall."

"Yes, I hope so," she replied, looking at Ben for agreement. He nodded. She smiled back. She usually had to travel with escaped slaves by night from one safe house to the next, and hide up in the woods by day. She hadn't been back to the 'land of Egypt', as she called her homeland, for many years, and even then most of it would have been traversed at night with guidance of the Pole Star. But travelling with white people she hoped to get away with an excuse. Once they were out of the local area they could pretend they were part of the household servants for Oliver and his children. '*Moses*', as she was known by her own people, was coming home.

"Little Tree has fed and watered your horses for the journey."

"Thank you," she said to the big man standing next to the chief.

"Are we now going to get your sister?" asked Charlie.

"If dat's all right with you three?"

Ben stood up and handed his bowl to a little girl with a shy smile standing behind him in moccasin

247

shoes and a light-brown leather dress. She was a bit shorter than him with long black hair as straight as the flight of a bullet. The smile on her face said she liked the look of Ben – but he didn't notice. Boys don't usually do that noticing thing, unless it's really obvious!

"I reckon so," he said.

Charlie stood up eagerly. "Yeah, if we can't do anything for Oliver, let's go and get your sister."

"It's not quite as simple as that! But I do have a plan. It'll need all of you 'cos I can't just march up to the door and ask for her and her children!" Rachel's children Benjamin and Angeline worked in the kitchen and garden while their mother worked as a chambermaid. Mrs Worthington was a short fat woman with a round face and an unfortunate wart the size of a marble on the right side of her chin. Her nose was thin and very pointy and it sat awkwardly below narrow beady eyes. It would be fair to say… she was ugly! Rachel, on the other hand, in her early thirties, was beautiful. Mrs Worthington had – more than once – seen the way her husband had looked at the chambermaid and the kind and generous treatment he afforded her had not gone unnoticed either. At any opportunity Mrs Worthington would viciously punish Rachel – sometimes just with her tongue but often enthusiastically with the whip.

"You be careful, Harriet," said Little Tree, "I heard you are a wanted woman."

"I know, I will. These wonderful little'uns, though, are goin' to 'elp me and dey know some people would take me if dey could. Don't we, Charlie?" She smiled at Charlie, he grinned back. Harriet was not known for getting excited but the thought of seeing her sister, who she'd not seen for many years, was making an emotional impact.

Little Tree looked a little surprised that she was placing her trust in the children – by now she was well known to be a slave smuggler and it was a dangerous game. Many people owed their freedom to Harriet and her tenacity for evading capture. Although he knew she would have the help of the Underground Railroad conductors and safe houses too if she needed them. If they needed it there was one not far from the village, where they could rest up in safety on their return.

At that moment Ramukata approached them. He asked to speak to Harriet by herself and they walked away. "He's worse than I thought; I've tried the usual potion I use and something the great spirit Orenda had said to do – but he's not getting any better. Orenda also cast a resting spell on him last night and used his healing hand magic but this morning when he should have awoken he remained asleep – even when I wiped the waking water on his lips he still remained silent. It's not as simple as we thought; I think he's been bitten by the wakadida fly."

Harriet's heart sank. No one she knew had survived a bite from the wakadida fly and Oliver was only in this condition because he'd come to help her. A wakadida fly bite was thankfully rare but it carried a disease that had symptoms similar to a combination of the Black Death plague of olden days and diphtheria. A truly nasty illness would be induced into the victim, from which there was no known cure. A long, slow and painful illness – inflamed boils grew under the armpits and groin, and the neck of the victim became swollen both inside and out – preceded almost certain death. After about a week the boils would burst and the remaining wound and skin surrounding the area would turn black and the tissue would die. Blood poisoning followed, which was ultimately the cause of death.

"But you will be able to save him, yes?" she sighed.

"I don't know. I'm going to call on Orenda again later – but he will only come after dark. I just hope it will be in time."

"There's nothing we can do, then?"

"No, it's just a matter of time and the goodwill of the gods – so you may as well go and see if you can get your sister and leave me to tend to this man." With a heavy heart Harriet returned to the children, yet at the same time concealed her worry from them. She had total faith in her God taking care of her but was not so sure that these other spirits and gods that Ramukata spoke to could do the same for Oliver.

She told the children it would be all right in the most positive way she could and then, with her back to them, said a little prayer before they set off.

Chapter 22

For the next few hours they rode along deserted tracks apart from passing through one small hamlet named Sparksville, which was no more than a collection of randomly placed wooden shacks either side of the main street with a general store and a saloon at the centre where another road branched off to the side. Other than two men sitting outside the saloon, who watched them pass like a slow-moving ball at a tennis match, they saw no one.

About a mile from the town they entered a forest of mainly tall black oak and grey dogwood bushes and after fifty metres or so, it was like the batteries of the sun were running down. The temperature dropped and an eerie silence surrounded them too. The tunnel of trees seemed to go on forever but in the distance brightness illuminated the exit and just before they reached it Harriet left the wagon to wait for their return. Although she was desperate to see her sister, it was not safe for her to continue to the place of her sister's servitude and, having explained what to do, she hid in the undergrowth. The woodland darkness gave way to fields of extensive agriculture on either side and dust rose from behind the wagon as Ben drove it down the lane past the sign that announced it was Peppers Farm – home of Mr and Mrs Worthington.

The house stood out like a bright white Bedouin tent in a desert oasis with a row of Doric columns supporting a porch across the whole front, shadowing an imposing front door in the middle. Wide steps led up to the door which, by contrast, was a dark oak colour with prominent brass door fittings. Ben hauled the wagon to a stop at the foot of the steps and jumped down from the box seat. He told Charlie and Olivia to wait in the wagon.

Ben climbed the steps and thumped the big brass door knocker against the door three times. A few moments passed before he heard voices inside and then a thin, wiry old man with grey hair and a stooped posture – but smartly dressed – opened the door. It was Abraham; he'd been a slave all his life and, for the most part, butler to the Worthingtons. "Good morning, young sir."

"Good morning," replied Ben courteously. Abraham nodded but said no more and expectantly waited for Ben to continue. "Ah… yes… I've come to see–" Ben's attention was distracted by a sight in the field to the side of the house. In the distance several people – he guessed slaves – were carrying large sacks and picking some sort of plant. His distraction was caused by the sound of shouting and a whip being cracked by a giant of a man standing behind them.

Abraham took no notice of the noise, "… to see?"

"Oh… yes, to see Mr Worthington."

"You'll find him down in the barn – they're busy bringing the cotton in, yer know." Abraham pointed to a cluster of farm buildings not far from the house.

"Thank you." As Abraham closed the door Ben heard a sharp-voiced woman shouting.

"Go and get Samuel from the field; that lazy good for nothing needs a lesson."

Ben winced, *Someone's in trouble.* He didn't hear any more as he jogged down the steps to the wagon.

"Is she there?" asked Charlie.

"I don't know – I have to find Mr Worthington first."

"Where is he?"

Ben pointed, "Over there." He leapt up onto the wagon seat and Charlie climbed over to join him. With a quick flick of his wrist Ben drove them towards the farm buildings.

There were a number of large sheds and one housed the cotton gin – the machine used to tease the cotton fibres from the boll. The others were for storage or drying the cotton bolls; Maryland didn't have the best climate for growing cotton and harvest time could be a very anxious time for the farmer. For the slave labourers it could be a very harsh time – whippings for not working hard enough were commonplace. At this time of year a cotton farmer never had enough field labour; those he did have were worked into the ground from the time the sun got up until it went to bed.

"Wooah!" said Ben and the wagon came to a halt outside a large barn. From inside, beyond the two wide-open doors, a noise like a dozen washing machines on slow spin could be heard. Voices were shouting to be heard and as one worried-looking man hurriedly left the shed with an empty sack, another approached with a full one. Neither took any notice of the children on the wagon.

Charlie and V followed Ben to the open doors. Inside, through gaps in the shed planking, rays of strong sunshine illuminated clouds of dust – it sparkled like a million tiny stars. In the middle stood some sort of contraption built of wood the size of a small truck, to the side of which a man – naked except for a threadbare pair of shorts – was struggling to keep a handle turning. His skin glistened like a wet road in sunlight and leaked like condensation on a bathroom window. To one side of the barn was a mini mountain of what looked like extremely fluffy, if slightly undersized, white tennis balls, whilst the other was stacked with bales of cotton lint wrapped partly in hessian cloth and tied with rope.

In front of the machine a man wearing a blue long-sleeved shirt and a wide-brimmed hat was standing with his back to them inspecting a wad of white fluff. As he was the only white man in the shed, Ben guessed it was Mr Worthington.

"Hello… excuse me!" Ben called. The man turned around, frowned and dropped the white fluff into a basket.

"Yes, what is it?" he replied, and approached Ben. Ben held out his hand and introduced himself and explained the reason for his visit. Charlie held his hand out too but the man ignored him.

"Your father's sent you to see if I have any spare labour? At this time of year! For goodness sake."

"He's not well, you see, and… well, it was Mother who sent us out really, to ask around. We're new around here and we, well… just wondered, that's all."

Charlie joined in, "We try and help, to do what we can and Mother had heard in town–"

"Heard what?" the man said abruptly, the man they now knew as Mr Worthington.

Ben put his hand on Charlie's shoulder, "Well, our mother overheard your wife say that she wanted to get rid of a woman called Rachel and her two children."

"Oh, she did, did she?" Robert Worthington knew his wife to be a gossip and knew his wife would like to get rid of the slave named Rachel if she could have her way.

"Yes… and any help right now – with our father not able to–"

"Yeah, yeah, well she works in the house and… Clem does have a problem with her, that's her affair." He sighed and shook his head.

A man shouted from inside the shed, "Boss!"

Robert Worthington put his hand up to the man, "Just a minute, Jessie." Jessie was like a foreman and kept the cotton gin running right. It was his job to see it produced the best-quality cotton possible. The machine was temperamental and often broke down.

255

During the cotton harvest Robert Worthington's mood was governed by the performance of the gin. Today was actually a good day – they were lucky. Otherwise Ben would have been met with the growl of a bear that had just had its dinner pinched.

"Hold on," he said to Ben, then went over to Jessie and chatted about something. After a short conversation Robert guided Ben and Charlie back towards the doorway where V was waiting. Outside in the yard he explained that he had no field labour he could spare but, for the right price, his wife, Clementine, may let Rachel go. In fact she would probably be pleased to see her leave and he could use the money to buy another field slave. He explained that Rachel had been on the farm since she was a young girl and worked fairly hard and he was used to her being around the house and would be sorry to see her leave.

"The problem is," he continued, "my wife runs the house as she wants and over the last few years she's taken a dislike towards Rachel. I'm not so fond of using the whip on a slave as my wife, but Rachel's back seems to be its second home where my wife's concerned."

"We'll be good to her," said V.

"It's no good being too good to a slave, missy – they gotta know their place. But sometimes…" Robert half-smiled and his mind drifted for a moment.

"We'll pay good money!" said Charlie.

"Ha!" Robert laughed. "Slave is as slave be, but if you give her a good home… not too good, mind, remember what I said, they gotta know who's boss. Cruel to be kind sort of thing, you know," he said looking at Ben.

"Yeah." Ben nodded naively.

They'd caught Robert Worthington in a good mood. Ben offered him a seat on the wagon and then drove them back up to the house. On the way Robert spoke well of Rachel and agreed a price of $1,000 for her and her two children. The mood in the wagon was good until they got closer to the house.

As they approached to the side they were shocked to see someone tied up to a post with their hands hauled above their head. The person had been stripped to the waist and the man they'd seen earlier cracking the whip in the field was now thrashing it across the back of the poor victim tied to the post. Olivia shrieked and put her hands over her eyes. Before Ben had stopped the wagon Robert jumped off and marched towards the whipping post. Ben told Charlie to wait with V and then cautiously followed Robert Worthington to the scene of the punishment.

Even before he got close, Ben could see blood oozing from swollen red stripe marks across the person's back. Another lash was greeted with another squeal of pain from the victim. As he got level with the back of the house Ben could then see two children among the other adult witnesses – watching silently and motionless. For a moment Ben turned his head away. He'd read about the treatment of slaves in his history lesson but now he was seeing it for himself, he couldn't believe this really was the way they treated people.

"What's all this about?" shouted Robert. His words were directed at a short, portly woman standing with her arms folded and displaying a sneer that would melt steel.

"I caught her at it, Robert. I told you she did; she was mouthing off about me again. Well, I won't have it – she has to learn."

The tenth lash was laid as feistily as the first. Samuel knew how to hurt with the whip and knew he had to do it well or he'd receive it as well.

Robert grabbed his arm, "That's enough!"

"What are you doing?" protested Clementine. "I said she should get twenty-five lashes; he's not even half done."

Robert stepped forward, pulled out a knife and slashed through the rope binding Rachel's hands to the whipping post. Her head and arms flopped down as she collapsed in a heap on the ground. Robert handed her a handkerchief to wipe the tears that streamed down her face, which she took gladly in one hand. The other she used to gather up her dress and cover her naked chest. Ben stood dismayed and checked behind him that Charlie and V hadn't followed.

"I've sold her!" Robert shouted. "You should be pleased. Any more damage from your whipping and they might not take her."

"Sold her to whom?"

Robert nodded in Ben's direction, "That boy over there."

"You'd better have got a good price or Samuel can start again," Clementine barked.

None of the witnessing staff had moved, or even changed the expression on their faces. Jessie knew better than to show any emotion when the masters were having a disagreement. Samuel just stood still waiting for further instructions and the other house staff, Hannah, Lottie and Rebecca's two children, stood as if at prayer in church.

Clementine gave Ben a look of indignation and then flicked her head in the direction of the crumpled slave, "How much, then, for this... this thing?"

Ben looked a bit coy; he wasn't sure whether he was supposed to answer.

Robert had moved up closer to his wife. "A thousand dollars, including her kids."

Clementine shrugged her shoulders and pursed her lips. "Be glad to get the insolent trash out of my house."

Robert nodded Samuel away and waved the others back to the house. Rachel's children, Benjamin and Angeline, went over and helped her to her feet.

"Where's your money then, boy?" asked Clementine.

"It's... it's in the wagon," stammered Ben.

While Robert followed his wife to the back door he told Ben to meet him at the front door with the money. Firstly, though, embarrassed and with a pained expression, he approached Rachel. She'd wiped the tears but the agony of her experience was still etched on her face. Ben had never seen anyone whipped before and the wounds on her back looked like she'd been clawed by a tiger. Rachel clutched her dress to cover her modesty while Angeline dabbed, with the handkerchief Robert had given her, at blood running from the ripped open flesh on her back.

"Is that all you've got to clean up with?" he asked.

"Yessir," said Angeline.

"Is it true, sir? You have bought us?" stammered Rachel.

"Yes, but it's better than you think. I can't tell you right now – but things for you will be different from today."

"Anyting 'tis better den here. She hates me. I never done nuffin, sir, honest. She thinks I have but I haven't."

Ben held his hands up, "Really, it will all be better soon, I promise." In Rachel's son's eyes he could see a look of anger and revenge building.

"I'll get her one day," the boy muttered.

"Come on, follow me." Ben led the way down the side of the house back towards the wagon. Ben turned and offered his hand to Rachel's son; the bare-footed boy dressed in little more than rags to cover his fragile frame stepped back and hesitated. No white boy had ever offered his hand to him to shake before. "I'm Ben."

"Really?" the boy replied.

"Yeah. Guess you're Benjamin."

"How did you know?"

"I'll tell you later – come on," he smiled. Angeline comforted her mother as she helped her follow the two boys who were a little way in front. Charlie jumped down, smiled at Benjamin and introduced himself, but his expression changed to shock when he saw Rachel's hunched figure get closer. V stood up in the wagon and screeched when she caught sight of Rachel's back as she was led to the rear of the cart.

Charlie looked quizzically at Ben but before he had a chance to say anything, Ben thumbed over his shoulder. "The man with the whip."

"'tis Miss Clementine that orders it be done – she's always been horrible to Mamma," sneered Benjamin.

After helping Rachel into the wagon Ben rummaged through the bag to retrieve the money pouch and walked back to the house. He settled the deal for Rachel with Robert Worthington on the porch – Clementine, satisfyingly and rather smugly, looked on from behind a window.

As Ben turned to leave he felt a hand on his shoulder and heard a quiet voice speak to him, "Take care of her, son, she's a good worker really but my wife has had it in for her for years." Ben nodded but thought, *Surely you could have done something to stop it.*

On his return to the wagon Ben climbed in the back and told Charlie to go up front and gently drive the horses with V sitting alongside him. He replaced the money pouch and pulled out a shirt from the bag, which he used to help Angeline mop the blood from Rachel's back. *How, how could one human being do this to another?* he thought.

Charlie gave the reins a gentle flick and the horses jolted the wagon into life. V looked over her shoulder but then squeezed her eyes tightly shut on sight of Rachel's back and turned back quickly before burying her head in her hands. Slowly but surely Charlie drove the wagon away from the farm.

"We'll have more help soon – you'll see," said Ben.

"How's that?" asked Angeline, as the cart turned out of the farm drive and towards the wooded area where they'd left Harriet.

Ben pointed, "Her sister Harriet is up there."

"Harriet! She's here?" exclaimed Rachael, who'd been silent since they'd left the Worthingtons.

"Yes, it's her who brought us here."

"But why–"

"Don't worry, you'll be all right now; Harriet will know what to do."

"Where will you be taking us… to work?" asked Benjamin.

"You won't be working for us."

"We won't… who will–"

"Don't look so worried, you won't be working for anyone around here. We've come to get you away from this place."

A feeling of relief and excitement engulfed the former slaves but it was tempered with caution – they'd known several slaves who had been terribly treated following recapture after initially escaping from a slave master.

"But what if we're caught?" asked Benjamin.

"No one is going to be looking for you – we've paid for you – you're ours! But you're not; I mean,

262

you don't belong to anyone – you're free now and we are going to help get you to a place of permanent freedom."

Benjamin was struggling to make sense of their situation – in his little world he'd never witnessed any white person be this kind to a black person before. He still looked worried. Ben put arm around his shoulder. "Just relax, really, everything will be fine." Instinctively Benjamin tensed up at the feeling of a white boy holding him. Ben smiled.

Then Rachel spoke up again, "But Harriet is a wanted woman – everyone knows dat."

"That is true but we've got her in disguise!" Rachel shook her head; she couldn't believe what was happening.

It took another ten minutes before they entered the cover of the wood and Harriet was able to get her first glimpse of the rescue party. She clutched her face in excitement and rushed out from her hiding place to greet them. On seeing her run towards them Charlie pulled on the reins and the horses obediently came to a halt.

"Rachel! Rachel!" Harriet cried out. Even as strong as she was, Harriet's eyes welled with emotion as she hastily leant over the side of the wagon and wrapped her arms around her sister who she'd not seen in years. She quickly released her grasp, though, when Rachel cried out and Harriet felt the bare flesh of her sister's wounded back. Rachel turned slightly to show Harriet the effects of the punishment she'd just received, something Harriet had seen on too many occasions. The bleeding had almost stopped and now the streaks of open wounds were covered in lines of congealed blood. The ridges and furrows on her back showed that this was not the first time she'd felt the lash; at least this time Clementine Worthington had not had the opportunity to throw a mix of salt and pepper into the open wounds, which was a favourite thing for her to do after a whipping.

Now with tears in her eyes again Rachel leant forward and excitedly embraced her sister. Mindful of her injuries Harriet cupped Rachel's face in her hands and then passionately wiped the tears away. "I'm sorry I couldn't get you before, sis, but I bin caught up in dis war. Dey says it will make us all free if de Union Army wins."

"I do hope so," cried Rachel.

After their emotional reunion Harriet climbed into the back of the wagon to tend to her sister, whilst Ben replaced Charlie at the reins. Charlie and Olivia joined the others in the back as Harriet gave instructions to Ben for their return journey.

Chapter 23

The crunching noise of the wheels gave way to a rumble as Ben steered the wagon across the grass of the encampment past the two elegantly carved totem poles. Little Tree waved from outside his tepee and beckoned to another to join him as he walked towards the returning wagon. Meanwhile Charlie jumped down and began to run towards the home of Ramukata but a shout from Little Tree stopped him and he re-joined the wagon now parked outside the hut where they'd spent the previous night. Harriet and Angeline helped Rachel down and into the hut. On the far side of the camp the sun sat like a deep red disc of fire on the treetops above Ramukata's tepee.

Charlie could see the man gesticulating as if he were talking to someone but although he had eyes as sharp as a hawk he could not see who Ramukata was speaking to. He was desperate to find out how Oliver was – they all were.

"I was only going to see–"

"I know, boy, but Ramukata is busy right now – conversing. He's been waiting all day for them to come," said Little Tree. Charlie stared but all he could make out was a large bird sitting on the wind-chime frame and what he thought was a dog by the man's side.

★ ★ ★

"Quaayayp says that Hawenniyo will come tonight," squawked Aral.

"You did describe what I told you?" asked Ramukata.

The owl flicked his head indignantly from side to side. "Yes! And Orenda told him too," he huffed.

"Well?"

"He agrees with you and believes your man is suffering from the bite of a wakadida fly, as well as the other condition you thought," replied Aral. Ramukata lowered his head and closed his eyes.

Then his earthbound familiar (a past spirit in living form that communicates with people like Ramukata) spoke up, "Take these," said Ayam. The porcupine by his side reached up and handed Ramukata a small bunch of spines. "They will keep him strong until Hawenniyo comes."

Ramukata gratefully took the spines and held them tightly – he knew what to do with them. It was a rare gift; someone had to be in special favour with the high god Hawenniyo to be allowed the gift of spines from the body of Ayam. *Why is this man so extraordinary? I know he's come to help Harriet-the-Moses but there must be something else about him.*

Ramukata had never known the gods to be so keen to offer so much help. Oliver would, more than likely, be dead by now if it had not been for the shaman's intervention, but he was still far from safe. Ramukata could not heal him on his own. Oliver's breathing was shallow, with a pulse like gently rippling waves on a pond, and his skin had turned the colour of spring catkins. Thin skin covered the boils under his arms and neck that were now the size of oranges, under which dark green pus was growing all the time.

Hawenniyo very rarely turned up in person; normally the spirit of well-being, Orenda, would be powerful enough to aid Ramukata's patients where his herbal remedies were insufficient. According to tradition, Harriet and the children would have to wait until daybreak to speak to Ramukata after a visit from Hawenniyo – who would only visit at night.

Aral stretched his wings. "I will return before Hawenniyo arrives." Then he disappeared into the forest. Ayam sniffed the air, blinked, rubbed his head against Ramukata's leg and scurried off into the undergrowth.

★ ★ ★

Harriet left Angeline and Rachel and closed the door behind her to speak to Little Tree outside.

"He's no better, I'm afraid," Little Tree explained; "he may be even worse." V starting crying. Ben and Charlie longingly looked across to where they knew Oliver was lying in pain.

"De Lord will not take 'im if 'tis not his time," Harriet pronounced with her hands praying.

"But what if he does, it's all our fault!" cried V. Charlie hugged V, trying to be brave himself.

"Can we go and see him now?" asked Charlie.

"No, he's best left alone. He's in the best hands," said Little Tree.

"He really is, Master Charlie," said Harriet.

Ben joined Charlie in comforting V. "I'm sure he'll be better in the morning, squidge." (Another, occasional, affectionate name he used for his little sister.) The warrior standing next to Little Tree held out a hand and led them towards the campfire. Benjamin followed behind until Ben wrapped an arm around his shoulders to join the family.

Harriet asked Little Tree if he would get some herbs from Ramukata so she could make a dressing for Rachel's wounds. Sumac and fenugreek were good with others to make an antiseptic poultice to place against the open wounds on Rachel's back. He agreed and Harriet went off to the forest to find some devil's claw to make a herbal tea, which would ease some of the pain from the inside. Meanwhile, Angeline was gently removing the blood-soaked cloth and carefully bathing the scars of her torment.

★ ★ ★

The feathers fluttered a little but the wind chimes were not singing as Little Tree asked for the herbs Harriet had requested. Ramukata disappeared inside for a few moments, returning with a small birch bark pot containing the fenugreek and sumac.

"How is he now?"

"No worse but no better."

"Did I see Aral and Ayam with you?"

"Yes, we are going to get a visit from Hawenniyo tonight."

Little Tree's eyes widened, "Really?"

"Yes, so nobody must come to me 'til he's been. He will come tonight when you see the moon vanish. Aral will guide him and Ayam will keep watch."

Little Tree crossed his arms over his chest and tapped himself three times and then looked skyward and held his arms up as high as they would go. "Saydadio, Reneska, Onondaga!" Ramukata handed him the herbs, then went back inside the tepee.

After a supper of buckwheat and buffalo meat had been consumed, Little Tree took the boys to his home and the girls went with Harriet to the hut. Little Tree wanted to keep the boys with him as he knew what was going to happen later.

Chapter 24

Oliver lay on the wicker bed drifting in and out of consciousness; he was barely aware of Ramukata using Ayam's spines as acupuncture needles. A few moments earlier he'd viewed himself from above – floating in an out-of-body experience. He thought he heard the voice of Jenny telling him to go back and imagined seeing Emilie standing in the entrance of the tepee. His mind tumbled over and over with visions and voices taking turns to confuse him; it was like watching a film but with a completely different soundtrack. Yet he felt peaceful. He jumped, as if falling from a cliff in a dream. He started to think of the boys, and Charlie asking where Emilie came from – he hadn't had time to tell them – now time was running out.

★ ★ ★

It made him think of the time he'd first met Emilie. He'd travelled back to 1625 and to the town of Arndell, about twenty miles from Rosemie Common, to help the local inhabitants overcome an epidemic of the Black Death. According to local records he'd been researching at the county archives, that year nearly three-quarters of the population was reported to have died from the disease. The records also mentioned that soon after the outbreak in the town, the remaining population had retreated within the walls of the town's castle that overlooked the River Arn. At the time it was unknown what caused the terrible blisters, boils and black patches to appear on the skin of the victims. Death was almost inevitable for anyone who contracted the condition – a slow, painful, disgusting way to die.

The swellings normally appeared first around the groin and under the armpit before spreading to the neck and other areas of the body. They gradually grew in size and then oozed pus before turning black in colour as they killed the body tissue. All manner of reasons were blamed for the plague, from someone's religious belief and stinky air, to the position of the planets; everything except the real reason! From his research Oliver knew the likely cause was the bite of a flea, which carried the bacteria, that lived on the brown rat. Obviously, Oliver couldn't help everyone but he also knew that cramming everyone into a rat-infested castle was probably the worst thing to do. He didn't have a particular plan but reasoned to either try and clear the place of rats or convince people to leave the castle grounds.

He prepared for the trip and used Jenny to transport him back in time as he'd done several times before, although these were the early days of his mercy missions. He'd arrived a short distance from the town and began the walk towards Arndell but was greeted by a sight he hadn't planned for. As he approached the town, on the road leading to the river bridge to the castle, he was greeted by the sight of the local sheriff, Thomas Cole, ordering his men to secure a woman in the town pillory.

The pillory was a medieval wooden structure for securing the hands and head of a convicted felon, who would then be subjected to further punishment dictated by the court magistrate. Oliver mingled with the milling crowd and discovered that the woman was due to be put in the pillory overnight before her execution on the following day, whereupon she was to be burnt at the stake for witchcraft. He stood next to a man dressed in a grey smock and wearing clogs and asked, "What's she supposed to have done?"

"Arh, no suppose 'bout it. It's her and that cat o' hers."

"What is?"

"This 'ere plague of death we a gettin'," replied the rugged-looking man with hands the size of dinner plates.

"'tis 'er heathen ways dat gets us punished."

"Why… what the–"

"Her witchcraft, dat what'll be. Her witchcraft brought the Black Death upon us," the man interrupted.

"Oh!" Oliver replied. *Witchcraft, mumbo-jumbo*, he thought.

One henchman pushed the woman's neck down into the middle part of the pillory and another pulled her hands down into the outer sockets. Then the top beam, pivoted at one end, was pulled down and secured with a primitive-looking large metal lock on the other end.

The sheriff stepped up onto a box, unrolled a length of parchment and calmly announced: "Emilie Bracket, by the power invested in me you are to receive twenty lashes for raising spirits of the dead and spend one night in the pillory. At midday in the morrow you will be taken from this place to Horse Bridge Common Green where ye shall be burnt at the stake for witchcraft. The result of which hath brought the Black Death to our town. Many good people have already suffered but you will suffer a lesser fate to please the Lord."

Lesser fate? thought Oliver, raising his eyebrows. Being burnt alive, for their belief that she caused the coming of the plague! It is hardly less painful – maybe a bit quicker, but. It made him sick at the thought. He made a decision there and then to save her from that awful destiny, although he didn't know anything about her, or very much about witchcraft, or if indeed such a thing existed; he knew, however, that it wasn't the cause of the plague. His plan had suddenly changed.

The sheriff stood down from his box. "Mr Guthroe, if you would commence with the lash."

One of the henchmen, a giant of a man with very broad shoulders and a harsh mean, merciless face, flicked the whip in his hand and made a cracking sound a couple of times before laying it hard across Emilie's bare back. She thrust her head up and yelled out in agony. Pain shot through the whole of her body. The crowd cheered. Some townsfolk at the front were also already throwing rotten, stinking food at her. Oliver lowered his head – he couldn't bear to look. She was a pretty woman who, he thought, looked around her mid-twenties. Her long jet-black hair flicked forward with each jerk of her head as she flinched with each strike.

Not wishing to stand out by walking away, Oliver endured the proceedings but winced in sympathetic pain as each lash was delivered and she let out screams of pain. After six or seven lashes the whip cut into her back causing open wounds to bleed and trickle down her back. It seemed to take forever and it gave Oliver a knot in his stomach to see the way the whipping man appeared to enjoy and take pleasure in his duty.

"Thank you, Mr Guthroe," said the sheriff on completion of the punishment and he turned and walked in the direction of the imposing Norman castle – followed by his aides. The crowd slowly dispersed with the last few manky missiles lobbed in Emilie's direction along with many insults. Oliver desperately wanted to shout at all of them of their ignorance and cruelty. But there was a time for talking and a time to remain silent. This was the latter. He could feel the intensity of the hatred of the crowd as well as their verbal anger. He realised he would have to bide his time.

Oliver left with the crowd who were mainly making their way towards the three-arched stone bridge that crossed the River Arn and led to the castle's south gate. From the south gate a trackway led down to the small wharf on the south side of the bridge for landing the supply boats that came up from the coast. Oliver paused for a moment on the bridge and reflected on what he had just witnessed and took a sideways glance back towards the pillory. Emilie slumped motionless with her head bowed. He vowed to do whatever was necessary to free her that night and take her away, far from this place of persecution.

He continued towards the castle. As he tried to enter the south gate he was stopped by a man in an official-looking cape. "Excuse me, sir," he said, holding up his hand, "you are not local to these parts by my recognition. From where do you come, sir, and what is your name?" As well as the purple cape the warden also wore a wide-brimmed cloth hat. In one hand he held a board with parchment attached and a cane in the other. Behind him stood a shorter, stockier man, bearing a servant-looking appearance.

"Nathaniel Hodge, from Cheshampton, sir," Oliver replied, bowing his head.

"Have you had reason to be in the city of London recently, sir?"

It was well known that there was an outbreak of the plague in London and the provinces feared that people coming from the city could also bring the disease to the town.

"No, sir, I have never been to London."

The warden looked Oliver square in the eye to look for deception. "What is your business here?" He had to think quick as his plan had changed. He was originally going to say he had come from London with news of new discoveries in avoiding the plague.

"To seek work, sir. I am fit and willing. If you know of anywhere I might find some, I would be most obliged, kind sir," Oliver grovelled.

"No, Mr Hodge, I'm sure I don't," the warden curtly replied. "Check him over, Stephen."

The short man stepped forward and began to study Oliver's skin more closely and asked him to undo his jerkin. After a few moments he turned to the warden, who had taken a couple of paces back, "I can't see anything, sir."

"Okay, Mr Hodge, you may go." The warden made a note of the name and Oliver continued into the castle grounds and surveyed the layout inside. The boundary walls enclosed a large area with gardens, some cottages, a few shops and a tavern. Towards the back of the enclosure a small hillock was surmounted by a tall, square, stone building with its own massive timber door. It was a second defensive keep. There were two other entrances to the castle – the north and west gates; both side of each gate were surrounded by large stone buildings of at least four storeys high. The doors of the gateways were set back in these structures with an outer portcullis that could be lowered for defence. Entry to the castle was controlled by appointed wardens who checked everyone entering was plague-free. Oliver knew that within a few weeks the castle would be ravaged with the Black Death and it would have nothing to do with Emilie.

For the rest of the afternoon he busied himself with the whereabouts of the man called Guthroe. He had the keys to the pillory. After chatting to one of the storekeepers he found out that Guthroe, almost without exception, spent the evenings in the Wild Boar tavern. And most likely before the evening was out, would not be in full control of his faculties due to his consumption of ale.

★ ★ ★

A mixture of laughter and arguments reverberated off the walls as Oliver entered the dimly lit tavern; the smell of oak burning in the grate was overpowered by strong tobacco piercing his nostrils and stinging his eyes. Some were eating, all were drinking. He felt his way across the low-ceilinged room to where he thought the bartender would be.

Then, having successfully navigated his way to the landlord, he ordered a drink, which was delivered in a wooden tankard. At the end of the bar he saw the man he was looking for – Jed Guthroe.

"So," asked Oliver, leaning on the wooden bar with one arm and raising a tankard in the other, "you're quite an important man round these parts, then."

"Well, yeah. Some would say that. Me being second to the sheriff and all that is. Get the wrong side of the sheriff and yous be the wrong side of me."

"Ah, I see."

"Yous not be getting the wrong side of the sheriff, are yers?" he said swaying like a child's spinning top that was slowing down.

"No, no, not me! I'm just glad we've got people like you to look after us. You being so strong and… er, bright too, probably," said Oliver through clenched teeth.

The pillory keys dangled teasingly from the giant's leather belt and well within Oliver's reach but there was no way he would be able to get them from him whilst he was conscious. The drinking continued late into the evening, and others came and went with the conversations. They moved from the bar to nearby the large open fireplace and sat by it for a while, stoking it with logs from time to time. Oliver ensured throughout that Guthroe was never wanting for beer and talked about anything he could think of, just to stay and humour him.

"You says yous be lookin' for work like mine. Wiv the sheriff an' all?"

"Well, yes," replied Oliver. "I need some sort of work and I was just wondering if…"

They were now seated at a crude table with the sheriff's officer propping his head up heavily in his hand and his eyes were more shut than open.

"Maybe I could put in a word for yers. You seem like a…" His voice trailed off as his head hit the table and his arms splayed out in front of him. He groaned.

The tavern keeper laughed, "Hah, look, old Jed's dun gone."

A mate of his at the bar wandered over and lifted his head by his hair, then let it go and the numbed skull crunched back onto the table. He laughed. Jed partially woke with a grunt and lifted his dribbling mouth from the table and as he licked his lips a confused look spread across his weary face.

Oliver sensed his opportunity. "He'll need some help getting home," he proffered.

Noticing Oliver's slim, if fit, stature, "He's gonna need more carrying than you can give him," said the barman.

Jed's friend, the other burly assistant of the sheriff, slipped an arm under Jed's and lifted him awkwardly from the table.

"Here, I can at least give you a hand," said Oliver and he shoved his shoulder under Jed Guthroe's other armpit. This instantly gave Oliver's nose a body-odour overdose and although he turned his head away, his face looked like he was chewing a lemon! Staggering from one side to the other they stumbled out of the tavern and towards Jed's home – which happened to be near the south gate of the castle. On the way, the ring of keys Oliver was after dug into his side.

"Come on, we'll shove 'im in 'ere for now. I'm not trying to get 'im up them steps." He indicated a stairway leading to a door in the south gate keep wall.

As they entered the alternate choice of an open doorway, a horse tied up in one corner took a moment's interest in them, then carried on chewing its hay. In another was a wheelie-bin-sized pile of straw – the two of them dragged the comatose bailiff and almost collapsed with him onto the makeshift bed.

Oliver had secretly already been able to unhook the large metal ring that secured the keys to Jed Guthroe's side. As he was dropped to the floor Oliver held onto the keyring and hid it behind his back.

"'e'll wake up when he's ready," said Jed's mate.

The two of them left the stable. "Where you be staying then, stranger?"

"Oh, the tavern keeper said he could find me a room."

"Right, yeah, well, I'll probably see yer in the morning, then. We gotta burning tomorrow," he said cheerfully.

Not if I have my way, thought Oliver.

The man headed for another doorway further up the south wall, while Oliver pretended to head in the direction of the tavern. As soon as the man had disappeared through the door Oliver made an about turn and hurried back towards the stable. He quietly untied the horse from the metal ring fixed to the wall and led it outside. Luckily for him Jed was dead to the world and heard nothing. Apart from a couple of men arguing outside the tavern, some way across the castle courtyard, there was no one about. Oliver walked slowly but purposefully out through the open south gate – clutching the keys tightly to stop them jangling. The gate warden and his aide had retired at sunset as travellers rarely arrived after nightfall.

After passing through the gate and down towards the bridge he broke into a jog, pulling the horse with him. Dark reflections shimmered off the river as he crossed the bridge on his way to the pillory. As he approached Emilie from behind, he saw the stripes of pain and dried blood standing out on her back. Hearing footsteps and fearing another attack Emilie raised her head and tried to look round at the visitor but was restrained by the pillory block. There was a fence nearby where Oliver tied up the horse and then he approached Emilie.

"Hello," he said in a soft voice and walked around the pillory to face her. She didn't respond. "Hello, how are you?"

Emilie eyed him cautiously. She knew most people in the town and did not recognise him. If fact, she'd helped many people in the town but now they'd turned against her.

"My name is Nathaniel... I mean, Oliver."

Emilie scowled and sighed but still remained silent. Oliver had decided that this was one case where he felt he could use his proper name as his mission had somewhat changed.

"I'm Oliver, Oliver Bramley, and I'm going to get you out of here." He started to fiddle each key on the ring into the padlock to find which one would release it.

"Why? Why would you do this? You don't know me."

"I know this is wrong and that's good enough for me," he replied.

"You'll be in great trouble if they catch you. They'll burn you with me."

"Well, let's hope that doesn't happen!" he smiled, as at last the lock released. He lifted the top bar up over her head and dropped it quietly down the other side. With great relief Emilie stood up and shook her head and shoulders.

"Who are you? Who sent you?"

Oliver took a length of material he had tucked in his belt and wrapped it around her shoulders. She winced, bit her lip and closed her eyes as the cloth touched her back. Oliver assisted her tying a loose strap around her chest to hold it in place, then held her hand gently.

"Come on, we need to leave here," he said leading her towards where he had tied up the horse.

"Is this yours?" she asked. In the bright moonlight she thought she recognised the white markings on the bay horse.

"Well, I've sort of borrowed it."

"Who from?"

"The big man. Mr Guthroe."

"Oh, God. I thought it looked like his; he'll kill you if he finds out, and not in a nice way."

"Is there a nice way?"

"Well he'll chop a few bits off first and then think how slowly he can make you die!"

"Yeah, well, he's got to find me first, hasn't he?" smarted Oliver. "Come on, let's get you up on this horse." He bent over and cupped his hands together for her to use as a step. Emilie was thankful for the rescue but was afraid it wouldn't last long – Jed Guthroe would be as mad as a wasp trapped in a jam jar. The first sting would be when he found his horse gone, the second when he learnt that Emilie had escaped the pillory. He would be answerable to the sheriff for that, who was a corrupt and vindictive official. Thomas Cole had been trying to prosecute Emilie for ages and finally when the plague arrived he concocted a case of her offending God by witchcraft. Many people had testified against her in court, some with inducement from Cole and others because they had been witness to her powers.

"I can't go without Postal," she said, as she settled on the horse.

"What?"

"My cat, I can't go without my cat; he's my only real companion. He relies on me, and I on him."

"Where do we find him?"

"My cottage. He'll be asleep in the kitchen, waiting for me. It's just on the outskirts of town down this road." She pointed in the direction of the Cheshampton Road.

"That's good; that's the way I was planning to go," replied Oliver leading the horse onto the track. A light breeze began to drag grey shapes overhead, twinkling stars disappeared and the overhanging branches of the trees cast eerie shadows across their path. The smell of bonfires – lit to ward off the plague – encircled them.

They went past two houses with white crosses painted on the doors and the words, 'Lord have mercy on their souls' crudely written alongside.

"This is it," said Emilie as they reached a small flint cottage with a thatched roof. The front door was never locked and Oliver went in and found Postal, as Emilie had said, curled up asleep by the fireplace. His little black face looked up at Oliver and he twitched an ear. The only part of him that wasn't black was the white tip to his tail that Postal flicked up as Oliver got closer.

"Come on, you," he said picking up the moggie. Postal let out a little meow and tucked his head under Oliver's chin affectionately. He held the cat out for a moment and smiled at the creature. Somehow, Oliver thought he could read an expression of gratitude on the old moggie's face and once more held him close to his chest.

"Have you got him?" Emilie called softly from outside at the moment Oliver appeared with Postal in the doorway and handed him to her.

"Is there anything else you need before we go? Anything we can take with us, I mean, because you won't be coming back here."

"You still haven't told me where we are going," she said, stroking Postal in her arms.

"Well, I know someone in Cheshampton who will look after you and make sure you're safe and help nurse your wounds."

"I went there once, to the market, with my father when he was alive, to buy some pigs. It took three days to get them back here."

"Where is he now?" Oliver asked.

"He died four years ago from the plague, as did my mother, three days after him."

"You didn't catch it?"

"No. I er... managed to get sort of... protected," she said, affectionately stroking Postal's head.

Oliver patted the horse on the neck. "Well, is there anything else because we need to get going to make it to Cheshampton before daybreak."

"There's a cloak hanging behind the door and... a special possession of mine." *Can I really trust this man?* she thought.

He was a mystery to her, a man whom she had seen in the crowd during her ordeal at the hands of Jed Guthroe, but one she'd never seen before. Normally she would only take people into her confidence once she had got to know them well – their background and religious beliefs and, if they had come to her for help, she would also check out the members of their family. But now she was the one in need of help and didn't want to imagine what would happen if her family secret was found and fell into the wrong hands. No, she would have to trust him.

"Okay, but where will I find this possession?" asked Oliver.

"It's hidden, behind a loose brick in the wall of the kitchen. A woollen cloth hangs on a nail in the beam that extends above the fireplace; behind it you will find one brick that is loose. Wriggle that out and put your hand inside. Above the nail hanging from the ceiling is a length of string with a bulb of garlic tied to it; pull that and the book will be raised into your hand. Otherwise you will find nothing."

Oliver raised his eyebrows and took a deep breath, "Right, hidden away in the wall, okay!" *Must be something very valuable*, he thought. Jewels, perhaps, or money... but a book?

Emilie sat hunched up on the horse holding on tightly to Postal as the pain in her back reminded her of what had happened to her earlier in the day. Stabs of pain kept shooting across her back along the lines of torture. Oliver entered the kitchen again that was dimly lit by a few burning embers in the grate and the intermittent moonlight through the open doorway. He picked up a candle from the windowsill and lit it from the fire. Around him dark shadows were cast from the flame but he could clearly see the woollen cloth hanging on the wall where she had said it would be. He lifted it off and threw it on the table, then held the candle up to the wall. He ran his fingers over the rough brick, found the loose one and gripped it with his fingertips. A few seconds later he'd wriggled it free from the wall.

Slowly he pushed his arm through the hole up to his elbow but could feel nothing, and then he remembered about the string above his head. He placed the candleholder on the large wooden mantelpiece beam that reached over the top of the open fire. Then, reaching up, he pulled down on the garlic string and felt something come within his grasp. Gripping it tightly he then pulled it out through the wall and let go of the string. Placing the object on the table he grasped the candle to have a closer look. In front of him he saw a dark-coloured rectangular casket, made of a material that was unknown to Oliver, with a leather strap and copper clasp securing the lid. He briefly looked towards the door – his fascination was getting the better of him –

he released the clasp and opened the lid. Inside was an old book. Embossed on the leather cover were the words:

The Divine Runes and Sigils
of the
Ancient Order of Solomon

Not knowing what that meant he opened the cover and held the candle over the text inside. The first inner page was illustrated with strange symbols and hieroglyphs at the top and some Latin text underneath. Although Oliver's Latin was limited he could work out that it mentioned 'spells for the good'. *Spells for the good*, he repeated in his head. *Spells?*

He heard a call from outside, although he didn't hear the detail. Oliver closed the book and refastened the lid of its container, blew out the candle, gathered up the cloak and left the room with the box in hand. Before he closed the door he remembered what the smell of the room reminded him of – the strong aroma of his grandmother's herb garden. She'd used many herbs in her cooking but was also a strong advocate for their use in medicinal remedies and she shunned modern medicines. More than once when he'd been ill as a child, his grandmother had created a remedy from plants in her garden. One day in her garden, when he was very young, she'd told him that some plants had magical powers that had been forgotten. He'd just remembered.

287

He latched the door quietly and held the box up to show Emilie he'd found it. After handing her the box he led the horse to a large stump of a tree which he used to mount the horse behind Emilie and wrapped the cloak around her neck.

"Right, let's get a move on," he said and gave the horse a gentle kick.

"Thank you, sir, thank you again for your kindness," she said holding on to her most prized possessions. The smell of the smoke receded into the distance.

Chapter 25

The sun was just getting up as the tower of the church of St Cuthman came into view in Cheshampton above the ancient elms.

"Nearly there," said Oliver.

"Is this where you live, sir?"

"Sort of," he smiled. "We're going to see a good friend of mine." Before entering the village, to keep from prying eyes, Oliver left the main road and followed a pathway he knew well across the brooks to the west. On their way to the local river many streams crisscrossed the low-lying meadows around the back of the rise on which the church sat. The locals called the area the 'Shooting Fields' because at certain times of the year commoners were given rights – by the Duke of Norfolk – to hunt the wild boar over the fields when they came out of the woods to forage near the streams. Now was not one of those times.

Alongside the imposing Norman church stood an impressive half-timbered Elizabethan house. To the rear, a high wall surrounded a kitchen garden the size of two basketball pitches. Oliver jumped down from the horse and led it up the small incline to a gateway in the rear garden wall.

With a different look of pain on her face Emilie asked cautiously, "Who lives here?"

"The vicar – Francis Cripps."

"Vicar!" gasped Emilie, but not with complete surprise. "But–" Oliver put a finger to his lips.

"It's okay, he's very understanding and tolerant, not like many of the other hypocrites," suspecting there was maybe more to Emilie than met the eye, but he was not one to judge without finding the truth first. She knew that most of those with strong religious convictions were hostile towards anyone of Emilie's talents and she was about to be introduced to a God servant and enter a second-division house of God. Every muscle in her body tensed as Oliver helped her down from the horse, and not only from the strain pulling on her wounds.

Postal jumped down and curled his body and tail affectionately around Oliver's leg.

"Wait there," he said, while he walked the horse into a nearby stable. "Come." Oliver led Emilie to a door where a bell hung on a bracket to one side. There was a chain to pull and make it ring, but instead of pulling the chain Oliver delved into an old chimney pot standing beside the door and pulled out a stout stick. He then held the bell with one hand and proceeded to tap the bell. First he struck it quickly three times, then slowly three times, then three quick taps again. As the last dull ring faded an upper-storey window opened slightly and a face peered down. Oliver held the stick above his head and the face disappeared, then he replaced the stick in its hiding place.

As the bolts on the inside of the door could be heard operating, Emilie tucked the box in her hand under the cloak she wore. The door creaked open to reveal the face of a short and stocky man smiling at them, "Oliver, how good to see you." He held out both hands which Oliver grasped happily and returned the smile.

"And… good to see you too, Francis!"

Emilie avoided eye contact and looked for Postal but he'd shot off and was hiding behind a small bush with his tail tucked under him.

"I'm sorry, do come in, come." Francis backed into the room behind him and waved them in.

Oliver offered Emilie first but her gaze was fixed on Postal's hiding place.

Sorrowful, she turned to Oliver, her face that of a child asking with their eyes.

In a moment Francis read the body language and spotted the feline stranger, "Yours?"

"She won't go anywhere without him," apologised Oliver.

Francis smiled, "If it's with you, then bring him in too!"

Emilie whistled and flicked her fingers. Her beloved Postal crept out, tail still tucked under his belly and his ears angled back as if to make his head streamlined, and slowly tiptoed towards her. She bent down and gathered him up.

"Come, tell me what I can do for you, my good man."

The rectory stood in the early morning shadow of St Cuthman's Church but enough light was penetrating the diamond-patterned windows to illuminate a well-furnished parlour.

"Is there anything I can get you first, a drink perhaps?"

Oliver looked at Emilie with a face of encouragement.

"A drink of water would be nice, thank you."

Francis took a jug and glass from a side cabinet and poured her a drink. Then turned to Oliver. "Well, my boy, what will it be for you this time?"

"I need to ask a really big favour." Oliver asked Emilie to stand up and turn round. The holy man flinched at the sight of the wounds on her back and for the next twenty minutes or so Oliver explained the situation. Francis rocked back in his chair and folded his arms. "Is there any way you could find her a position to work for you in the gardens, or the church?"

The vicar frowned and studied Emilie carefully. "Well, young lady," he said scratching his chin and then curling his hand over his mouth apparently deep in thought. Expectantly, Oliver leant forward. Emilie dropped her head. *No church man will help me*, she thought.

After what seemed an age and some searching looks in Emilie's direction, but in reality was only a few moments, Francis spoke, "Is there anything else you couldn't leave behind, young lady, as well as your cat?" he asked inquisitively.

Under her cloak, the box with the book sat hidden on her lap.

Oliver cast a glance at Emilie. "It's okay, I think he's guessed already," nodding in the direction of her lap.

Emilie slowly and purposefully placed the box on the table and pushed it towards Francis. He picked it up and opened the lid. "Hmm," he murmured and raised an eyebrow. "Well, this proves that they were right in one thing," he said as he read the cover, "but this book provides for the good of people not the evil."

"That's what they don't understand," said Emilie. "I've never used my power for evil; maybe mischief," she said with a wry smile, "but never evil."

"What do you mean, Francis?" asked Oliver.

Francis picked up the book and flicked through some pages. The introduction was written in Latin followed by three sections: the first in Hebrew; the second in Sanskrit; and lastly hieroglyphics. Scattered throughout were notes in the margins written in old English. "This information is very powerful, and in the wrong hands could lead to the Devil's work, but in the right hands heal and provide help for those most in need, except the owner and conjurer of the spells." Oliver was muted by the revelation.

Francis looked at Emilie. "Where did you get this?"

"My mother; she gave away its lair with the last words she spoke, and her mother had given it to her when she died. We only used it for good, to help people; with potions and, at times, spells; before she died I was never allowed to read it without her being there. We never used it for our own benefit. And Mother said that if we used it in a bad way – to do harm to anyone – the next time we removed it from the protection of its case, the words would start to disappear from the pages and our power would be lost."

"She was quite right, unless you only used it from within the protection of the case."

"What's so special about the case?" asked Oliver.

"It's made from an ancient crystal called Sealonite – it's very rare. It's only been known to be found in the Holy Land, during the time of the crusades. And it is mentioned in the Book of Kings and, in particular, in connection with Solomon's First Temple as having mysterious shielding properties. Some believe it was from a falling star, cast down by an angry god."

"Quite something, then!" exclaimed Oliver, scratching his ear.

Holding the book in his lap Francis read some more. "I've heard of the lost books of the Old Testament – the Deuterocanonical scripts – parchments written almost before time began. These pages mention some of the names in those scrolls but my Hebrew is rather scant and the rest – I would just be guessing." He closed the book and returned it to the casket.

"Can you read it, my dear?"

"Yes, sir; I struggle with some parts, that's why the notes are there – to remind me."

"What do you think then, Francis?" asked Oliver.

"I think you should be very careful with this." Emilie bowed her head, resigned, and stroked Postal.

"I had heard rumours from Arndell, of strange but good deeds going on, for some time, so I had my suspicions. However, I never heard of any bad work from the same sources, just a bit of jealously from the parish priests because they weren't getting all the credit for the good fortune of their parishioners!" Francis stood up and handed the casket containing the book back to Emilie.

"It is my belief that you should remain the operator of the book and continue, perhaps with more caution, your work, when needed."

"Thank you, kind sir, if able, I always will," she smiled.

Oliver smiled too and held out a hand for her to hold.

"As it happens, Oliver, I do have a position Emilie could fill for me; that of church warden. The previous one died of the plague here three weeks ago but I have had no offers to replace them as it would mean living in the house where they died from the disease. If Emilie has no objections, she could live there, help me and have use of the gardens."

"What do you think, Emilie?" asked Oliver. She nodded.

"First, young lady, we need to get you patched up, eh, Oliver?"

"Yes, yes, of course."

"I have some linen you could use," Francis smiled.

Emilie was still unsure of her saviour's friend, members of the church were normally amongst her biggest enemies, but here was a member of the clergy who appeared friendly towards her. Not only that, he was prepared to conceal her true identity. Postal looked up at her, perplexed, and then leapt from her lap and ran to the door. He anxiously pawed at the door. Animal instinct told him they should leave. He'd only witnessed men of the cloth being mean to his mistress.

Francis went to her side and rested his arm gently around her shoulder. "Do not worry, Emilie, I'll make sure no one finds out who you really are. We can help one another, secretly, for the benefit of all our neighbours."

Postal leapt back on to Emilie's lap and hissed at the man.

"He doesn't seem to like you much!" laughed Oliver.

Emilie stroked him. "He's just protective, that's all. Ever since... well, ever since I helped him get better – after the accident."

"It's no matter; if this man thinks it's a good thing to save you, then I will continue what he started."

"Thank you, Francis."

"Come, let us get you properly clothed," said Francis and he led them away.

★ ★ ★

Oliver and Emilie spent some weeks together after the rescue as she recuperated but the time came for him to leave and return to his normal life in the twentieth century. During his time with her they had got to know one another very well but he'd managed to remain very illusive and vague about his origins. She had begun some of the simple duties of a church warden which pleased her because, although her practices might have been perceived as pagan, she was passionately Christian. She and Francis had also formed a common bond and worked well together. Once he'd accepted their new home, Postal had been particularly proficient at driving out any rats in the house, which removed the risk of contracting the plague.

Her tied cottage had a private path to the rectory and was only a short walk down the lane to the church. On Sundays she would sit at the back of the church and listen and learn the woes of the parishioners. Together with the prayers of the vicar her spells conjured up the help the less fortunate needed. Of course the church always got the praise for good fortune falling upon the needy. That didn't bother Emilie, though, as she did not do it to get thanks. Seeing people change from their demeanour of sadness or ill-health to one of happiness was reward enough.

It had been a selfless act that had nearly got her burnt at the stake before, so the less people knew of her talents the better. She trusted no one except Oliver and Francis Cripps. However, she not only trusted Oliver, she had fallen in love with him. Not that he noticed the subtle signs she gave him. No, for Oliver to read them the signs would have to be the size of a battleship. And then it would have to have all guns blazing for him to take notice! He had, though, developed affection for Emilie but knew his calling was back at Pegasus Ride with Jenny.

The day came for him to make his excuses and leave. After a semi-formal embrace Oliver turned around and left the cottage and disappeared down the lane towards the field outside town where he had left Jenny. He did not see the tears stream down Emilie's face, a stream that became a river of sadness. It felt like her heart was being ripped from her chest; it made her gasp for breath. The pit of her stomach emptied and felt hollow for days after his departure. She sought solace with Francis, who assured her it was for good reason and that he would be back. Several years later he returned and found her very settled into community life and she was an accepted part of the church.

There had been one scare some months after Oliver had originally left – the men from Arndell came to town after getting a tip-off from a traveller – but after Francis's intervention they left town empty handed. Oliver would normally stay for a few days before moving on again. As the years went by she commented that whenever he visited, Oliver didn't seem to age but she was growing old. At first he dismissed it but when on one visit he returned with some spectacles for her, as her eyesight was giving her trouble, he decided he'd better sit her down and tell her his full story. But first he wanted to know how her cat was still alive. "Postal must be more than thirty years old and doesn't look a day older than when I first saw him," he said.

"Well, you two make a good pair! I could have told you but I just didn't get around to it," she smiled. "He was actually killed when my mother was alive, by a post horse rider galloping over him. I carried him into the house and my mother showed me a spell to use to bring him back to life. Well, not fully to life – only in body and spirit. He's what is known as a familiar. Not fully alive or dead."

"Ah, well that sort of explains things."

"What is it you want to tell me?" she asked.

He wasn't sure how she was likely to take his true story, so he asked her to sit down. Would she go mad and hit him? Would she understand why he didn't take her with him? She had pleaded that at the time he left a few weeks after her rescue. But he'd concocted a story of why he had to go alone and of course not the real truth.

"I too have a gift. Well, not mine exactly, but one endowed on a friend. A very close friend."

"Ah, I see, now I understand," she said, jumping to the wrong conclusion. "You don't need to explain any further," and then got up and walked to the window. Peering down the lane she said, "Is she with you now?"

"Well, er… yes, she's waiting on the edge of the shooting fields."

"Oh, the way you brought me here," Emilie replied rather caustically and dodged Oliver as he approached her.

"No, Em, you don't understand."

All these years of waiting and hoping – now she felt sick. *One day he'll stay* she'd thought. She popped

299

on her glasses to see him clearly. "Oh I do, Oliver, I do understand. Has she… got a name, then?" looking him straight in the eye.

"Yes, she does have a name; it's Jenny."

"Oh, very quaint, very nice. Jenny."

Oliver was numb; he'd not handled this very well and had never seen Emilie react like this before. She stood stiffly in front of the fireplace with her arms firmly folded. Oliver sighed.

"Well, don't let me keep you from – Jenny! The door's over there."

Oliver slowly approached her. "Look, if you'd just calm down, I can explain."

"Yes, I'd like that. I've been waiting for you all my life when you should have just let me burn and saved me the pain of all these years that you have just gathered up and thrown in my face."

"What do you mean, Em! For Christ's sake, what are you on about?" Oliver rarely swore but he couldn't work out why she was reacting in this way.

"I've loved you from the day you saved me, not that you noticed! And all these years I've been waiting for you and now you introduce me to… Jenny!" she said, almost spitting the name out.

Oliver stood motionless for a second while his brain computed the sentence.

"Jenny's a bloody aeroplane, you…" Oliver struggled for words, "not a woman. And anyway I didn't know you loved me. Why didn't you say something?"

"Would it have made a difference?"

"Yes, 'cos I… I feel the same about you!"

Emilie creased her nose and squinted, "An aeroplane – what's that?"

"Oh God, never mind, I'll try and explain in a moment."

"So she's not another woman, yet you referred to her, it, as a she?"

"It's just something I do; it's a machine… that I think of… as female, okay? Where I come from, it's what we tend to do."

"Where exactly, then, do you come from?"

He hugged Emilie and then she hugged him back. "I'm sorry, Em, I've been a bit of a fool. I never realised you… well, felt like that about me." She hugged him even more tightly and passionately kissed him.

"Come sit down and I'll tell you my story."

Having explained everything as best he could, "So you see I couldn't take you with me because, according to the message in the hieroglyph, you wouldn't survive the journey alive."

Now she understood, or thought she did! He left in Jenny the next day, promising to return sooner next time. However, he got delayed again and on his next visit he found her confined to her bed. She was desperately ill; in fact, terminally ill with not long to live. He could do nothing to help and she begged him to take her with him, even though she knew what the consequences were. The script in the floor of the aeroplane explicitly said that no one would survive transport from the past to a future date not of their time. So he'd never taken anyone back. Even he wasn't sure what would happen if he defied the ruling of the gods.

After spending a couple of days by her bedside, he gave in to her request. To transport her to Jenny he used a wheelbarrow; the failure of a similar mode of transport when it reached Cheshampton was rumoured to have been the reason for St Cuthman founding the church there. He wrapped her in some blankets for the journey and carefully placed her in the barrow. The only other item she took with her was her special casket. When he reached Jenny he lifted Emilie into the passenger compartment and secured the door.

As he turned around to climb up to the pilot's seat he saw Postal bounding through the grass towards them. "Of course, we can't forget you," he said and lifted the moggie, opened the door and popped him in. Emilie smiled in a resigned way. He pushed the barrow into the hedge before climbing aboard himself and asking Jenny to return them.

During their journey home he passed through the dark clouds as usual and was illuminated by flashes of lightning. But today they were brighter and more intense than usual. He glanced down through the little window into the passenger compartment below and saw an intense light in there too. Emilie was surrounded by a halo of electric blue and all but her face was obscured. Her head was tilted back and she was smiling. Oliver squinted against the glare. She opened her mouth and a white mist steamed out and cascaded onto the floor. In an instant Oliver's heart raced, he clenched his fist and thumped the sides of the aeroplane and screamed at the dark sky. He tried to turn the aeroplane around but he was not in control – it continued through the cloud.

"Jenny!" he screamed. But for once there was no response. He thumped her again. He was just about to rip off his helmet and goggles when he felt a warm glow inside, a strange tingling feeling shooting through his body, flowing one way then the other. It made him feel a bit light-headed but it was a feeling of happiness and pleasure. It made him feel the way he had when he'd first met Emilie, and the time she'd said she'd loved him all her life. He peered down through the porthole to the passenger cabin, the blaze of light had gone and he could see Emilie sitting comfortably and relaxed. He sighed with relief.

After landing back at Rosemie Common he jumped down and opened the cabin door. There was Emilie still sitting upright and quietly smiling to herself, Postal on her knees, with none of the pain in her face that she had previously displayed. For a moment she didn't move.

"What is it?" he asked.

Without a word she bent forward and gracefully stepped out of the cabin. There was no sign of assistance being required and she stepped quietly past him. He shut the door and turned around to face her. He gripped her by the waist to lift her up into his arms. It was then the reality and shock hit him. Emilie's form was solid enough but there was no weight to her. She flung her arms around his neck.

"Thank you," she whispered, in a slightly hissing sort of voice. "I can be with you always now."

His realisation was instant. She was with him in mind, body and spirit, but in a completely different way to a normal living person.

"But…" he began.

She put her fingers on his lips.

"I'm here with you now, without any pain; that's all that matters, my darling." Her voice was different too, somehow vacant and not full-bodied as it was before, but it was still unmistakeably Emilie. He now knew what happened if he brought someone back who he wasn't supposed to.

"Come on then, Em, let me take you to my house."

"Yess, I would like that," she replied, with a slight hiss to her voice.

He led her to the garden and in through the back door. She twisted and turned, staring at the modern unfamiliar fixtures inside his home. Oliver pulled out a chair for her to sit at and helped himself to a drink and a piece of cake. Emilie declined the offer of refreshment herself. In fact, from that day on she was never to eat or drink again. Oliver left Emilie in the kitchen while he went upstairs to change into clothing more suitable for the twentieth century.

"Gosh, Em, don't do that!" he shrieked. She had appeared behind him without a sound.

"Sorry!" laughed Emilie with a wry smile.

"How did you do that?"

"I've just discovered that I only have to think of going somewhere and I just appear there."

"Well, try and make some noise when you come up behind me. Please! Or I'll be having a heart attack and be joining you!"

"I'll try, I promise." She laughed and hugged him dearly.

Over the next few days together Oliver came up with a plan for Emilie and her situation. He had heard that the old antique shop in the nearby market town of Cheshampton was up for sale. It was somewhere he regularly visited to buy items for his trips into the past and was concerned that it would be closed down for good. Of course, it was a town well known to Emilie, although in another era. The antiques shop was in an extensive fifteenth century timber-frame building, a converted manor house. The top floor jutted out over the front of the ground floor and the roofline sagged in the middle. The roof was covered in large flat stones, rather than tiles or slates, quarried locally. Inside there were many small rooms and a network of passages and three staircases to the upper floor. The windows were mainly all ancient diamond-shaped leaded-light style, except for two of the shop windows that were made up of many larger square panes of glass about the size of an average book.

The building was known as the 'Old Workhouse' and it sat just off Church Street in Cheshampton, opposite a piece of common ground called Chantry Green. In fact, it was not far from where Emilie had lived more than four hundred years earlier. Having agreed a viewing time with the estate agents – selling the property on behalf of the owner – Oliver drove into town by himself in Harry Hobbard's classic Morris Minor car. Suddenly he swerved and nearly ran the car off the road.

"I wish you would not do that!" he shouted.

A short way out of Rosemie Common, Emilie had decided to join Oliver, on his way to view the Old Workhouse, by materialising out of thin air, onto the front passenger seat! She chuckled to herself and stroked Postal sitting on her lap.

They pulled up outside on the gravel road. Oliver had arranged for the incumbent owner to show him round.

"It might be best if you stay in the car, Em," he said.

"Of course, my dear," she replied, and gave him a big grin. The grin of a child who had no intention of doing as they were told!

Ignorant of the thoughts in Emilie's head, Oliver headed down the path to the front door. Inside he was greeted by Angus Volk. Angus had owned the shop for over thirty years but at the ripe old age of seventy had decided to sell up. Angus had the face of an old log pile and a beard that he'd been growing since he bought the shop. He started by showing

Oliver through the labyrinth of corridors and rooms on the ground floor. He then led the way up the first of the three staircases; in the narrowness of two of them his broad shoulders almost brushed the sides.

Oliver suddenly felt a chill pass his face and instinctively turned his head and then jumped back and bashed his head on the side wall of the staircase. Emilie just stood there, at the bottom, grinning like an idiot.

"It's just great, Oliver, I love it!"

"Emilie, I told you…" Oliver gave Emilie a cross look.

She returned a sad face, which then broke back into a smile.

Angus twisted round in the narrow passage, by which time Emilie had disappeared.

"Pardon? Are you all right there?"

"Yeah, yes, I'm fine. I just slipped."

"Yes, they are a bit steep, aren't they? And I expect you felt it can be draughty too."

"Hmm," mused Oliver.

Upstairs, Oliver was shown around another group of rooms with different antiquities. At one point they were engaged in conversation when Oliver spotted Emilie over Angus's shoulder at the top of another flight of stairs. Oliver raised his hand to try and secretly wave her away, pretending to scratch his ear when Angus saw his action. As Angus turned around Emilie disappeared again.

When Oliver returned to the car Emilie was sitting there as if she'd never left – smiling! A few weeks later and the shop was theirs. Although Oliver had always confided in Harry and Beryl, so far he had not mentioned Emilie's arrival and that was the way he wanted it to stay.

It soon transpired that Emilie was very efficient at obtaining any old thing from antiquity that Oliver should desire. However, when Oliver couldn't go to see Emilie in person he would send Harry to make a purchase. Harry was not so impressed with the new owner; Emilie always spooked him. For the most part Emilie stayed in the Old Workhouse, which they had renamed Emilie Bracket's Emporium. However, when Oliver was away on a trip she would visit Pegasus Ride and look for his return from the attic window at the rear of the house. The room was simply furnished with a small table, cupboard and a rocking chair. So that he could access the room easily himself without anyone else knowing, he'd built a secret staircase into the wall behind a wardrobe in one of the bedrooms. Emilie, of course, had no need of the stairs but the room was somewhere for her to go if he had visitors to the house, where she would often sit knitting in the rocking chair. Now, as he slipped into unconsciousness, he wondered if he would ever see Emilie or the house again.

Chapter 26

They awoke to a beautiful morning and presently had a similar breakfast as before, around the campfire. There was a discussion between the visitors about the night-time noises, illuminations and chanting that had been going on around Ramukata's tent. But none had been allowed to closely witness the visit of the god – Hawenniyo. By the time he'd arrived Oliver's heartrate had reduced to that of a mammal in hibernation. This was not due to the illness but to the special powers of Ayam's spines used for acupuncture. A chemical released into the body from a spine slowed down the blood supply around the body which was carrying the deadly toxins and therefore slowed down the poisoning process. This was to give him time for Hawenniyo to arrive with a possible cure.

Harriet had taken breakfast to her sister in the cabin, whilst Benjamin and Angeline had eaten with the Green kids at the campfire, where Ramukata now joined them. Charlie stood first to ask him the inevitable question, "How is Oliver?"

"He's still very sick and will need to sleep for some time," replied Ramukata.

Oliver was actually in, what is nowadays called, an induced coma. They had put him into a state of hibernation but at this time Ramukata had no idea when, or indeed if, he would recover. Hawenniyo had prevented him from getting any worse but a lot of damage had already been done to his body before he'd arrived.

"Can we see him?" asked V.

"Just for a short time but he won't be able to speak to you."

V burst into tears and turned to Ben for comfort.

At that moment Harriet joined them and firstly thanked Ramukata for the remedies he'd given her for Rachel. She was feeling much better this morning, although still in some pain.

"And what of Mister Oliver?" she inquired.

He repeated what he'd told the children and said that Oliver would need to stay for some while yet and remain in Ramukata's care. There was still more work to be done with his associates from above and beyond this world to heal him.

Harriet discussed with the children that they should return to their mother and tell her about their father and she would take Rachel and her children further north to safety. Of course, Ben knew they should return home but he could not tell his mother about Oliver's condition or where he was – Charlie might have to come up with one of his stories!

Firstly, though, Ben, Charlie and Olivia were desperate now to see Oliver; Ramukata led the way.

"You can speak to him but he won't reply," said Ramukata, opening the flaps to his tent. Oliver lay motionless under a multi-coloured blanket, his yellow skin colour had been replaced by a deathly white and when V touched his exposed hand she recoiled because it was so cold.

"Ahh," she cried, "why's he so cold?"

The previous day he'd been boiling hot to the touch, now it was completely the opposite. Had any of them witnessed a dead body before, they would have now assumed he was dead too.

"He's resting," replied the medicine man. Ben took hold of Oliver's hand and felt the cold lifeless limb and then replaced it back further under the blanket.

Charlie began to weep – he thought the old Indian was lying to them. "Come on, Oliver, please, you must get better; don't die." By now he was in floods of tears, and V too. She just lay over Oliver and tried to hug him.

"He's not going to die – is he, Ben?" she cried.

Ben was trying to act the adult but was struggling to compose himself – he looked at Ramukata for support – but Ben privately thought that Oliver was as good as already dead.

"I'm doing the best I can for him," he said, in the most reassuring way he could.

A comment, Ben thought, that was less positive than before. With the younger ones in tears and nothing more to be gained by staying, Ramukata suggested it was probably time to leave Oliver to continue sleeping.

Harriet had been watching on from outside and gathered Charlie and V in her arms outside the tepee.

"Come on, you lovely children, let's get you off home to your mother," she said, eyeing Ben with a smiling stare. He knew what he had to do.

A little while later Charlie and V sat comfortably on a thick fur – given to them by Little Tree – in the back of the wagon and said their final goodbyes to their new Native American friends and Harriet and her family. They spoke of reunion at some time in the future but obviously without knowing from quite how far in the future the Green children had come!

Ben flicked the reins and the horses in front of the cart twitched into life and pulled them slowly away from the camp. As he drove them through the entrance and onto the lane he mused about the brightly coloured bracelet he now wore on his wrist, given to him by the pretty girl in the camp, and the tears she'd shed at his leaving. When he'd said thank you and then goodbye, she'd run off into her home so that she'd not see him leave. He'd never known a girl have that reaction to him – he felt a tingle in his stomach.

They made their way to Richmond, retracing their path, and joined a train southbound to find Jenny. During the ride back they talked a lot about Harriet and their encounter with Native American Indians – particularly Ramukata. Ben thought about the girl.

★ ★ ★

Harriet would travel north towards New York State – initially by night – to take her sister to safety. They would use the Underground Railroad network to go from one safe house to another – with the help of Little Tree who was accompanying them on horseback. Chief Deep River had insisted they borrow some animals from him to aid their journey, along with one of his most trusted warriors. To help them, when they got there, Ben had given them a substantial sum of money to start a new life. In New York, Harriet would use her contacts to find Rachel and her children somewhere to stay, and then she would take a Union boat south, back to Hilton Head and re-join the nurses at the hospital. Her work was not done yet. The war was far from over and she had more missions to complete.

Eventually the train brought Ben, Charlie and Olivia back to Bowville where they set off on foot to find Jenny. On the journey south they'd had a lot of time to discuss what to do about Oliver's situation and what they would say to their mother. Between them they had come up with a plan. During the last part of their train journey they'd acted it out and rehearsed what they would say when they got home. Their mother would be expecting to see Oliver – for lunch!

When they reached the aeroplane Charlie put on the pilot's flying helmet and told Jenny to take them home. She did enquire about Mr Oliver but Charlie made up an excuse. She whisked them dutifully and safely home to the old airfield behind Pegasus Ride.

With Jenny parked up once again in the hangar, the three adventurers trooped back into the garden. After a brief stop in the shed, for Ben to have one last check on the story, they marched on down the garden path. The noise of their entrance to the kitchen attracted their mother, who was in the hall on the telephone. Their arrival had also been noticed by an unseen, part-time occupier of the loft room. Neither she nor Laura was going to be pleased about the news coming to them.

Chapter 27

"Hi Mum!" they all replied to her greeting.

"Where's Oliver?"

Charlie and V both looked furtively at Ben. "Well," he started, "he's... err, had to go home, to the Hobbards. He... well, Harry came up and said he'd had a call."

"What, onto the airfield? A call?"

"Yes!" said Charlie, jumping in on the action. "He's got a sick relative apparently and Harry came to get him."

"Oh, I see," replied their mother.

"He said to say he's sorry not to come and say goodbye," said Olivia.

"Yes, he just had to go with Mr Hobbard. In the car," said Ben briskly.

Glances and comments were being exchanged between the children at a rate that made Laura suspicious. She knew when they were up to something and that seemed like now!

"Why didn't Mr Hobbard come to the house?"

"Err... I don't know," replied Ben.

"I expect Oliver had told him we would be getting some timber from there. He said the farmer told him we could have some," said Charlie, who was better at telling stories than Ben.

"Oh, I expect that's what it was," replied Laura, somewhat disbelievingly. "Anyway, whatever – sit down and I'll sort some lunch out." Laura wasn't overly worried about Oliver's peculiar disappearance but the unseen visitor, listening in, was. Although the back door had swung closed, it was not latched and suddenly a cool breeze ripped through the kitchen throwing open the door and knocking over a vase of flowers that Laura had only recently picked from the garden and stood on the table. Ben caught the vase but could not stop the contents spilling all over the table.

Laura swivelled round from facing a cupboard, "What on earth–"

She didn't feel anything as it didn't fill the room, just a narrow rush of air through the centre that went straight through V sitting at the end. A sensation that made little V's eyes pop out; it was as if someone had thrown a bucket of cold water over her.

She shivered for a moment and shook her head like a dog shaking off after a dip in the sea. Charlie got up, looked this way and that, and then closed the door. Sometimes if the front door was open at the same time, there'd be a sudden rush of wind through the house but this was not one of those times.

Laura told them she'd just come off the phone after speaking to George's mother, and his dad was going to be okay. He'd badly lacerated his arm and broken it in two places when it got caught in a farm machine but he would be home tomorrow.

In the afternoon Ben and Charlie rode down to the post office on their bicycles and told Harry and Beryl what had happened. Beryl got very upset but Ben and Charlie said they planned to return to hopefully collect Oliver in a couple of weeks' time. In the meantime the Hobbards would back up their story of Oliver having to go away to see a sick aunt – just in case their mother asked! There was someone else waiting in the Hobbards' kitchen, who was very upset to hear the news too, but none of them could see her. She left silently in tears with no one to console her but her cat. The thought of the worst happening actually scared her.

Will Oliver recover from an incurable illness? Charlie and Ben will be the first to find out in their next adventure in Jenny – the magical aeroplane!

Characters to Research and Places to Enjoy Visiting:

Harriet Tubman: Christened Araminta Ross, married John Tubman - a free coloured man - around 1844 and then changed her name to Harriet Tubman but was also known as Minty. Born into slavery, around 1820, she was the granddaughter of a slave imported from Africa and lived as such until 1849 when she heard that she was to be sold. At that point she decided to escape and she walked from her homeland of Maryland to Philadelphia where she found work. After saving a small amount of money she returned to Maryland and thereafter began her crusade to free enslaved people. As a young girl she suffered, at times, daily whippings at the hands of her mistress - often across the face. Much of the historical information for this story came from a book first published in 1869 - Scenes in the Life of Harriet Tubman - by Sarah H Bradford.

Harriet Tubman Memorials: There are a number of memorials to Harriet Tubman and the

Underground Railroad but in March, 2017 a new National Park Monument in Dorchester County, Maryland on an 11,750 acre site opened. There is a visitor centre and is a joint operation between the National Park Service and the Maryland State Park Service.

Underground Railroad: Was a network of secret routes and safe houses used by nineteenth century enslaved people of African descent in the United States in efforts to escape to Free states (states where slavery was illegal) and Canada. It relied on people sympathetic to the cause to help keep the travellers safe on their journey to freedom. Guides were called 'conductors' and safe houses 'stations'. Harriet was such a successful guide she was also known as 'Moses', after leading hundreds of people to freedom.

American Civil War: Began in April 1861, after a raid by Confederates on the US Fort Sumter, until May 1865. Around 750,000 people died as a direct result of the conflict, (soldiers and civilians) with hundreds of thousands wounded. The main driving force for the war was the difference in opinion over the slavery issue between the Northern Free States and the Southern slave states, although there were other compounding factors. Abraham Lincoln (the president at the time) decreed that it was against the constitution of the USA for individual states to break away from the union and become independent, therefore any that chose to do so would effectively be guilty of treason against the union. The first state to secede (leave) the union was South Carolina, where Charleston is situated.

General William T. Sherman: He served as a General in the Union Army, under Ulysses S. Grant, during the American Civil War and was one of the most successful commanders of the war. Although he did not perform well in the early stages of the war he developed into a clever tactician as the war progressed. As he marched his men through conquered states, one policy he employed was to tear up railway lines and then have them heated and bent around trees, leaving behind what became known as 'Sherman neckties', which made repairs difficult.

General Robert E. Lee: Initially he was appointed commanding officer of the Confederate Army of North Virginia and was a very successful tactician, often defeating armies of the north more superior in number. By the end of the war he was the supreme commander. Other prominent generals of the confederacy include P.G. T. Beauregard and James Longstreet both of whom served with distinction.

Cotton Gin: Cotton was a major product grown in the southern states of the USA and exported to other nations like the United Kingdom in bales to be processed and woven into fabric. Cotton grows on the plant as small ball of lint called 'bolls' and was picked by hand and then had to be separated from the plant head in a machine called a gin. Before mechanisation these machines were cranked by hand - usually by slave labour.

Morse Code Telegraphy: Samuel Morse is credited with the invention of the single wire telegraphy in the early 1800's and the development of the code of dots and dashes which enabled messages to be sent instantly over long distances. Other scientists in Europe also worked on similar systems to send messages using electricity and utilising the phenomenon of electromagnetism at a similar time. The Morse code system is still used today in some radio communications including in aviation, although it has largely been replaced by voice communication. As the equipment is relatively simple in construction and operation it would be quite feasible as a classroom construction project at school!

The Science Museum, London: Is home to thousands of artefacts including telegraphy and its development through the ages where the early types of communication mentioned in the story can be seen. Although in the UK two scientists, Cooke and Wheatstone developed an alternative type of electric telegraph to the Morse code system.

Richmond, Virginia: Served as the capital of the Confederate States of America for most of the conflict. It was a vital source of munitions and other supplies for the army and navy of the confederacy. It was attacked several times and finally fell in April 1865 with large parts of the city destroyed by fires set alight by the retreating soldiers.

Spratt and Winglet double action brass butt hinge!: Although fictional in name, an example of this type of hinge can be found in the Metalwork Gallery on the third floor of the Victoria and Albert museum in London, England, on a window shutter assembly dated c. 1600 from Belgium!